PROTECTING THEIR DESTINY

A BINDARRA CREEK MYSTERY ROMANCE

ERIN MOIRA O'HARA

O'HARA PUBLISHING

ALSO BY ERIN MOIRA O'HARA

STEELE OPS SERIES

The Kalista Diamond

Precious Gems

Jewel of the Kimberly

The Amethyst Code

Elusive Treasure

Silver Lies

SANTINI/DEROSA SERIES

Conspiracy in Emilia Romagna

DEADLY FORCES SERIES

Beat of the Jungle

BINDARRA CREEK SERIES

Tempting Fate

Date with Destiny

A Twist of Fate

Protecting their Destiny

Mistletoe Magic

CONTEMPORARY FANTASY

The Knight of Castle Kildare

Protecting their Destiny

Copyright © 2022 Erin Moira O'Hara

All Rights Reserved
ISBN: 9780648951063

Cover Design by Annie Seaton
Editor: Juanita Kees of Kees2Create

First published in 2022

O'Hara Publishing, Peatties Road, Cardiff Heights, NSW 2285 Australia

DEDICATION

To the Romance Writers of Australia Association. I wouldn't be here without your workshops, contests and support. It was through your annual conferences that I met so many wonderful writers, many who have become close friends. It was through this association that I found two great writing groups and more friends. I've entered, placed and won awards they have run. I've learned to judge competitions and participated in many workshops.

CHAPTER 1

*E*ach step brought Emma closer to her worst nightmare. Her heart pounded in her throat as she stepped onto the bottom stockyard rail and reached for the top one, her advanced pregnancy making her movements awkward. Cattle yards were her least favourite place in the world. Almost being trampled to death on her twelfth birthday had ensured a fear that didn't look like diminishing anytime soon.

She'd loved hanging around her grandfather's stockyards, absorbing the whistles, dogs barking, cattle bellowing. The sound of hooves thundering as stockman pushed the mob into the yards had been exhilarating. But not anymore. Not since that day. She hadn't been this close to a stockyard in years.

She didn't trust cattle, and she didn't trust Reid's huge stud rams either. Not even Stanthorpe, who had been raised as a pet for the first year of his life. The only animals on Tulachmhor she trusted were the horses and lambs. The horses had ideal temperaments, were easy to manage and obedient. Lambs were cuddly and gorgeous. She didn't mind ewes either, as long as they were out in the paddocks.

From her position on the rail, Emma could see the cattle being herded down the valley towards her. Perspiration dampened her forehead. She gripped the rail tighter.

I can do this. I can't hide away forever. If I'm going to help Reid run Tulachmhor one day, I must overcome this fear.

It would get easier, the Sullivans were gradually reducing their Hereford numbers as they turned Tulachmhor back into a Merino stud.

Two riders at either side kept the cattle from breaking. Another brought up the rear, cantering back and forth. From a distance, the mob looked docile. Emma shuddered. Draft the cows from their calves and it would be another matter.

As the riders got closer, she identified Jerry Eckford, the Sullivan's jackaroo. A nice guy she planned to introduce to her best friend. He rode his dapple-grey gelding to the right of the mob. Hunter Sullivan, her soon-to-be brother-in-law, spurred his bay gelding and blocked a calf's escape on the left.

Her attention shifted to the rider at the back of the mob. Her fiancé. In fifteen days, he'd be her husband. Reid was totally absorbed in moving the mob towards the yards. Sitting relaxed in his saddle, his Akubra shading his face, one hand resting on his thigh, as he whistled up his dog, Gypsy.

Emma took a moment to admire his broad shoulders and easy posture. How she loved this man and his calm way of going about life. His patience and gentle hands as he worked his horse or trained his blue heeler never ceased to impress her. She wouldn't be here now, if it wasn't for a twist of fate and the amazing connection they shared. She could only be grateful for his concentrated effort in pursuing her.

She shivered as the thundering hooves drew closer. If Reid's grandmother hadn't twisted an ankle, she wouldn't have been here this morning. And after all Kathleen's generosity, it was the least Emma could do to drop off two flasks of coffee and a basket of egg and bacon rolls. If she could just get Reid's attention, she'd hand them over and be on her way to her morning clinic at the hospital.

"Morning, Doctor Fahey. Do ya need a hand climbing over that rail?"

Emma flinched. She hadn't noticed the farmhand lurking in the shadows across the yard. The way he stared at her with an unblinking intensity sent shivers scuttling across her stomach. He had to be in his mid to late thirties yet lumbered about like a 60-year-old. He always seemed to be watching. Calculating. She couldn't put a finger on it, but the less she saw of him the better.

"Why on earth would I climb into a yard where a mob of cattle are heading, especially as I'm heavily pregnant?"

He grunted. "Who knows what ya thinking of doin'?"

She watched warily as the lean man sauntered across the yard, his thumbs hooked through the belt loops of his jeans. His sleazy gaze fixed on her chest, making her skin crawl. "Shouldn't you be outside the yards, Bob? Don't you need to open the gate?"

"I reckon the boss would rather I kept an eye on you, sweet cheeks."

Emma narrowed her eyes. "Do *not* call me sweet cheeks. It's offensive and bad-mannered. I am perfectly safe here, so please go away."

"Pride goes before a fall, sweet cheeks." He spat on the ground then sauntered away, opening the far gate for the cows and calves streaming down the hillside.

Emma looked over her shoulder to the high ridge in the distance, easily seen from all over the district. A Morgan ancestor had planted a row of hickory trees along the top, hence the name Hickory Ridge. The golden acres and rolling

3

hills had been in the Morgan family for generations. It shared a boundary with Tulachmhor, which had belonged to the Sullivans just as long. As a child, she'd loved holidays at Hickory Ridge, watching her grandfather and uncle work their stock. Since her near death experience, she preferred to take a quiet ride as far away from the cattle and stockyards as possible.

Her fear of cattle had made no sense to her maternal grandfather. Morgans had been breeding cattle since they settled in Bindarra Creek back in the 1800's. And even though Gramps had been the one to save her life, leaving him with a permanent limp, he'd continued working with cattle until his heart gave out.

She still missed her tough-as-leather grandfather. Before his death, Gramps had often told her he was proud of her achievements but insisted she'd have made an incredible jillaroo. Emma smiled. Apparently, a jillaroo outweighed a gynaecologist any day, at least in his eyes.

Reid's shout brought her back to earth with a start. She watched in fascination as he leaned forward out of the saddle to chase a calf that had broken away from the mob. Reeling his horse left and right, he headed off the nervous animal.

Emma turned back to the yard and froze. Bellowing cattle, breathing hard, streamed in. She coughed as their hooves churned up the dirt and covered her in dust. Terrifying flashbacks of that awful day bombarded her, locking her fingers to the top rail. She couldn't move.

"Get off the bloody fence, Emma." Reid's shout broke the trance holding her in its grip, enabling her to unlock her fingers. His thunderous scowl sent a shiver down her spine. Within one breath and the next Reid had gone from calm and controlled to aggravated and angry.

She stepped down from the rail, shaking as she tried to

stem a different kind of fear. One she hadn't encountered since leaving Sydney. A fear she refused to face ever again.

Her breath caught as an agitated cow charged the fence. It veered away at the last moment but left Emma's heart pounding in her chest. The cow forced her way through the entering herd and out of the yards again. Emma watched as Reid wheeled his horse around to chase the runaway, shouldering it to turn the beast back. The runaway kicked up her heels then followed the last of the cattle into the stockyard.

Hunter rode forward and shut the gate. He was as tall and broad as Reid, and they shared the same brown hair and green eyes. From all accounts, he'd mellowed since marrying Emma's cousin. Yet right now, he looked savage as he yelled at Reid, who yelled back. They were too far away to hear but their body language spoke volumes and it scared her much more than a herd of cattle ever would.

"You okay, Doc?"

Emma dragged her eyes from her fiancé and his brother to Jerry Eckford, as he drew his snorting gelding up outside the fence. She nodded. "I'm fine." Her gaze flicked to Bob Farrell, smirking at her from the other side of the yard. "I do not like that man. He's rude and obnoxious."

"I agree, Doc. Reid wouldn't have hired him if we weren't shorthanded. He won't last long, take my word for it. Best you stand well back. With a herd this size, they can be unpredictable."

"I know. I just froze for a moment."

Jerry removed his hat and wiped his shirt sleeve across his sweaty forehead. He had a rugged complexion and gentle hazel eyes. "I reckon you've given Reid a few white hairs today. He almost fell off Zeus when he saw you at the rail. I've never seen you at the cattle yards."

"Kathleen asked me to bring down breakfast, but I see you've still got a lot to do."

"Yeah. Today, we're drafting the cows from their calves. Deciding which heifers to retain as breeders and get the culls into the forcing pens before the trucks arrive."

Reid cantered up and dismounted. He was covered in dust. "What the hell are you doing here, Emma?"

Jerry frowned at Reid before spurring his horse and trotting away.

"I brought breakfast." Emma turned on her heel and stalked over to a tree stump table and chair setting where she'd left the basket of egg rolls and coffee flasks.

Reid followed, leading Zeus behind him. "Emma, I appreciate the thought, but we had breakfast hours ago."

"It wasn't my idea." She picked up the cane basket. "Here." She shoved it into Reid's chest. "Your grandmother twisted her ankle this morning. She's fine but needs to rest. There's coffee too. I've done my good deed for the day. See you later."

"Emma, wait." Reid dropped Zeus' reins and placed the basket back on the table. "I'm sorry I yelled at you. I wasn't expecting to see you here. You scared me."

"The fences are solid, and I wasn't in any danger of falling into the yards."

"Yeah, but you're carrying a wide load and not as quick on your feet as usual."

"I beg your pardon?" She wacked his shoulder. "A *wide* load?"

He grimaced. "Baby. You're carrying a baby. Thanks for bringing us a second breakfast. We have worked up an appetite and coming to the stockyards took guts. I'm proud of you, Em."

"I'm proud of me too." Maybe she'd overreacted. "I didn't mean to scare you, and I'm sorry if it caused friction between you and Hunter."

"Don't worry about it. We're always having a go at each other." He walked with her to the driver's side of her Beetle, opened the door then kissed her. "Enjoy your last day at work."

"I plan to. What's on your agenda today?"

He sighed. "Once we get these vealers loaded, I've got to find out why one of our windmills is not pumping."

"Okay, don't overdo it." She climbed into her Beetle. "I'll see you after work."

"You will." He winked. "Every inch of me, if you want."

"Don't be naughty." Emma grinned as he closed the door then she took her time putting on her seat belt and starting the engine. She watched her soon-to-be husband call the other men over for breakfast. Apparently, they were going to eat before separating the cattle.

She exhaled and released the brake. She'd done it. Stood beside a stockyard crammed with cattle. It had taken every ounce of courage she possessed, but she'd done it. She'd overcome one of her biggest fears. Cattle weren't so bad, as long as she wasn't in the yards with them. In two weeks, she'd overcome another fear and marry the man of her dreams. She wouldn't be running away from this man a week before the wedding.

* * *

REID WATCHED the woman he loved drive away in her yellow Volkswagen Beetle. He really was proud of Emma, even though she'd scared him. She'd taken a big step today, coming down to the stockyard despite her crippling fear of the cattle.

He unpacked the basket, his thoughts still on Emma. It had been an almighty battle convincing her to move in with him two years ago. Her terror of cattle and cattle yards had only been one hurdle. He hadn't expected to fall in love with a woman who shared his aversion to marriage and children.

It hadn't mattered at first, but as time went on, he wanted what his brother and sisters had. And he wanted everyone to know Emma was his.

Getting Emma to choose a date had been his biggest difficulty. Her pregnancy hadn't swayed her an inch, and he couldn't figure out why.

He'd had a violent and neglectful mother who'd ruined his childhood. She created the trust issues he carried with him even now, but Emma came from a stable, loving home. He couldn't help but think that there was more to her aversion to marriage. Something deep that she wasn't ready to share with him yet.

Leaving Zeus to graze on clumps of grass, Reid set out four mugs on the roughly hewn table they sat around most mornings. He poured coffee into each then sat on tree stump to eat his egg and bacon roll.

Hunter sat on the next stump beside him. "Got something on your mind, Reid?"

He took a mouthful of sweetened coffee, savouring the taste as he met his brother's questioning look. "I was just thinking about our feud with the Morgans."

Hunter chuckled. "The ancestors would be turning in their graves."

"What feud?" Bob Farrell claimed a stump opposite, glancing between Hunter to Reid. "I thought you fellas got on well with Jake and Riley Morgan."

"They do now," chimed in Jerry with a laugh. "Not that long ago these two took every opportunity to outwit, outride, and outthink Riley and Jake Morgan. It's been that way between both families for generations."

"Why?" Bob's confusion had Reid grinning.

"I hear way back in the day, one stole the other's fiancée, and they fought over who owned an allotment of land fronting the river. The feud grew and lasted until six years ago."

"What happened six years ago?" asked Bob.

Jerry chuckled. "A pretty, green-eyed lady arrived in town. She was searching for her biological mother and ended up bringing the Sullivans and Morgans together. Now these guys are all best mates."

"The right woman will do that to a man." Hunter raised an eyebrow at Reid. "Isn't that right, bro?"

"You should know, Hunter. You fell the hardest."

"Look who's calling the kettle black." Hunter held up his cup. "To the women we love. May they always welcome us home with open arms and warm hearts."

Reid shook his head. "You've gone soft in your old age, mate."

"Nope. It's called domestic bliss." Hunter's lips twitched. "Except when the terror twins are teething. That's called sleep deprivation."

Reid laughed. In five weeks, he'd have his own son or daughter to cherish and keep safe. His smile faded. The thought terrified him. If his own father hadn't known his children were suffering, how would he?

CHAPTER 2

"*H*ello, sugarplum." Emma rubbed her stethoscope against her white coat to warm it up before placing it on the newborn's chest. The tiny girl's colour looked good, her heartbeat coming through nice and strong. This little angel and her mother were right to leave Bindarra Creek Hospital and go home.

With no other patients due in the next month, Emma could start her parental leave and concentrate on her wedding in … Goosebumps broke out over her arms. How had September crept up so fast? She still had so much to do.

The baby's delicate fingers curled around Emma's thumb. Another baby she'd brought into the world safely. Giving the precious little girl's tummy a gentle pat, Emma stepped away, rubbing her own pronounced abdomen. She'd always loved children and would soon get to cuddle one of her own. Nothing in the world would stop her from raising him in a safe and loving environment.

Thoughts of her approaching wedding triggered memories she'd rather forget. After escaping a narcissistic, two-timing bully, she'd sworn never to trust any man again.

Meeting Reid Sullivan had sent her life in a direction she hadn't dreamed possible.

What should have been a one-night stand, had somehow grown into something more. They'd been living together for over two years now and he hadn't changed. He didn't have a violent temper. He wasn't controlling. Reid was a hard worker, a generous lover, and she couldn't be happier. He'd overcome his own demons where marriage was concerned, and their future looked promising. So why was she so scared?

They'd been engaged for a year when fate had stepped in, and she'd fallen pregnant. She loved Reid with all her heart but setting a date had raised old fears. He'd finally worn her down and in two weeks, she'd be taking the biggest step of her life.

She ignored the prickle of apprehension. It wasn't as if she didn't have family around if she needed them. Her cousin Ryan was the Senior Police Sergeant in Bindarra Creek. His twin, Jake, the vet. Her uncle and aunt owned Hickory Ridge, the cattle property next to Reid's family property, Tulachmhor. And her parents were an hour away in Armidale. She'd never be caught in a distressing relationship without the support of family again.

Reid is nothing like Glenn. Stop with this paranoia.

"Doctor Fahey, is everything all right?"

"Perfect, Scarlett." Emma turned to smile at the fiery redhead, who marched across the nursery. Although Scarlett had transferred from Tamworth Hospital only two months ago, already the midwife had become a trusted colleague. "Just wool-gathering. Have we got a name for this little cutie-pie yet?"

"Yes. I was about to write it on her board." Scarlett popped the cap off a black marker and wrote *Maia*.

"That's unusual. I like Maia."

"I do too. It's nice she has parents who have taken the time to pick a name that suits her and won't make her the butt of jokes." She pointed at her own hair and raised an eyebrow. "I mean, really? Scarlett Stark ...what were they thinking? Have you decided on names yet?"

"Not quite." Emma wasn't about to tell anyone her baby was a boy. Reid would be over the moon, but surprises weren't her thing. She liked as much information as possible, so she could make sound decisions and be prepared for any outcome.

"I hear there is a darts final tonight." She checked her patient's notes. "Our jackaroo is a finalist. Jerry sees himself as Bindarra Creek's next champion."

"Jerry? What's his last name?" Scarlett dropped her marker and bent to pick it up.

"Eckford. He's been practicing every spare minute he gets. Do you know him?"

"I'm ... I'm not into darts. Rally driving is more my thing. Next weekend I'm competing in a race out Dubbo way."

"Oh, goodness, Scarlett. The thought of you skidding around dirt corners scares me."

"I've been doing it for years, Doc. My birthday is coming up and thanks to a generous family member, I've finally got the money to buy a new rally car. It's very exciting."

"Aren't you afraid of breaking down or getting lost out in the wilderness?"

The colour drained from Scarlett's cheeks. "Not anymore." She touched the bulky ring hanging on a black cord around her neck. "I have a satellite GPS tracker."

"Is that it?"

"Yes."

"Why do you wear it to work?"

Scarlett shrugged. "I like it, and when I'm not at work, it's on my finger."

"Fair enough. Just be careful out there on those dirt roads."

"I will. Oh, Deidre King is on her way. She thinks she's in labour, again."

Emma exhaled. "I've never known anyone to get such strong Braxton Hicks contractions, so early. She still has seven weeks to go. If it's the real thing this time, we'll need to transfer her to Armidale neonatal ward. I'm going to check on Jillian Cooper. She and Maia are right to go home today, but make sure Gillian has an appointment to see my replacement in a month."

"Yes, doctor." Scarlett smiled down at Maia then began setting out what she needed to change the baby's nappy.

As there were no other babies in the nursery, Emma left to check on Maia's mother. She hurried along the quiet corridor, mentally listing all the things she needed to do for her wedding. *Finalise flowers. One last fitting. Check on the cake. Ring Brenda and make sure her roster hasn't changed.* She'd love to talk her best friend into moving to Bindarra Creek. Midwives with Brenda's experience were in high demand in Sydney, but the tree change would do her the world of good and with luck, she'd meet the right man here.

Her mobile phone vibrated in her pocket. The caller ID made her smile. "Hello, handsome."

"Hey. You're not overdoing it, are you?"

"No, darling. I only have one mother and her baby to keep an eye on, and they will be going home today. Once I'm finished the afternoon clinic I will be officially on maternity leave. You sound tired, Reid. What's up?"

"I've got two broken windmills, which means they are not pumping, and the troughs are empty. As if that's not bad enough, sixty cows and young calves got out on the road. Did you accidentally leave the front gate open this morning?"

"No, I didn't. Someone else must have come through. Did you get the cattle back safely?"

"Yeah, but it put me behind. Emma, I don't mean to harp on this, but no vehicle came through the gate between yours and the cattle trucks. Are you sure you put the slip ring over the bolt?"

"Yes. Shutting gates is second nature to me, Reid. Did you miss your tax appointment?"

"Yeah, but I've rescheduled for next week."

"Good." She took advantage of a chair in the corridor to ease off her runners and rotate her ankles. Her feet were a little swollen. She should have gone on parental leave a week ago, but Jillian Cooper had gone over her due date, and Emma hadn't wanted to let her down. "Are you still there, Reid?"

"Yeah, sorry, I've just pulled up to another windmill and two of the buckets are on the ground. They were only recently replaced. Jerry must have pulled them off. What time will you be home?"

"Around four. I want to pick up some milk and sourdough. Ouch."

"What is it?"

"I dropped my shoe on my sore toe. Wait! I stubbed my toe this morning when I was latching the gate. It's not my fault the cattle got out."

"Sorry, I'm tired, dirty, and grumpy. I shouldn't have moved them into Minnie's field before it was fenced off. It must have been a delivery driver I missed. It was bound to happen. I'll get Hunter and the boys to help me fence off Minnie's field tomorrow."

Emma frowned and placed her feet on the cold tiles. "We're going to Armidale tomorrow for lunch with my parents and sister."

"I've got a lot on my plate this weekend. If Dad and

Antonia weren't away, I might have been able to go with you, but with a man down, I don't have a choice."

She sighed. "You've always got a lot on your plate, Reid. One day off wouldn't hurt."

"This is life on Tulachmhor, Em. We breed cattle and sheep and grow crops to feed them. You don't need me to work on wedding stuff with your mother and sister."

"I know, but I wanted you to have a say in things."

"I'll go with whatever you want."

"Okay. I'll bring leftovers home, so you don't have to suffer my cooking."

"Great. I'll see you later?"

"Bye." She ended the call and stared at the ceiling. Reid usually said something nice when she mentioned her woeful cooking attempts. Some really had been woeful, but she was getting better. He must really be out of sorts today.

Maybe I didn't slip the gate ring over the bolt properly.

The frustration in Reid's voice hadn't been hard to miss, but at least he hadn't lost his temper. She was so emotional at the moment, if he'd turned his frustration on her, it would probably bring on a meltdown.

Damn hormones.

She pulled on her runners then made her way along the hall to the nurses' station. It was entirely possible she had baby brain. Yesterday she'd misplaced a bag of groceries. That or someone had stolen it, which was ludicrous. She'd especially bought spelt flour to make sourdough, a skill she'd mastered with Kathleen Sullivan's help. She'd have to get more flour on her way home if she wanted to surprise Reid on Sunday morning. If all went according to plan, she'd welcome Antonia and Jack back from their holiday with a beef casserole and gramma pie.

A nurse looked up from her screen. "Doctor Fahey, there's a call for you on line two. It's a doctor from Sydney."

Emma stared at the phone as rising panic froze her in place. Why would a doctor from Sydney want to speak to her? She was being paranoid, there could be any number of reasons.

"Thanks, Ishya." She reached for the handset, her hand shaking. This was ridiculous. Gritting her teeth, she pressed line two. "Emma speaking."

She was met with silence then a dial tone. *No, please don't let it be him.* A rush of fear bombarded her, leaving her trembling.

"Is everything okay, Doctor?" Ishya touched Emma's arm, making her jerk away.

"The line dropped out. If he calls back, can you ask for his name and take a message?"

"Sure. Scarlett is settling in well, isn't she? I only just heard she grew up in Bindarra Creek and that Valma and Vince Stark are her parents. Rhonda from the cafeteria said Scarlett left town when she was sixteen. Just disappeared without any explanation."

"Scarlett's past is Scarlett's business." Emma picked up her folder. "I'm just grateful to have her skills and that she's such a nice person."

"She is nice." Ishya ambled around the counter. "Ready for your morning clinic?"

"Right after I see Mrs. Cooper. Lead the way."

Two and a half hours later, Emma finished typing up her notes at the nurses' station and pulled out her mobile. She rang the florist to check if they'd received her request to add a sprig of rosemary to the baby's breath and deep-red rose-buds for the men's corsages. Then she checked on the cake's progress. With the urgent things out of the way, she retreated to her office to call her best friend.

"Emma! I was going to ring you over the weekend. It's

been bedlam at work. I haven't even had time for a good run in … weeks."

"Wow, that's not like you. No marathons on the horizon?"

"No, but I did put in for a couple of weeks leave."

"Great." Emma put Brenda on speaker and sank into her chair to remove her runners again. "Does that mean you're coming to Bindarra Creek early?"

"Seriously, Emma, you expect me — the Queen of Bondi Beach — to pass up the chance for a few more days of early morning runs? I've almost forgotten what it's like to hit the pavement at the crack of dawn."

"Okay, enjoy your down time. What else is on the agenda?"

"I want to drive to Cobar and spend a few days with my parents. As I also have a wedding to attend, I need a day or two to find a drop-dead gorgeous dress, get my hair done, and find a present for my friend and her hunky fiancé."

"Woohoo." Emma picked up her bottle of sparkling water and poured herself a glass. "So, when can we expect you in Bindarra Creek?"

"I plan to drive across next weekend, so you have a week to show me why it's the best country town in the New England region."

"Fantastic. I can't wait to see you."

"Same. I do have some other … news."

"Oh?" Brenda's hesitation gave Emma goosebumps. A sixth sense told her who it would be about, but why her old friend thought she'd care was new.

"Glenn Hanson has been suspended. Two nurses from the orthopaedic ward complained he was bullying them and there's allegations that he's been under the influence of drugs at work. I also heard he's been asking around about you, and now he's disappeared."

A shiver ran down Emma's spine. "Are you serious?"

"Yeah, Glenn has a big ego, but to be honest, the nurses who made the complaints are lazy cows, and I've seen them attempting to flirt with him. It could be a case of sour grapes, because … since you dumped him, he's become very anti-social, or so I've heard. I find it hard to believe he's taking drugs though."

"Whatever he's doing, it's not my concern." Emma's hand shook as she took a gulp of water.

"You're right, but I thought you should know in case the police contact you."

"Wow, wait a minute. Why would the police want to talk to me?"

"It's only a rumour, but from what I've heard, Glenn is either stealing drugs from the hospital or buying them from a dealer and it could be put into the hands of police."

"That doesn't make sense. Glenn could write his own scripts."

"I'm just telling you what I've heard, Emma."

"Hopefully the police won't need to speak to me, but if they do, I'll tell them the truth. Glenn was a controlling, narcissistic bully who became verbally abusive. I left him because his moods were escalating."

"And he was having an affair with a nurse."

"I didn't know that at the time, but if I had, I would have left sooner. The rat had the audacity to accuse me of flirting with a colleague. I can't believe you didn't tell me."

"I didn't believe the rumours, Emma. I'd never known Glenn to look at another woman once he met you."

"Me either. It shocked a lot of people when I cancelled the wedding." She glanced at the photo of Reid on her desk. "Now I'm about to marry a much better man."

"You did the right thing, hon. Anyway, I thought fore-warned is forearmed. With luck you won't get dragged into this."

"Let's hope so. I'm so happy you're coming a few days early. Are you sure you don't want to be a bridesmaid? It's not too late to change things."

"No way, hon. Always a bridesmaid, never a bride. I'm happy to be a guest and I'm glad you're happy, Emma."

"I am happy, Bren. I'd like you to be as happy. You won't get it working crazy shifts in Sydney and spending all your spare time sleeping. There are some great running trails through the Akuna National Park that I can personally recommend."

"I'll certainly check them out. Pity you can't run with me."

Emma laughed. "Ever seen a duck run? It's not pretty, but seriously, Bren, we are looking for skilled nurses here and there's a nice guy called Jerry, who I would like you to meet. Come check out the hospital and the community. You will love them."

"So you keep telling me." Brenda gave an exaggerated sigh. "I'm seeing a guy I dated years ago, before I met you. He's everything I've ever wanted, Emma, and I'm confident we can make it work, if his ex would just butt out of his life."

"How come you never told me about him?"

"It hurt to talk about him, and it ended before I met you. No use crying over spilt milk."

"You can tell me all about him when you get here. Ooh … the baby just rolled."

"I still can't believe you're pregnant."

"I wouldn't be if the condom hadn't broken." Emma finished her water and filled her glass again. "Neither of us regret it."

"You've told me many times." Brenda huffed. "Don't mind me, I want what you have."

"I want that for you too, Bren. I have to get back to work. I'm monitoring an anxious mother who has the worst case of

Braxton Hick's contractions I've seen in a while, and I've got an afternoon clinic today."

"All in a day's work for you, Emma. See you soon, bye."

"Bye." Emma ended the call and dropped her phone in the pocket of her lab coat.

Her afternoon flew by. Deidre King had returned home after another false alarm and the afternoon clinic had been a breeze. With nothing else on her agenda, Emma replaced her runners with knee-high boots then locked her office and made her way out of the maternity wing. She waved to Vince Stark, their Monday to Friday dayshift security guard, and Scarlett's father. His wife, Valma, worked on reception. No wonder Scarlett knew everything that went on in the hospital and Bindarra Creek.

Emma crossed the pedestrian crossing to where she'd parked her car, shuddering as a blast of cold wind hit her.

"What the?" She stared at the lopsided bonnet of her Beetle. "Oh no." She hurried to the passenger side and groaned. "Two flat tyres. You've got to be kidding me."

"Got a problem, Doctor Fahey?" Vince came jogging across to her car, his face red with the exertion. "Oh, that's not good."

"I know. Who carries two spare tyres?"

"They might just need air. When did you last have them checked?"

"We checked them a few weeks ago." She exhaled. "I'll ring, Reid. He has a battery-operated pump, and he'll get me a spare tyre if I need it."

"Righto. Don't wait for him out here, it's freezing."

"I won't. September is supposed to be a lovely month to get married."

"Ah well, you've still got a couple of weeks for a beautiful spring day. This won't last."

"I hope you're right." Clutching her coat about her more

firmly, she dug her phone out and called Reid as she trailed Vince towards the warmth of the hospital's reception area.

She was about to hang up when he answered. "You have to deliver a baby, right?"

"No, but I am still at the hospital. I've got two flat tyres."

"Two? At least you're not stuck on the road. I'll need to have a shower. I'm covered in mud and sheep sh… poo. Bob Farrell brought his dog to work today. It chased Stanthorpe and another ram into a drain, and they couldn't get out."

"That man gives me the creeps, Reid. Did he help you get the rams out?"

"I couldn't contact him. He was supposed to drop off a few bales of hay to the cattle over at Eckfords then come back and help me. Stay put, I'll be there as soon as I can."

"I can call Jake or Riley. Surely one of my cousins can help me."

"No, those two won't let me live it down if I don't come to your rescue. Aside from that, I want to be your knight in shining armour. Wait inside the hospital for me."

"I will. See you soon." So much for leaving early. She'd make a pot of herbal tea in the doctor's lounge and put her feet up. She'd been so looking forward to spending tomorrow with Reid and her family. Life on the farm didn't allow him much time off and at the moment she wasn't a great help. At least Reid wasn't a narcissist or a bully. He appreciated everything she did for him. She had to stop expecting him to change or it would affect their relationship.

Movement drew her attention to the dark shadows near the Men's Shed. She could make out the silhouette of someone standing there. It was odd for anyone to be hanging around the community organisation so late in the day. The thought of someone breaking in to steal or damage tools and machinery had Emma quickening her pace, only to slow down again when sharp pain took her breath. Touching her abdomen, she found it rock hard. After a couple of slow breaths, it relaxed again, allowing her to continue. Entering the hospital, she was relieved to see Vince leaning on the reception counter, talking to Valma.

"Sorry to interrupt, but someone is hanging around the Men's Shed."

"I'll go take a look." Vince pulled his shoulders back and sucked in his impressive gut. "Leave it with me, Doctor Fahey."

As soon as he was out of earshot, Valma chuckled. "Poor Vince. He has a heart of gold, but he's got no chance of catching anyone up to mischief." She passed Emma a huge bunch of pink, red, yellow, and purple flowers. "I was afraid I'd missed you. These are from all the staff."

"They're beautiful, Valma." Emma buried her nose in the perfumed bouquet. "I love gerberas and chrysanthemums."

Valma smiled. "Just a little something to start your maternity leave with a smile and show you how much we value you."

"That's lovely. Please thank everyone for me."

"I will. How are the wedding plans going?"

"Good. Tomorrow I'm off to Armidale to finalise everything with my parents and sister."

They were still talking weddings when Vince stumbled through the front door. The shoulder of his shirt was soaked with blood. He wobbled then collapsed.

Valma screamed.

"Call Casualty." Emma dropped her bag and flowers on the counter and ran to the security guard. Kneeling by his side, she checked the head wound. It would need stitching. She felt for his pulse, which was erratic then examined his pupils. They were dilated. "Vince, it's Emma. What happened?"

His eyes fluttered. "He snuck up behind me, Doc. I tell ya, my head hurts like I've been on a weeklong bender."

"There's blood everywhere," Wailed Valma, clinging to her husband's hand.

"It's okay, Valma. We'll get Vince straight into emergency."

"What happened?" called Doctor Frobisher as she ran down the hall towards them.

"He was attacked from behind." Emma shifted back so Jessamine Frobisher could take her place. Two nurses and a wardsman pushing a gurney were with her. One of the nurses put her arm around Valma and ushered her towards emergency.

The other nurse, Shaun, helped Emma up. "You're looking a little flushed, Doctor. Go have a cup of tea. We'll take care of Vince."

"Thank you. I appreciate that. I'll ring the police and admin. They'll need to replace Valma." Emma glanced out into the carpark and shivered. Did the attack on Vince have anything to do with her flat tyres? Had that person intended to mug her? Nausea churned as she splayed her hands over her abdomen. Her precious baby might have been hurt. Bindarra Creek was supposed to be a safe haven. What in the world was going on?

CHAPTER 3

*S*omething wasn't right. An urgency to reach Emma as soon as possible gnawed at his gut as Reid straddled his quad bike. She had a lot on her mind with the baby coming soon and making sure her patients were taken care of before she went on parental leave. He could understand how she might get one flat tyre. But two flat tyres? Especially after all the odd things happening at Tulachmhor. He hadn't thought much of the rancid horse feed or the tractor's broken axil shaft until now.

"With me, Gypsy." As soon as his Blue Heeler leaped onto the back tray, he gave the bike full throttle and sped across the field. They both stank like they'd been wrestling in a sewer pit, which was close to the mark.

Where the hell Bob had disappeared to, he couldn't guess. He cursed the farmhand. If he'd been where he was supposed to be, the rams would have been rescued much quicker. Getting the two rams out of the drain alone had been a battle he'd only won through sheer determination, along with a lot of swearing and numerous landings on his butt in the putrid mud. Bob shouldn't have a dog if he couldn't control it.

It was a shame Jerry Eckford had needed the rest of the day off. He would have jumped into the drain and helped Reid get the rams out without a word of complaint. Gypsy only worked cattle. He couldn't trust her with the sheep as she'd nip their back legs. She'd stayed put on the bank today like she'd been trained to do, watching all the action with what could only be described as a grin on her face.

Reid screwed up his nose at the smell coming off his clothes. Emma would wait inside the hospital for him, so he had time to clean up, and Vince would still be there. Reid and several others had badgered the hospital board into employing extra security guards. Expecting staff to leave the hospital in the early hours, after a long night on shift might not worry the bureaucrats, but it worried Reid.

He parked the quad at the back door of his stone cottage. Unlike his estranged mother, Emma never complained about its rustic appearance. Instead, she'd put her warm, colourful touch on it. Not once had she suggested they move up to the main homestead, which had plenty of room. Like him, Emma valued their privacy.

How things had changed in the last five years. His siblings had found happiness and his father was now married to a wonderful woman. It had united two families after more than a century and a half of animosity.

Gypsy flew off the quad to check on the hens scratching in the dirt. Leaving her to it, Reid jogged to the back step and dragged off his muddy boots. He dropped his filthy pants and stripped off his shirt, throwing them in a bucket outside the laundry door. Emma drew the line at foul smelling clothes in the clothes hamper, which he'd never worried about before she pointed out the error of his ways.

It still amazed him that a strange turn of events had brought him and Emma together. He'd meant it to be a short fling, but their physical attraction and her fragile grace had rivetted him. She had a gentle, caring nature; nothing like his mother. What most impressed Reid was her love of children and the babies she delivered and cared for at the hospital. She was made to be a mother and her unexpected pregnancy had put her in seventh heaven, and driven Reid with a single-minded focus to make her his wife.

Enough daydreaming, time to clean up. He grimaced at their external laundry, which also housed the bath-shower combo and a spare toilet. He was running out of time to build Emma a proper bathroom before the baby came. He had to make it a priority.

After he had a thorough wash, Reid quickly dressed then shut the back door and ran to his Landcruiser, whistling for Gypsy.

"With me, girl."

Gypsy came tearing around the side of the cottage, skidding to a halt to sit in front of him, her tongue hanging out, her eyes alight for the next adventure.

"We need to go rescue Emma."

Gypsy barked, her tail wagging with her excitement. There was only one thing better than a day on the farm with her master, and that was to welcome Emma home.

"Crazy girl. Let's go." He opened the rear hatch and stood back. "Come up."

Gypsy leaped into the rear of the Landcruiser and waited for him to attach a lead to her harness that would keep her safe on their journey into town. "All done." He ruffled her head then shut the door. He was about to open his own door when he caught a whiff of smoke.

"Fire!" He tore his door open and jumped in, gunning the engine and spraying gravel as he hit the accelerator hard. A spiral of grey smoke wove its way above the hayshed.

Reid skidded to a stop beside the shed. Ignoring Gypsy's frantic barks, he leaped out and grabbed the fire extinguisher from the back compartment, before sprinting into the shed. Bob lay against a bale, snoring his head off, an empty bottle of whisky beside him. Reid pulled the extinguisher's pin and foamed the flaming bales by the door. He'd got there in the nick of time.

With the flames out, Reid tossed the extinguisher aside, strode over to Bob, and dragged him up by the collar, shaking hard. "Wake up, you drunken sod."

"Wha… What's happening?" Bob's slurred words only enraged Reid further.

"You almost burned the hayshed down. You're done here, Bob. I'll pay what you're owed, but I never want to see you on Tulachmhor again, and don't expect a reference. If anyone enquires about you, I will tell them you're a lazy menace."

"Yeah, yeah, whatever." Bob staggered to his feet and lurched out of the shed, making for his battered utility.

"You're in no condition to drive, Bob." Reid strode after him. "I'll drop you and your dog in town. Jerry will bring your utility in tomorrow."

"I'd rather hitch a ride." Bob gave Reid the bird then stumbled down the uneven track.

"Don't forget your dog. He's tied up near the main barn."

"Useless mutt. I should've put a bullet between its eyes months ago. Save me feeding it."

"In that case, leave him here. My sister-in-law will see he goes to a good home."

"Hell, if I care. You think you're better than me, with that stuck-up doctor and your prize rams, but good things don't last forever, mate. It can all be gone like that." He clicked his fingers then spat on the ground before stumbling away, leaving Reid shaking his head in disgust.

Tomorrow, he'd take Rob's dog to Chelsea. She had a knack for finding good homes for unwanted animals. Today had been one step forward, two back.

Adding to his filthy mood, the jolting trip to the front gate reminded Reid he needed to grade the drive. These holes had to be responsible for Emma's tyres going down. He added the task to his mental checklist of things to do asap. Running a property the size Tulachmhor gave him a new respect for all the years his father had run it on his own.

Reid drove to the hospital's parking lot and pulled up beside Emma's car. It lacked air-conditioning and easy access to the back seat, which she needed for the baby. He didn't care if she kept the Beetle, but they needed to buy a new car suitable for transporting Emma and the baby in comfort.

Gypsy howled like a wolf, her gaze glued to the hospital's entrance doors.

Reid chuckled. "I don't think they'd welcome you in there, girl."

He strode to the back and opened the rear hatch. It was getting dark, and several drops of rain hit his face. He noticed lights blazing in the Men's Shed and a police wagon parked outside. *Hope it wasn't a break-in.*

He pulled on his jacket to block the chilly breeze. *Hell, it wouldn't hurt the hospital board to approve undercover parking for their staff and visitors.* Steel beams and a metal roof would do the trick. He'd put a petition together and get as many signatures as he could.

Gypsy panted patiently as he released the lead from her harness. Once free, she leaped out of the rear compartment and took off like the hounds of hell were chasing her, straight to the glass entrance doors. She sat down to wait, tongue lolling, tail twitching as the doors opened and closed, all due to her proximity.

Grabbing his electric pump from the Landcruiser, he inflated one tyre only to watch it deflate again. Two sharp barks drew his attention back to the hospital. Emma hurried towards him with a huge bunch of flowers, looking about as if checking for cars. He was pleased to see her rugged up in a coat, knee high boots and a beanie. Not so pleased to see Gypsy jumping around Emma excitedly. He whistled. "Steady, girl."

The dog immediately calmed to trot by Emma's side.

Reid took the time to appreciate the willowy blonde he'd fallen in love with. Her pregnancy only made her more beautiful. Her dark, chocolaty eyes glowed with vitality and amusement. There was a serenity about her that always soothed his emotions.

"I wish Gypsy would do that for me." Emma stretched up to kiss him. "Hello, darling. Thank you for coming to my rescue." She placed the flowers on his bonnet then wrapped her arms around him and squeezed tight, their baby nestled safely between them. "You're so warm."

He hugged her just as tight; gratitude settling over him just from having her in his arms.

She glanced over towards Men's Shed and shuddered. "There was someone over there earlier. Vince went to check and was attacked from behind."

"Hell. Is he okay?"

"He has a nasty contusion on his head and will probably spend a couple of days in hospital under observation. After I gave Abby Taylor my statement, I popped into emergency, but Vince was having an Xray. I can't believe someone attacked him."

"Sadly, it happens." Reid kissed her forehead. "I've inflated one tyre, but it's gone down again. The other has a tear, so you're going to need new tyres."

"Do we have time to get them now? I want to get away early tomorrow."

"No, it's too late and those clouds are going to dump on us any minute. You can drop me at Hunter's house in the morning and take the Landcruiser to Armidale. I'll fit new tyres then head home to work on the fence with Hunter and Jerry."

"Thank you, darling. I appreciate you giving up your car."

"It's a small thing compared to what you do for me, Emma."

She scoffed. "What do I do for you? I'm hopeless around the sheep and cattle. I can't stand the smell of manure and I'm a terrible cook. You should be marrying a woman who can help you run Tulachmhor."

"Hey, what's all this about?" He hugged her tighter. "You've made our cottage into a beautiful home, and you spoil me. I can always count on a smile and a kiss." He opened his passenger door. "You might not be comfortable around cattle, Emma, but you've brought me more happiness in the last two years than I can ever remember."

"You make me happy too, darling. I'm sorry it took so long for me to commit to a wedding date. It wasn't that I don't love you. It was because I kept expecting you to … to realise how unsuitable I am. I don't want you to regret marrying me."

"Never." He pulled her woollen beanie lower, covering her ears completely. "You've changed my life for the better, Em."

She smiled. "I'm glad. I want a wonderful, happy child-hood for our baby."

Reid rolled his shoulders. Talking about his mother always left him edgy, but Emma deserved to know the truth. He handed her into the car. "I'll tell you about my childhood, as long as you tell me what's really bothering you."

"I'm an open book. What you see, is what you get."

"Then why do I sometimes feel like you're walking on eggshells around me? Why do you withdraw when I'm having a heated conversation with Hunter or Dad?"

She wriggled back in the seat. "I don't like confrontations, especially between people who are supposed to care about each other."

Reid frowned. When he'd first met Emma, she'd told him she'd moved to Bindarra Creek for a break from the stress of working long hours at a frantic pace. He wasn't so sure. If anything, she was extremely composed under pressure. He knew her previous relationship ended because the guy had an affair. He suspected that was the reason she hadn't wanted a serious relationship. Luckily, fate had intervened.

"Does it have something to do with your last boyfriend?"

"No. Not at all. I … I just don't like nasty confrontations."

"Fair enough, but I can't help feeling you're afraid of me sometimes." She was hiding something, he knew it. "I will never raise a hand to you, Emma. My mother was a violent person. She physically and verbally took her temper out on us. I will never forgive her for the fear she instilled in us as children. It had a lasting effect on us. But you and our children will never face that. You will always be safe with me."

"Thank you." She squeezed his hand. "I don't want walls between us."

"I agree. Now stay in the car where it's warm. I'll put your flowers in the back and I won't be long." He closed the door and zipped up his jacket. The bitter wind cut into him as he strode to the front of Emma's Beetle and checked the air pressure in her spare tyre. It was fine but wouldn't have been much help if she'd been stuck on Reservoir Road. Anyone could have come along. A shiver ran down his spine. If anything happened to Emma or their baby, he'd never recover. They'd become more important to him than anyone else or Tulachmhor, and that was saying something.

CHAPTER 4

*A*fter a relaxing bath, Emma cuddled up to Reid on their lumpy sofa. Another thing she planned to update in the near future. She needed to find a comfortable three-seater as Reid liked to lean back and stretch out his legs or lay with his head on her lap. He loved it when she ran her fingers through his hair or massaged the tension out of his neck.

Gypsy curled up in front of the fire, content to have her people where she could keep an eye on them. It was a small cottage, but Emma's flowers looked beautiful on their dining table. This was her favourite time of the day. Knowing Vince would recover without any lasting ill effects was a bonus. As often happened, her gaze lifted to the huge print above the fireplace. Reid, wearing his Akubra and holding a trophy, sat astride his powerful, grey gelding. Both man and animal radiated an air of confidence, command and controlled energy. The photo had been taken after Reid had won a camp drafting competition six or seven years ago. The photographer had undeniably captured the essence of Reid.

Emma cuddled closer to the love of her life. During

dinner they'd discussed the multitude of problems Reid had faced over the last week. They laughed over the antics of Stanthorpe as Reid tried to get him and the other ram out of the drain. And afterwards they sat on the front porch, rugged up as they watched the sun go down. Once a week they had dinner with Reid's entire family, which included Emma's three cousins and eight tiny tots. Quite often her grandmother, Aunt Hannah and Uncle James joined them too. It always ended up a great night. This coming Christmas Day lunch would be a huge gathering as Emma's her parents and sister had promised to come.

Emma loved working at Bindarra Creek Hospital, with the capable and friendly staff. Being welcomed into the Sullivan clan had been the icing on the cake. She'd never felt so content, happy or safe. All she needed now was to vanquish the nagging fear that Reid might one day change or come to despise her the way Glenn had.

She glanced from their joined hands to Reid's handsome face. He was dead to the world, exhausted. He worked hard to make Tulachmhor a successful Merino stud as well as helping his father breed healthy Hereford cattle.

Emma chewed her lip. As Reid had sacked Bob Farrell today, and his father was on a well-earned holiday, the last thing he needed was the extra work of building a fence. At least Hunter would help, but he still ran the stock and station real-estate office.

A sigh escaped. If she could do more, she would, but her pregnancy put a lot of things off limits. Her fear around cattle would have to be worked on.

A low growl erupted from Gypsy's throat.

"What is it, girl?" Emma eased her hand from Reid's. "Is it a fox?" Emma froze. She hadn't put the hens in their chook shed.

Gypsy trotted to the back door and whined.

"I'm coming, girl." Emma glanced at Reid. He was sound asleep, and she really didn't want to wake him. If a fox was hanging around, Gypsy would chase it away. She prayed it wasn't a wild dog or that any of her hens had been taken. She'd raised all six from day old chicks. A major achievement in her book.

She grabbed Reid's Akubra, the torch and his oilskin jacket off the wall hooks then shoved her feet into his huge gumboots, thankful for her thick, woollen socks. She still had way too much room, but she didn't fancy sinking her runners into oozing mud. With all the rain that had fallen over the last few hours, it would be a quagmire out there.

As soon as Emma opened the back door, Gypsy took off into the darkness, sounding more like a ferocious guard dog than a happy-go-lucky Blue Heeler. The back awning only just gave Emma enough shelter to button up the oilskin jacket. She planted Reid's Akubra firmly on her head then stepped out into sheeting rain, gasping at the cold sting against her face and hands. She trudged across the soaked grass to the hen's enclosure, shining her torch about, fearful of coming face to face with a fox or a dingo. They'd be wary of humans, which should relieve her mind. It didn't.

The gate was shut and bolted. Relief surged. Reid had put the hens away. To be sure she shone the torch at the hen house. All was quiet, so what disturbed Gypsy?

A high-pitched yelping had Emma swinging around. She cried out as Reid's boots stuck in the mud, sending her careening off balance into the gate as a loud crack of thunder boomed overhead. Something pinged loudly in her ear. She'd probably broken the gate's hinges, but at least she wasn't now sitting in the mud with a bruised bottom. Taking a shaky breath, she pulled the boots free, checked the gate, which appeared sturdy then made her way back to the house.

The back door swung open, and Reid stepped out. "I heard Gypsy yelp. What happened?"

"I don't know. We came out to put the hens away, but you'd already done it. Gypsy! Come on, sweetie. Time to go inside."

Gypsy slinked around the side of the cottage, her head low, her tail between her legs.

"What made you yelp, girl?" Emma rubbed the dog's head. "Are you okay? Did you chase a naughty fox away?"

Gypsy sat at Emma's feet, licking at her hind leg. She suddenly stared out into the dark, her teeth bared, and growling low as if she sensed something still out there.

"Come on, girl." Reid held the door open for Emma and Gypsy then shut it firmly, locking out the cold night air.

Emma pulled her freezing feet out of Reid's gumboots then hung his oil-skin coat on the hook. "It's so cold out there."

Reid's gaze shifted to Gypsy, still growling at the back door. "Something is upsetting her. I'll look around." After pulling on his oil-skin coat and Akubra, he pushed his feet into the gumboots. "Leave the chooks to me from now on. You need to take things easy."

"You were tired, I didn't want to wake you."

"Doesn't matter. You and our baby are too important. Wake me next time? I'll be back in a minute." He took the torch and opened the door. "Stay, Gypsy."

The Blue Heeler whimpered, but did as Reid instructed, leaving paw prints and droplets of mud across the rug as she slinked to her bed by the fire.

Emma put the kettle on and scooped a couple of spoons of milo into two cups. Once the kettle boiled, she filled the cups, added milk then carried them to the coffee table. She glanced at the back door, wondering what was taking Reid so long.

The ominous sound of retching had her whirling around. "Gypsy, what's wrong?"

Her fur baby panted and drooled over a pile of vomit in her bed. Tremors racked her muscular frame. There was a pool of blood beside the dog bed.

Emma ran to the back door and screamed, "Reid, Gypsy's hurt."

He came striding from around the side of the cottage, brushed past her then ran to his dog, leaving chunks of mud and boot prints on the wooden floor and rug.

Emma covered her mouth, trying not to cry as she sank to her knees beside Gypsy, watching as Reid examined his faithful dog. This was her fault. If she'd shut in the hens earlier, it wouldn't have happened. "That's blood on the floor. I heard her yelp."

"She's bleeding, but there's too much blood for a snake bite. I found fresh boot prints all around the house. They're not mine."

"What?" Emma shivered. The thought of a stranger or vagrant hanging around their cottage on a night like this had her stomach clenching. "Should we give her milk and make her vomit again?"

"No, but she does need a vet. The vomiting could mean she's been baited." He ran his hands over Gypsy. "What the blazes? There's a hole in her hind leg." His startled eyes pinned Emma. "It looks like a bullet hole."

"It can't be. I would have heard the gunshot."

"Maybe the thunder disguised it." A crack of thunder gave credence to his words. "Gypsy must have heard something. She could have eaten the bait then caught someone's scent and gone after them."

"Who would do something so evil?"

"I can only think of one person who might have a grudge

against me. I'll talk to Riley tomorrow. It's times like this, I'm glad my sister is married to a cop."

"You think it's Bob Farrell?"

"I can't think of anyone else. Can you?"

Someone with a grudge against her. Yes. Although she couldn't imagine *him* baiting or shooting a dog. He wouldn't even have come to mind, except Brenda had mentioned him.

"We'll know soon enough." Reid picked Gypsy up and turned for the door. "Bring your phone. Once we're in the Cruiser, ring Jake and Ali. Tell them Gypsy might have been baited and shot, and that we're on our way to the clinic. Then ring Jerry … no not Jerry, he'll be in town at the darts competition. Ring my grandmother and tell her to lock her doors, and ring Hunter. Tell him what's happened and ask him to spend the night up at the main house." He ran out the door.

Emma pushed her feet into her runners, not bothering to untie the laces first. It didn't matter. What mattered was getting Gypsy to Jake and Ali. She snatched a jumper, her bag and Reid's phone off the kitchen counter and ran after him, locking the door behind her.

"Yuck." She sloshed through the thick mud, cringing as it sucked at the soles of her shoes. Rain mingled with her tears as she reached the Landcruiser. Reid laid Gypsy on the back seat, jumped in the front seat, and had the engine running before she closed her door. "I'm so sorry, Reid."

"You're not responsible, Emma. We can be grateful the Cruiser locks automatically, or it might have been stolen. Buckle up then make those calls."

"Okay." She had Ali's number in her close contacts. The children would be asleep, but with luck Jake and Ali were still awake. The ringing went on and on, seemingly forever until a gruff voice answered. "Jake Morgan here."

"Jake, it's Emma. Reid thinks Gypsy's been baited and shot. Can you meet us at your clinic?"

"Are you serious? Who did it?"

"We don't know, but Reid found footprints. I took Gypsy outside with me to check on the hens. I didn't realise she'd been hurt until she vomited, and I saw the blood."

"Calm down, Emma. I'm on my way."

"Thank you." She turned to Reid. "Jake will meet us at the clinic."

"This isn't your fault, Em. I would have let Gypsy out before we went to bed."

Emma gasped. "Then she'd have gone to her bed by the fire and died, wouldn't she?"

"Maybe not. She's a clever girl. I'd like to think she'd let us know she wasn't well."

"I hope Jake can save her." Emma glanced between the seats at Gypsy, still drooling as tremors racked her body. "When you're feeling better, I'll get you the biggest bone I can find."

Gypsy whimpered and closed her eyes.

"Hurry, Reid. I think she's unconscious."

He had the wipers going flat out, yet still had to lean over the steering wheel, squinting through the windscreen. How he could negotiate the twists and bends of the road, she didn't know. All she could see through the headlight beams was a solid wall of rain coming at them in gusts.

After Emma spoke to Kathleen Sullivan, she tried Hunter's phone twice. It kept going to voice mail, so she rang her Uncle James, who agreed to drive over and check on Kathleen.

Twenty minutes later, Reid slid to a stop behind Jake's van, outside J & A Morgan Veterinary Clinic. The lights were on and the front door wide. Emma climbed out, shut the car door, and ran after Reid.

Jake met them at the door and waved Reid past. "Take her through to the operating theatre. I've got everything ready." His glance swept from Emma's dripping hair, over her damp jumper, down to her mud-splattered leggings and filthy shoes. "This could take a while, Emma. You're shivering. Ali has spare clothes in the locker in her office. Take whatever you need."

"Thanks. I might have a quick shower to warm me up if that's okay."

"Good idea." Jake shut and locked the front door then turned back to her. "After your shower, have something hot to drink." He gave her a stern do-as-I-say look, which made him look even more like his identical twin. No wonder most people couldn't tell them apart. He pointed to the door with the sign that read *staff only* before striding into an examination room and closing the door firmly behind him.

Despite the warmth of the clinic's central heating, a cold chill seeped into her bones. A hot shower, dry clothes and a cup of tea would do wonders and keep her from catching a chill.

Twenty minutes later, hair dry and wearing Ali's warm tracksuit pants, thick socks, a T-shirt and woollen jumper, Emma sat at the clinic's kitchen table, sipping herbal tea. Reid had stuck his head into the bathroom earlier to check on her then gone back to Gypsy. A yawn escaped. There was no way she'd be driving to Armidale tomorrow.

A fire engine screamed past with its siren blaring. She hoped it wasn't a car accident. This was a terrible night to be on the road. She sent off a text to her parents, explaining what had happened. Maybe they could bring Lindsay and the baby to the cottage for lunch on Sunday. Afterwards her father could help Reid, while she sorted the final arrangements out with her mother and sister.

She jumped at the ringing of her phone. It was almost

eleven. She checked the ID and swallowed. It was her uncle. She prayed all was well with Kathleen.

"Uncle James?"

"Hello, love. Can I speak to Reid please?"

"He's still in the operating theatre with Jake." Her heart raced. "Is everything okay?"

"Not really. Your cottage caught fire."

"What?" Emma clutched her free hand to her chest. "Are you sure?"

"Kathleen saw the flames from her window. She'd already phoned Jerry and the fire brigade before I got there."

Emma's phone shook as a sense of dread invaded her veins. Too many things were happening to be brushed aside. Bob Farrell wasn't a nice man, but to shoot Gypsy and burn down their cottage was seriously deranged. What else was he capable of?

"I loved that cottage." A sob escaped. "Reid's going to be devastated."

"I know, love. Thank heavens Jerry was home. He managed to get some water onto the flames before the fire brigade turned up."

"My hens?"

"They're fine. How's Gypsy?"

"I don't know. Reid popped out earlier to check on me. He said Jake did an X-ray, which showed a bullet, but I don't know any more. Did you check on Tom's kelpies?"

"Don't worry about the dogs, they're inside with Kathleen. I don't know what condition the cottage will be left in, Emma."

"I'll ... let Reid know." She hung up then leaned on her arms and sobbed. Their beautiful stone cottage. All the hours Reid had spent sanding back and staining the cradle for nothing. It had been passed down through several generations of Sullivans. Their baby's hand knitted jackets, bonnets, blankets, and booties, all made by the dotting great-grand-mothers. Were they all destroyed?

"Emma?" Reid scooped her into his arms and sat on the chair, cradling her in his arms. "Gypsy's going to be fine. Jake removed the bullet and has her on intravenous fluids. We got her here in time. It's all good."

"I'm … so … glad." It was too much to deal with. She shook her head, blubbering into the T-shirt Jake had lent him. "The … cottage … A fire."

"What?"

"My uncle … just rang. Our cottage … is on fire."

"How? All that was left of the logs were embers, and the metal screen would block them from falling out anyway." He scowled. "The door was locked. It must be an electrical fault. If we'd been there, I could have put the fire out. To lose the cottage … It means … meant so much to my family."

"This is all my fault. You've lost everything because of me."

"Emma. We haven't lost everything. We have each other. Our baby is safe, and Gypsy is on the mend. You are not to blame, love. It's just been one hell of a day."

"But the cottage? Where are we going to live?"

"There's plenty of room up at the main house. Dad and Antonia won't be back from Darwin for another week. Gran will be glad to have us stay with her. Or Hunter can find us somewhere to rent if you want to live in town." The lack of enthusiasm in his voice drove another arrow of guilt through her heart.

"I don't need to live in town, Reid. I was happy with you in the cottage."

"We can build a new cottage, Emma. It's not the end of the world."

She tried to smile, but it was more of a grimace. "That

was your great-great grandparents' home. It had historical and sentimental value to your family."

"I know, but we've dealt with far worse disasters over the years. It's just one of those things. At least Gypsy will recover."

He was taking the disaster awfully well. He hadn't yelled at her once. Would he stay calm and controlled? Was he reining in his temper because of the baby? Would he one day turn on her the way Glenn had?

His arms tightened. "We have insurance, Em. Hopefully, once the fire investigators have done their job, we'll know how the fire started."

"What if it's not Bob Farrell? What if it's someone with a grudge against … me?"

"Who? You don't have an enemy in the world."

She squeezed her eyes shut and buried her face against his chest. *I might. A narcissistic control freak who swore vengeance on me.*

CHAPTER 5

*W*ithin minutes of leaving town, Reid looked for the orange glow of fire in the direction of Tulachmhor. Jake had offered to take Emma back to his place, where no doubt Ali would pack her off to bed. Emma had hugged her cousin and stubbornly refused the offer.

Since leaving the clinic, Emma hadn't said a word. The wall between them had thickened. She sat stiffly beside him, her hands clutched tightly in her lap, staring out the windscreen into the misty rain. Only a deluge would put the fire out.

How had their happy life turned into turmoil and uncertainty? He couldn't comprehend why Emma would think someone had it in for her, but the fact she'd suggested it had him worried.

"Emma, talk to me. Why would anyone hold a grudge against you?"

She shuddered, flicking him a quick glance then dropping her gaze to her hands. "Five years ago, I was engaged to a doctor named Glenn Hanson."

"Engaged?" Reid's gut clenched. Why had she never told him that? "What went wrong?"

"Everything. We became friends during our internships at the same hospital. We started dating and a few months later, he suggested we get married. He was my first serious boyfriend. I wasn't ready to get married. I suggested moving in together would be a good way to make sure we were compatible."

Jealousy streaked through Reid, leaving him restless and aggravated. He knew he was being hypocritical. He'd hooked up with his fair share of women, but he'd only ever had a real relationship with Emma. He'd only ever wanted to marry Emma. Tension pulsed through his body as he negotiated several bends on Reservoir Road. "What happened?"

"He pushed and pushed until I agreed to a date." Emma expelled a shaky breath. "Then he started complaining about trivial things. How I made the bed. The cushions I bought to brighten up the sofa. Not telling him I'd had lunch with Brenda in the hospital café. His jealousy got worse. He didn't like me spending time with Brenda or driving to Armidale to visit my parents. I never seemed to say the right thing. He was under pressure at work, and I tried to be mindful of that, but so was I. My unpredictable hours annoyed him. I threatened to call off the wedding if he didn't change his attitude. He apologised and promised to try, but it left me on tenterhooks."

"I can see why."

She shifted in her seat, rubbing her belly. "A week before the wedding, I came home late from shopping with Brenda. He grabbed my arm and twisted it behind my back because I smelled of perfume. I'd gone to help her choose a dress and a nice perfume for a date. He refused to believe me and accused me of cheating on him."

Emma smoothed her hands along her thighs, lost in the past for a moment.

"Go on, Em. What happened?" Reid concentrated on the road, looking for their turn onto Wallaby Flats Road.

"I told him we were over. He threw me against a wall. He said I belonged to him and no one else. And all the time he'd been seeing someone behind my back."

Reid's hold on the steering wheel had tightened until his fingers ached. He flexed them to get the blood circulating again. This was why she hated confrontations and raised voices. Why she'd taken so long to commit to a wedding date. "How'd you get away?"

"I waited until he fell asleep then sneaked out. I applied for immediate stress leave, cancelled the wedding, and hid at Brenda's apartment. She suggested I apply for a job outside Sydney, somewhere he wouldn't think to look for me."

"Bindarra Creek." Reid reached for her hand and squeezed. "Great choice."

"At first my parents and sister were devasted I'd cancelled the wedding. They really liked Glenn. They changed their minds when I told them how he'd been treating me. My mother rang Uncle James, who told Aunt Hannah and my cousins. Chelsea started emailing me ads for jobs in this region. Jake and Riley offered to warn Glenn off from ever contacting me, but I didn't want them to get into trouble, or for him to discover my whereabouts."

"Wise decision." Reid could well imagine the Morgan twins heading to Sydney to threaten a bully away from their cousin. He and Hunter had tangled with Jake and Riley enough on the football field to know it wouldn't be pretty. "So, you applied for the job here."

"Yes. The hospital board did a phone interview, checked my references, and offered me the job two days later. I only told Brenda. Once we knew Glenn was at work, we went to the apartment to pack my things. I left the engagement ring and a note that I'd cancelled the wedding and never wanted to see him again. The rest you know."

"Did he try to contact you?"

"Yes. I wouldn't answer his calls, so he sent texts, demanding I return to the apartment, and he'd forgive me." Her sarcastic laugh was so unlike Emma, Reid flinched.

"He sent texts promising retribution for stringing him along and being deceitful."

"You're kidding." Reid wanted to throttle the guy. "He sounds like a nut case."

"He was lovely when we met but he changed so drastically, he could have been another person. Even Brenda thought I was exaggerating. In the end, I got a new number."

"Glenn Hanson." Reid filed the name away. "What kind of doctor is he?"

"An orthopaedic surgeon." Emma reached out and lay her hand on Reid's thigh. "I had a call from Brenda today. She said Glenn has been put on leave, pending an investigation into verbal abuse and being under the influence of drugs while on duty."

Reid raised an eyebrow. "Hell, if the allegations are proven, there goes his career."

Her fingers tightened on his thigh. "I should have told you all this a long time ago, but I'd lost so much self-esteem in Sydney. Here I became the person I used to be. Happy and carefree. Independent and respected. It's because of my trust issues, I decided to stay single. I never wanted to feel vulnerable or frightened again." She drew her hand back and placed it on her belly. "I won't allow any person to put me in that position again."

Her warning sent a shiver down Reid's spine. "Emma, arguing is normal. Tempers get heated, especially between me and Hunter. That doesn't mean we get into physical altercations. Think of it as a heated discussion to get each other's point of view across."

Reid slowed for the final bend. The rain had stopped. "Rest assured, Emma, I will never verbally or physically abuse you, no matter what." He lay his hand on her knee. "We may have the odd disagreement, or heated argument, but I swear I will protect you and any children we have until the day I die. Having said that, I need you to talk to me if something is bothering you."

"I heard you and Hunter have had physical altercations with Jake and Riley in the past."

He huffed. "That was because of the feud started by our great-great-great grandfathers. We have riled each other and competed against each other since we were kids. Most of our school holidays were spent trying to outdo each other. We made sure we were on opposite teams on the football field, so we could target each other. As I've been told many times, if not for the feud, we would have been best friends."

"Which you are now." She placed her hand over his. "I've been looking forward to our wedding so much, then today all these old anxieties bombarded me. I know I didn't shoot or bait Gypsy or start the fire, but I keep expecting you to blame me."

"Everyone needs to let off steam, Emma. I do it when things go wrong, or I'm frustrated." He'd been expecting to see the glow of fire as they turned into Tulachmhor and was surprised not to see it. Maybe the rain had spared part of the cottage. He could hope. He drove through the open gate, relieved he'd decided to move the cattle before they'd started on the postholes.

Emma sniffed. "Why would Bob Farrell want to hurt Gypsy?"

"To get even with me. It's possible he hadn't expected her to track him and when she did, he panicked. Most likely, the

fire is due to an electrical fault. We'll know soon enough."
The hairs on the back of Reid's neck bristled. If not, they had
a major problem. Bindarra Creek was a long way from
Sydney, but he'd ask Riley to make some discreet enquiries
about Doctor Glenn Hanson. As Senior Sergeant, Riley could
check into Hanson's whereabouts. Being a narcissist was one
thing, if the man was unhinged, Emma and the baby could be
in danger. Five years had passed. It seemed unlikely he'd be
targeting her now, but who knew how the man's mind
worked?

Reid glanced across at Emma. She'd closed her eyes and
had one arm protectively wrapped around her swollen belly.
It had been a rough night for her. He drove up Tulachmhor's
front drive then branched off towards their cottage. He
noticed Jerry Eckford's utility out front of the cottage. Riley's
patrol car and the fire engine were round the back. All the
vehicles' headlights lit up the cottage.

His breath left him as he stared at the burned-out shell of
the weatherboard laundry. The flames had been extin-
guished, although spirals of grey smoke rose from the wet
ash, where the add-on used to be. The sandstone bricks on
the back wall of the hundred-year-old cottage were
completely blackened, but salvageable. The guttering and
part of the roof had melted into a twisted mess. The kitchen
window had shattered. There would be smoke and water
damage. Unbelievably, the rest of the cottage looked intact.

Reid killed the engine and let out a thankful breath.
Losing the cottage would have devasted the whole family. It
could have been so much worse. He would extend and build
a new internal bathroom, laundry, and a larger bedroom
with an ensuite. He'd give Emma a bigger kitchen to practice
her cooking skills and a wraparound verandah where they
could sit and watch the sun go down. He'd take a leaf out of
her book and turn this near disaster into a positive outcome.

"It's like a bomb hit it." Emma's broken voice had him pulling her into his arms.

"We can fix it, Em."

A tap on his side window had Reid opening his door. Riley ducked to look past Reid to Emma. "Hey, cuz, how you doin'?"

"Hey, Riley." She sniffed.

"Can you tell how the fire started?" Reid climbed out to stare at the mess.

"The chief's on it, but it's early days yet. Could be electrical, could be something else." Riley shrugged. "Kel said the fire took hold extremely fast and there's several locations of localised burning, which *may* indicate an accelerant of some kind. We'll know more once the samples he's taken are examined. You're lucky Kathleen saw the flames and Jerry Eckford got here so quickly."

Emma marched around the front of the car to stand beside Reid. Her hand over her mouth as she scanned the back of the cottage. He put his arm around her waist then returned his attention to Riley. "You're saying it *is* arson?"

"No, I'm saying it's a possibility." Riley pulled out his notebook. "Jake told me Gypsy was shot. Talk me through what happened tonight."

Reid opened his mouth, but Emma got in first, detailing everything that had happened until Reid woke up then he took over. When they both fell silent, Riley glanced about. "Have you had any trouble with pig or roo shooters on Tulachmhor recently?"

"None."

"I hear you sacked a farm hand today?"

"I did. Name's Bob Farrell. He was always late, often hungover, and lazy. Today his dog chased two of my rams into a deep drain. Bob disappeared when he knew I needed help. He hid out in the hay shed, smoking, and drinking until he passed out." Reid ran a hand through his hair. "If I hadn't seen smoke, he would have been badly burned, possibly dead. He almost cost me a shed full of hay."

"I don't know the man. Is he the type to bait and shoot a dog, or start a fire deliberately?"

Reid exhaled. "I don't know. He blew into town, desperate for a job a few weeks ago. When I dismissed him, he made a comment about me thinking I'm better than him and everything I have could disappear with the click of his fingers. I suspect he baited Gypsy, and then shot her because he thought she was about to attack him, but to set the cottage alight is extreme, even if he knew we weren't home."

"I'll talk to him. You're lucky it's only the laundry that got destroyed. Any chance either of you left the dryer on?" Riley directed his question at Emma.

"No, we haven't used it for a couple of days, and it's always switched off at the plug."

Riley scribbled in his notebook. "What time did you head into town?"

"I'm guessing just after ten o'clock," answered Reid.

"Okay." Riley's gaze flicked from Emma to Reid. "Dad checked around the main house and spoke to Kathleen. No sign anyone has been up there. Jerry told me Bob Farrell is living at the caravan Park, so once Kel and his team are done, I'll head into town and speak to him.

Reid squeezed her hand. "We'll get to the bottom of this, Emma."

"You bet we will." Riley's serious eyes settled on Emma. "Kel will have a good idea what started the fire. Aside from that, until we catch the person who shot Gypsy and the person who attacked Vince Stark, I want you both to be careful. They're probably not connected, but don't take any chances. We have a nut on the loose with a gun. I want him locked up."

CHAPTER 6

*E*mma opened her eyes to a dark room, although slivers of daylight peeped through the sides of the drapes. She reached out only to find the sheets beside her empty. Reid rose early every morning, but she'd thought he might sleep in today. He'd tossed and turned most of the night. They'd barely spoken after leaving the smoky, water-damaged cottage. It needed airing and cleaning before they could move back in, which meant they'd be living with Kathleen for the next week, at least.

Tulachmhor's homestead was a stunning ancestral home. Emma looked forward to every celebration hosted in the beautiful house, but it wasn't her home. She knew too many women in one house didn't work. Her mother had always ruled the kitchen, dispatching Emma, and Lindsay to set the table or cut flowers whenever they came together for a family meal. Vanessa Fahey liked her furniture, cutlery drawers and linen cupboard a certain way. Washing was done on a Wednesday unless it rained. Thursday was shopping day. Monday was for cleaning the house. Sunday lunch was always a lamb roast.

As for Emma's dad, John Fahey still taught secondary school Mathematics and ruled over his vegetable garden with his treasured fork and shovel. As long as he ate his rolled oats every morning, saw the evening news and his dinner was on the table at seven, he was a happy camper.

Emma and her sister, Lindsey, didn't work that way, which is why they'd left home to follow their dreams. Her younger sister couldn't care less when things got done or if they got done at all. She spent most of her day on her potting wheel or in her shop, selling what she created. Being married and having a baby hadn't changed anything. Luckily, Otis was a placid baby and went with the flow.

In Emma's case, she was a minimalist. She liked a few scatter cushions but wasn't into frills and ornaments. She liked her house clean and tidy, but she had no special days to do specific jobs. Everything got done around her working hours. Reid didn't seem to mind. He was happy to cook dinner if she was late home. He made his own breakfast through the week, as he rose so early. On the weekends they cooked breakfast together, taking their time to enjoy the slower pace, often sitting on their tiny porch to drink their coffee as they watched calves frolic or a mob of kangaroos grazing. Some mornings they'd see one of Tulachmhor's eagles circling high above, searching for a tasty meal to take back to the nest.

With a sigh, she pushed the covers aside. She loved Tulachmhor. The peace and quiet called to her. Living here with Reid in their little cottage had been a healing experience. Now the cottage would need extensive cleaning and drying out before they could even begin to repair the damage. They had no choice but to stay with Reid's family, who were wonderful, but it wouldn't be the same. They'd have little privacy.

"I'm thinking like a spoilt brat. We are alive. Gypsy is

alive. The baby is safe. We can fix the cottage. I love Reid's family." She padded over to the window and drew the vertical drapes open, taking time to look out over a field of sheep to Eagle Rock, a silent sentry overshadowing Tulachmhor's rolling acres. Five horses grazed leisurely in the paddock next to the stables. Everything would work out. Hopefully, it wouldn't take too long to fix the roof, replace a few windows, and rebuild a laundry.

Her phone trilled from inside her bag. She groaned on recognising her father's number. She'd have to put her parents off coming to Bindarra Creek tomorrow. "Hi, Dad."

"Emma, we've just had a call from Lindsay. She said Reid's dog was shot and an arsonist set the cottage alight. Is that true?"

Emma closed her eyes. She'd forgotten about Bindarra Creek's notorious grapevine. Its tentacles reached far and wide extremely fast. "Reid's dog was shot, but we don't know the cause of the fire yet."

"Right. Well, your mother and I think it best you move back home until the wedding."

"No, Dad. I'm staying with Reid at the main house. Riley is investigating the shooting and the fire."

"I don't like it, Emma. We had a call from Glenn a few days ago. He asked for your phone number and address. Your mother refused and told him not to call again."

"Did he say why he's looking for me?" Emma's heart hammered in her chest.

"No, he didn't, love."

A shiver ran down her back then her phone beeped with another call. It was Reid. "I have to go, Dad, I've got another call coming through."

"Righto, love. Be careful."

"I will. Bye, Dad."

She ended the call and swiped at her screen. "Reid?"

"Hi, Emma. I'm over at the cottage with Riley. You're on loudspeaker."

"Is everything okay?"

"I've got some bad news."

Emma sucked in a breath. *What now?* "Tell me."

"Dodge Myers checked on your Beetle this morning. It's been vandalised since last night. It could be teenagers, who thought slashing your other two tyres would be funny, but Riley doesn't think so." There was a graveness in Reid's voice that worried her.

"Is it only my tyres?"

"Your windows were smashed, so there's water damage from the storm last night, and your bonnet and roof have been graffitied."

"Graffitied as in their tags or words?"

"The words are not important, Emma," barked Reid. "What is important is you are not to go anywhere on your own."

"What did they write?" Emma sank to the bed. "Tell me."

"Your time is coming," answered Riley. "It's a threat we are taking seriously, Emma, especially after what happened here last night and the attack on Vince. After Abby took your statement and Vince's statement, she walked around the Men's Shed and your car. Only two tyres were down, and your Beetle wasn't vandalised. That was done later."

She shivered. "Someone was standing there, watching me. Maybe vandalising my car was payback for reporting them to Vince?"

"Possibly," muttered Riley. "Until we catch the person responsible, you are not to go anywhere alone. Promise?"

She clenched her teeth as fury coiled. "I promise."

"There's one more thing, Emma." Reid's tone softened. "I know you were wearing my oil skin coat, Akubra, and gumboots, but can you take us through your exact move-ments when you left the cottage to check on the hens?"

"Uh, sure. Gypsy ran off into the dark, so I sloshed over to the hen house. I didn't realise you'd already shut the hens in."

"So, you went all the way to the hen house?" asked Riley.

"Yes. Why?"

"Did you hear anything unusual?"

"The rain and thunder were too loud to hear much. I checked the bolt was across and shone the torch at the hen house. I heard Gypsy yelping and turned around. Oh, Reid's gumboots got stuck in the mud and I lost my balance."

"Hell, Emma. You didn't tell me that." Reid's grumbling concern warmed her heart.

"It slipped my mind."

"Did you get hurt when you fell?"

"No, the gate broke my fall."

"When you checked the bolt was across, did you notice if it was warped in the middle?" Fear, almost tangible, put an edge on Reid's question.

"It was perfectly straight. Why?"

"Riley found a bullet wedged into the post. It … it bent the bolt."

"A bullet?" A rush of terror seized Emma, as black dots floated across her vision. "I did hear a loud ping." Nausea rose in her throat. "Someone shot at me."

"Maybe." Riley didn't sound convinced. "Did you call out to Gypsy before you fell?"

"No, but I did once I got myself unstuck. She came slinking around the side of the cottage, growling. I didn't know she was hurt. We met Reid at the door. He went to see why Gypsy kept growling."

"I didn't see anyone," snapped Reid. "Whoever started the

fire must still have been lurking close by. Why didn't he take another shot when I went outside?"

"That's what I'm worried about," Riley sighed. "Especially after examining Emma's car. I'll put out an alert to pick up Bob Farrell for questioning."

"I could have been shot. Our baby could have been killed." Shock followed closely on the heels of the realisation. Emma took a deep breath, quashing her need to vomit. She wanted answers. "Riley, do you think it could be Bob targeting everything and everyone important to Reid?"

"It's possible, but I can't say for sure until we've questioned any witnesses and possible suspects. We are talking attempted murder and arson. Baiting an animal is a jail sentence and carries a huge fine. *If* Bob's the culprit, he'll be going away for a long time."

"*If?*" Emma held her hand to her chest. "You think it could be someone else?"

"Reid told me about your conversation last night. I intend to check up on Glenn Hanson."

Glenn. She shuddered. "I haven't seen or heard from him in five years. Dad said he rang a few days ago, asking for my phone number and address. Why would he do something like this now? He doesn't even know where I am."

"When the hell did you find that out?" demanded Reid.

"I was talking to Dad when you called. Even if Glenn knows where I am, there is no way he would risk his career by murdering me."

Riley sighed. "People do crazy things, Emma. It's possible he heard you're pregnant and about to get married. If he's unhinged, it might have been enough to push him over the edge."

"Brenda is the only person from my old life who knows those things and she wouldn't tell him. However, my name did come up when the police asked her about Glenn. They're looking into allegations he's using drugs. Oh, and a doctor called me at the hospital yesterday, but when I picked up the phone, there was no one there."

"Damn." Reid cursed a few unsavoury words. "Are you sure Brenda hasn't told anyone where you are? Someone who might repeat it to Glenn Hanson."

Emma lifted her chin. "Positive. She's a loyal friend." Towards the end of their relationship, Emma had been frightened of Glenn. Scared his rages would turn physical, which had happened that last night. It had been five years since she'd seen him. Could the man she'd almost married be capable of baiting animals, setting fire to a cottage, murdering a pregnant woman or Reid? Could he have been Vince's attacker?

"You still there, Emma?" Reid's voice cracked. "I won't let anything happen to you."

She clenched the phone so tightly, her fingers hurt. "What about you? Who is going to protect you when you're out in the paddocks, or building fences?"

"We will electrify all the external fences. It's only a matter of flicking a switch. All the gates will be padlocked from now on. We have external cameras up at the main house, which I can access on my phone. No one will get onto the place who isn't welcome."

"Reid, someone got on to Tulachmhor last night. Gypsy could be dead. You could be dead." Her voice rose. "Our baby could be dead."

"Calm down, Emma. Once Riley questions Bob Farrell, we will know if he is responsible, or if we are dealing with someone else."

"My father wants me to move back to Armidale until the wedding."

"I'd rather you stayed here where I can keep you safe."

"I agree," came Riley's hard voice. "I'll speak to a few key residents, so everyone in Bindarra Creek is on the lookout for strangers in town. Damn, we have the Organic Festival and Scavenger Hunt Challenge next weekend. The town will be overrun with strangers from all over the district and further afield. You can't electrify the fences, Reid. Scavenger hunters always end up lost in Akuna National Park, and the surrounding properties."

Reid cursed again. "Not to mention a clue is usually planted on Tulachmhor and Hickory Ridge. Riley, can you talk to the organisers and ask them to bypass our properties?"

"Sure, but you should probably move into town for the weekend. I can't imagine a safer place to hang out than my house. Sam and the kids would love having you there and—"

"No." Emma interjected. "I am not putting Samantha or your three children at risk. I won't stay with Chelsea and Hunter or Ali and Jake either. I would never forgive myself if something happened to any of you or your precious babies. I will stay at Tulachmhor with Reid and the dogs and cameras. Kathleen should go stay with Therese Morgan on Hickory Ridge. Give me a rifle and I will defend what's mine."

Riley groaned. "Emma, you don't have a gun license. You can't touch a firearm. Plus anything bigger than a .22 kicks like a donkey when it goes off. It'll knock you off your feet. Do you want to risk that?"

"Fine. I need a shower and breakfast. When you're done, come up and have some coffee and scones."

"We will." Reid sounded so relieved, she wanted to throttle him. What if he got hurt and she needed to protect him?

"Sounds good. Take care, cuz."

"Bye, Riley." She placed the mobile on the bedside chest of drawers, her hand steady, her mind focussed. She would not tolerate anyone hurting those she loved.

A light knock had her turning to the open door. Kathleen Sullivan stood there with a tray in her hands. "I made you some cinnamon toast and a cup of tea."

"Thanks, Kathleen. It's just what I need."

"I heard your side of that conversation. We need to talk. A woman needs to know how to defend herself, especially living on a property this size with a nutcase on the loose."

"I agree, but Reid and Riley aren't about to give me a rifle."

"No, but I will. I have my own Lithgow 22LR rifle. It was given to me by my husband many years ago and I keep it in pristine condition."

"You shoot?" The thought appalled Emma. No way could she shoot an animal.

"Emma, I was raised on a cattle property. I married a cattle breeder. In dire times, rabbits and stock are what fed the family. I have never shot an animal for the fun of it. However, I am a member of Bindarra Creek Women's Target Rifle Shooting Club. A mouthful I know. I still have a good eye and my bolt action rifle is very accurate. It takes a five shot magazine and I'm happy to teach you how to use it."

Well, this was serious. Emma brought babies into the world. She did everything possible to deliver healthy babies and take care of their mothers, or women with gynaecological problems. Taking a life was the furthest thing from her mind. Yet, if someone really did intend to kill her baby or Reid, could she raise a rifle and stop them? She swallowed. *Yes.*

Kathleen laid the tray on the beside set of drawers. "I can show you the basics. It's up to you whether you ever take a shot. For me, a bullet finding its mark meant a long happy marriage with my husband. Otherwise, a wild boar would have gored him to death."

"You shot the wild boar?"

"Right between the eyes, seconds before his tusks would have pierced my husband's thighs."

Emma swallowed again. "You must be really calm under pressure, Kathleen."

"It happened so fast I didn't have time to think. I was on a bank higher than Frank. He was bent over, pulling a calf from between two rocks in the Akuna River. With the noise of the river, he didn't hear the boar charging."

"Wow, Kathleen, I want to be just like you when I grow up."

She threw her head back and laughed. "Well, we've made a start with the cooking. You want to know how to make my gramma pie?"

"Yes, please. Reid loves your gramma pie. He said it's a secret recipe."

"Only within the Sullivan clan. Eat up then have your shower and join me in the kitchen. You can drive me over to Hickory Ridge. I will organise for all the girls and babies to be there. You need a nice distraction then Ali, Chelsea and I will show you how to use a rifle, while the boys are building a new fence."

"I want you to move over to Hickory Ridge, where you will be safe."

"Poppycock. This is my home. I'm staying to defend it." Kathleen straightened her slightly rounded shoulders and marched out the door. "I may be in my eighties now, but Sullivan women stick together. No one takes what is ours. Ever. Remember that. We fight tooth and nail to protect what's ours. You are one of us now."

Emma shook her head. Kathleen was a force to be reckoned with, so were the rest of the female clan. Emma appreciated Kathleen's vote of confidence. She would do her best to make the Sullivan women and men proud of her, which meant learning to cook well, getting close to cattle, riding a horse and … shooting a rifle. Maybe.

She shivered as she looked out the window. Was Glenn somewhere out there watching her? Or Bob Farrell, determined to destroy Reid's life? It was so far outside her realm of comprehension she couldn't get her head around it.

Emma picked up her phone and selected Brenda's name from her close contacts.

"Hey, Doc. What's up?"

"Hi, Bren. Can you talk?"

"Yes. I've done a huge run and now I'm drinking a healthy smoothie while I procrastinate over whether to clean my apartment or drop into my favourite café for bacon and eggs. You sound … odd."

"Glenn phoned my mother. He asked for my number and address."

There was a splutter on the other end of line. "You're joking?"

"Nope. My mother didn't give him any information."

"Good. It's best you have nothing to do with Glenn."

"I'd prefer it that way, believe me. I was wondering if you'd heard anything about him?"

"No. I'm on leave so I'm not privy to the hospital grapevine. You're planning something. What is it?"

Kathleen's words came back to Emma. *Sullivan women stick together. No one takes what is ours. Ever. Remember that. We fight tooth and nail to protect what's ours. You are one of us now.* "I'm thinking of threatening him with an AVO if he comes near me."

"That's not a good idea, Emma. I don't imagine Reid would think so either."

"He wouldn't, but I'm afraid Glenn is out to make trouble."

"Don't you dare contact him, Emma. You haven't spoken

in five years. Leave it that way." Brenda sounded so annoyed Emma backed off.

"I knew talking to you would set me straight."

"Damn right. Is there something else you're not telling me? I'm getting this weird vibe."

Emma hesitated. She didn't want to worry Brenda or turn her off coming to Bindarra Creek, but they'd never kept secrets from each other. "We had some trouble on Tulachmhor last night."

"Trouble? Come on, girl, spill. What happened?"

"Someone baited then shot Reid's dog. They also took a shot at me."

"What the …?"

"I know." Emma rubbed her forehead. "It's possible they thought I was Reid. We think the same person tried to burn down our cottage while we were at the vets."

"Tried?"

"Yes. Luckily only the laundry was destroyed. There's some smoke and water damage inside the cottage, but thankfully we can fix that."

"Good God. What about the dog?"

"She's okay. My cousin, Jake, saved her life and is looking after her."

"Who would do something like that?"

"We think it might be a farmhand that Reid fired yesterday. My cousin, Riley, is searching for him."

"Riley? Is he the cop?"

"Yes. He's the senior sergeant in Bindarra Creek. Once he brings Bob, the farmhand, in for questioning, we will know if he's responsible, or …"

"You think someone else could be?"

"I did consider it might be Glenn, but I'm a bit paranoid at the moment. As the wedding gets closer, I … I'm terrified something is going to happen to burst my happy bubble."

"Nothing is going to happen, hon. Sounds like wedding jitters to me. Do you need me to come out there earlier? I can put off my parents if you want some girl time."

"No, Bren. Enjoy your down time. Kathleen is taking me over to Hickory Ridge, where we are having lunch with the girls. All the children will be there too, so they will keep me too busy to dwell on negative thoughts."

"Sounds like you've really found your niche. Now go kiss your fiancé. I need a shower before I hit the café."

"Okay. Bye, Bren."

Emma ended the call and picked up her cup of tea. Maybe she was jumping to ridiculous assumptions. Still, if Glenn was facing disgrace, he might blame her for his downfall. If so, how far would he go to get revenge? How far would Bob Farrell go to avenge a grudge?

Her resolve hardened. It didn't hurt to be prepared. Against all odds, she'd landed a great job in a town she'd always loved. She'd made wonderful friends and fallen in love with an amazing man. She would soon hold their precious baby in her arms.

Sitting straighter, Emma gritted her teeth. She'd fight tooth and nail to protect her baby and those she loved no matter who or what she had to face.

CHAPTER 7

*S*weat ran down Reid's face as he set the post hole digger on the marked cross, ready to bore the next hole. If he kept busy, he didn't have to think about some bat-shit crazy person who had got close enough to almost kill Emma and their baby. He'd had a horrendous nightmare last night, leaving him in a lather of sweat, the top sheet twisted around his torso, while Emma lay shivering on the far side of the bed. She'd never slept so far away before.

The engine of a car slowing to turn into the drive had Reid narrowing his eyes. He relaxed on recognising his brother's Range Rover. Better late than never, he supposed.

Hunter pulled up in the dirt, climbed out of the car, and strolled over. "Why are you scowling at me? I'm not that late."

Reid reigned in his temper. "If you hadn't turned your phone off last night, you would know."

"Hey, it was that or risk another night without sleep. Joel and Ellie are teething and they're an irritable little pair of nine-month-old tyrants. Chelsea and I were desperate for sleep. Did something happen to Bob?"

"It will if I get my hands on him." Reid gave Jerry a nod and stood back as the auger barrelled into the ground. "Bob Farrell no longer works for us. Yesterday, I caught him out cold in the hay shed. An empty bottle of whisky beside him. A discarded cigarette set fire to a bale of hay, which is what caught my attention."

"Bloody idiot."

Reid nodded. "He's never turned up on time and when he did, he often reeked of alcohol. I gave him several warnings to clean up his act. Yesterday was the last straw. Although, I might live to regret it."

Jerry took the digger out of gear and raised it out of the ground. "I'm glad he's gone. He always talked down to me and disappeared, leaving me with the worst jobs."

"You should have said something, mate." Reid knocked mud off the spiral blades then followed as Jerry moved the tractor forward. "We work as a team on Tulachmhor. Everyone pulls their weight."

"I told him that," called Jerry. "This is the best job I've ever had, and I appreciate everything you've done for me." He pulled off his Akubra and wiped the sweat off his forehead with his sleeve. "I don't have a mortgage draining the life out of me since you fellas bought my place, and I get to live in your shearer's quarters for free. Best of all, I don't have the stress of running my own cattle or worrying about crops and the weather."

Reid rolled his stiff shoulders. "I'm just thankful you were here last night to help put the fire out before we lost the whole cottage."

"Fire?" Hunter swivelled and stared at the old cottage. "What the hell?"

Jerry jumped down from the tractor. "While you two catch up, I'm going to head up to my place. I'm still getting over whatever side-lined me yesterday. Must have been something I ate."

"No worries, Jerry." Reid waved him off and turned back to Hunter. He gave his brother a quick rundown on the previous night's chaos then stared into the distance. "I suspect it could be Bob trying to get back at me for firing him. He did threaten me as he left." Reid picked up his shovel. It was days like this he envied Jerry Eckford. Selling his debt-riddled property to the Sullivans had given him the chance to start over. He didn't owe a cent. Wasn't responsible for another living soul. Wasn't being eaten alive with fear that the woman he loved, and his unborn child, could be taken away from him.

Hunter stared at Reid, his mouth hanging open. "What the …." He shook his head. "Did Gypsy survive?"

"Yes. Jake's keeping her for a few days. He says, she'll be fine. The bullet didn't hit anything major."

"That's a relief. I can't believe you didn't get Jake or Riley to come banging on my door. I'm your brother. I'm here for you, Reid. Teething baby tyrants or not."

"I had a lot on my mind. The fire, Gypsy, discovering Emma had an abusive ex-fiancé."

"Fiancé?" Hunter blinked at him. "I knew she'd been in a relationship back in Sydney, but Chelsea said Emma broke it off, because he'd had an affair."

"She dumped him a week before the wedding. Apparently, the guy is a nutcase with a temper and control issues. He is the reason Emma took so long to set a date for our wedding. He got physical and threatened to make trouble if she left him. Thank God, she had the guts to leave him, but after what happened last night, she is terrified it may be him and not Bob who caused the mess last night. I can feel her pulling away."

"No wonder the Morgans are so protective of Emma. Where is she now?"

"Gran is teaching her how to make gramma pie, and then they're going over to Hickory Ridge for lunch."

"That's where Chelsea is taking the two tyrants today. She said something about handing the kids over to her mother while she caught up with the girls. It will do Emma good to have her friends and family around her."

"I hope so. I went up to the house after meeting Riley at the cottage early this morning. Emma is not happy about us working out in the open today. She's terrified Bob Farrell will pick us off, one by one. Oh, and Emma reported seeing someone hanging around the Men's Shed late yesterday. The security guard went to investigate and got hit from behind. Then Emma's car was vandalised in the hospital car park last night."

"Hell. This amount of stress is the last thing she needs two weeks out from the wedding."

"Yeah. She was talking about keeping a rifle handy this morning. Riley and I freaked. She's never touched a rifle in her life." He frowned at his brother. "You don't think the girls will give her a rifle if she asks, do you?"

"Not without showing her how to use it properly. I'd be more worried about Gran."

"Good God." Reid shuddered. "You're right. I'll ring Riley. He can ban the girls doing any such thing."

"Are you sure? Riley might be a cop, but when it comes to protecting the woman in their lives, Morgans don't pull punches. Chelsea's father and brothers taught her how to shoot years ago, even though she refused to shoot anything with a pulse."

"Far out. I remember when our Ali and Chelsea out-shot us the year we set up the Sullivan-Morgan World Shooting Championship with cardboard targets."

"That's because our grandmother had been secretly training them for weeks beforehand."

Reid laughed. "I didn't know that. Grandpa would have had a fit if he'd known. I'd better have a serious word with Gran."

"Good luck, bro. If she defied her own husband, she's not going to listen to you."

"Then let's hope the idea hasn't crossed her mind, and Emma doesn't mention it."

"She won't." Hunter chuckled. "Emma wouldn't hurt a fly."

"Yeah, you're right. Let's get this fence built. Can you stay to check all the external fences? I want them all electrified asap."

"Sure. Did you check the cameras we installed all over Tulachmhor?"

"Yes. Nothing showed up and I didn't have one at the cottage. That will be rectified today too."

"What are you going to do about the cottage?"

"Dodge rang me before you turned up. Tessa is organising a working bee. She's already got a stack of names and donations from people wanting to help. I asked Dodge to thank Tessa, but I'd like to extend the cottage. Emma deserves an internal laundry and bathroom. I'd like to add on a master bedroom too. With luck it will be thirty years before we lose Dad and Antonia. I want to make the cottage big enough for those three kids Edwina Lette predicted."

"I totally agree. Chelsea's over the moon with the renovations we've done to our house. I'm not bad at drawing up plans if you need help."

"Thanks, I'll take you up on that. By the way, Gran and I decided not to tell Dad and Antonia about the fire. We didn't want them cutting their holiday short and rushing home."

"I agree. Thanks for the heads-up. Let's get these holes dug."

Reid gave a nod and took up his position at the digger, making sure Hunter lowered it on the white cross he'd sprayed there earlier. They worked their way along the crosses, digging another five holes before Jerry rumbled across the paddock in his utility.

After parking beneath the shade of an old gum tree, he ambled over and pulled on his work gloves. "Could be a twenty-four-hour gastro bug. Good thing, or I would have been in town last night at the darts final."

Reid glanced across the paddock towards the shearers' bunk house, a new addition since he'd brought Merinos back to Tulachmhor. "With the weather bureau forecasting rain Monday and Tuesday, it might be a good time to drain the water tanks. Do you reckon you could give them and the gutters a clean tomorrow then they can fill again naturally?"

"I can get onto it now, if you two can finish the post holes without me." Jerry grinned. "Although maybe I should stay. You two look to have been talking more than working."

"Smartass." Hunter gave Jerry the bird. "Betcha we have the holes dug before you finish cleaning the tanks."

"Like that's gonna happen. You pair are worse than Paddy Cullen on a slow day." Jerry rubbed his chin. "Put your money where your mouth is, big shot."

"Done," Reid grinned at Hunter, who was doing his best not to laugh. It was a challenge they couldn't knock back. "Jerry, you get a day off, fully paid, if the post holes are not dug before you finish the tanks. What are you willing to lose?"

"Not that I'm going to lose, but I'll agree to do that blind date thing being organised for the Organic Festival next weekend."

Reid couldn't hold in his laughter. When he could finally

breathe properly again, he raised his hand to clap it hard against Hunter's hand. "Deal."

Poor Jerry. When it came to contests, they'd learned a lot of dirty tricks in their battles with the Morgan twins.

Once Jerry had disappeared behind the main homestead, Reid pulled out his phone, smiling when his brother-law answered. "Hey, Jake, any chance you can take a few hours off to help your two favourite brothers-in-law?"

"You're my *only* brothers-in-law. What's happened?"

"Jerry Eckford just challenged us. He believes he can clean out the water tanks before we can dig about fifty post holes, using the post hole digger."

"You're dead in the water, mate. Why the hell did you accept?"

"Because, if he loses, he has to go in that blind date thing your wife, sister and sister-in-law are organising."

"I'll be there in twenty minutes. Riley's off today, I'll bring him too."

"I was hoping you would. See you soon." Reid ended the call and grinned. "Done."

A horn tooting had them waving as Emma and their grandmother drove past on their way to Hickory Ridge. It eased his mind somewhat. Emma would be safe at Hickory Ridge surrounded by women who would keep her mind on much more pleasant things than the fire and shooting.

Over the next three hours, Reid worked his butt off alongside his brother and the twins. It gave him plenty of time to dwell on his life and how it had changed for the better since starting a relationship with Emma. She'd impressed him four years ago, the night Ali and Samantha had both gone into labour and had their daughters. Cut off from town because of a truck accident on the bridge. What a night that had been. An unimaginable string of events that could have ended in tragedy. Luckily, Jake had been there and delivered his first human babies. It had been a worry as Ali's little girl had been premature.

On hearing Ali and Sam were in labour and unable to get into town, Emma had made her way through waterlogged paddocks, crossed the fast-flowing Akuna River in a tinny, and arrived just as the babies arrived. She hadn't complained to Reid once as he escorted her from the river to the house on a tractor that kept getting bogged.

She'd made a huge impact on him that night, yet he'd avoided her, determined to stay single, and steer clear of the beautiful, willowy doctor. Until that fateful New Year's Eve two years ago. Antonia's idea of throwing a big party in their barn for family and friends hadn't bothered Reid. But that night he'd fallen hard and fast for Emma, only to find she was as commitment-shy as he was.

He'd worked hard to change her mind. If she cancelled the wedding and left him, he'd be devastated. He needed to find a way to convince her she was safe with him. That he loved her and would always be there for her and the baby. That he'd never hurt them. She needed to know he cherished her more than anything else in the world.

They finished with the digger and had the new posts dropped in the holes when Jerry drove his utility over. He climbed out, looked along the line of leaning posts then narrowed his eyes on the four sweat-drenched men grinning at him. "That's bloody cheating."

"Hey!" Hunter held his arms wide. "You didn't state we couldn't ask for help."

"It was safer when you bloody Sullivans and Morgans were enemies." He shook his head. "Now I've got to go on a bloody blind date with God knows who."

Hunter smirked. "With Chelsea in the mix, I'd be worried too, mate."

They all laughed then Riley and Jake ambled over to Reid.

It was uncanny the way they were always in sync, as if they knew what the other was thinking or about to do.

Riley clapped Reid's shoulder. "We're heading over to Hickory Ridge now for a late lunch. I'll make sure the ladies haven't been up to anything shifty."

"Thanks, mate. I appreciate that. I … can't bear the thought of anything bad happening to Emma and the baby. I know I can count on you fellas to help watch over them."

"Count on it," added Jake. "Nobody is going to get near Emma."

Another weight lifted from Reid's shoulders. "Good to know. Thanks."

"Right, well we'll be off." Riley glanced at the line of posts. "You want help securing the posts and running the wire?"

"Sure, if you're offering."

"I hear there is a working bee here tomorrow. While the bees are working on the cottage, we can knock this fence over too." Riley looked out over the golden field of grass. "I've got everyone keeping an eye out for Bob Farrell, but I think he's done a runner. I've put out a state-wide alert."

Reid nodded. His throat had blocked up with emotion. The people of Bindarra Creek would always come to each other's aid. "Thanks." He waved his brothers-in-law off and turned to Hunter and Jerry. "Let's secure a couple of these posts then take a break. After lunch I want to check our perimeter fences and gates. They need to be live and sign-posted, and all our gates padlocked before dark."

"What about the scavenger challenge?" asked Jerry. "You're gonna have scavengers all over Tulachmhor next weekend."

"Not this year. It's off limits, and so is Hickory Ridge. I don't want Bob Farrell sneaking in a back way."

"He could already be here," muttered Hunter. "Hiding out on Eagle Rock."

Reid looked up at the mountain that towered over Tulachmhor, named for the eagles that had ruled it for the last century. It had a system of underground caves, which had been Reid and Hunter's secret, until six years ago. He hated thinking of the deadly fire that would have killed him, Ali, Samantha, Jake, and Riley, if they hadn't made it to the hidden access point. They'd also sheltered three men who'd turned out to be dangerous felons. Another night that almost ended in tragedy. Now the whole district knew of the cave system, which often drew kids looking for adventure or cavers from further afield, hoping to explore the mountain's hidden depths. Padlocks and signs only deterred people with integrity.

They worked solidly for fifteen minutes then Jerry yelled, "Smoke!" He pointed to a barely visible spiral, wafting its way up above trees, midway up the right side of Eagle Rock. "Looks like a campfire."

"Jerry, ring Riley." Reid ran for the farm ute. "Come on, Hunter. Let's get the bastard before he decides to burn us out."

"Stop by the house. I'm not going up there unarmed." Hunter clamped a hand on Reid's shoulder. "If that's Bob, he has a clear view of Tulachmhor. Perfect for a sniper."

CHAPTER 8

*A*ttempting to keep her face devoid of the guilt consuming her, Emma added a dollop of cream on top of the scone Elise had buried in blackberry jam. The little girl giggled then endeavoured to get her tiny mouth around the indulgent treat.

Riley folded his arms across his chest. "Should I be worried you ladies have gathered in such a large number?" His grin took the sting out of his words.

Emma needed a moment as she prepared to lie through her teeth. Thankfully, Kathleen beat her to it, the look on her face pure innocence.

"Gracious, Riley. What a suspicious mind you have. It must be all those years as an undercover cop in Sydney. We've been cooking scones and biscuits, not a witch's brew in sight. The only thing Emma asked us to help her with is the lamb and sweet potato pie she wanted to make for Reid's dinner tonight. It's there on the counter if you don't believe me."

Riley glanced across the kitchen, where several large, foil covered dishes were lined up. "That's it? You've been cooking? Nothing else?"

"Darling, what's this about?" Samantha walked into her husband's arm and hugged him. "You know when the girls get together, we love nothing more than to chat, cook, and play with the kids. Did you finish digging the post holes?"

"Yes, we did." Riley released her to pick up his twin boys, each trying to climb his legs. "Tomorrow we'll go back and set the posts. I'm hoping to gather a few extra volunteers from the working bee Tessa Myers has organised."

Jake, who had his arms full of his own wriggling, twin boys, grinned at Kathleen. "Reid is worried you might decide to teach Emma … how to defend herself."

Ali laughed. "Honey, we did that over a year ago."

"What?" Riley and Jake answered as one, their gazes locked on Ali.

This was Emma's cue and she dived in. "After what almost happened to Chelsea two years ago, we all signed up to do that self-defence course that Senior Constable Abby Taylor ran. Remember?"

"Right." Riley shared a look with Jake. "Okay, well, we need to shower." He lowered Brian and Aaron to the floor. "Did you cook pie for us too? We're starving."

"Daddy, I made you a cake." Elise slid off her chair and ran to Riley, offering him her half-eaten, cream and jam-lathered scone. "Eat it quick or the boys will gobble it up."

"Thank you, Lissy. You've saved my life."

Elise giggled and assumed her seat beside her cousin Jasmine, who was utterly absorbed in cutting out animal shapes with various cookie cutters. The flattened dough looked grey from all the chocolate covered fingers involved. The pair born on the same night; were so alike they were often mistaken for twins. Not surprising as their fathers were identical twins, and their mothers were half-sisters.

Aunt Hannah smiled at her sons. "We knew you'd be

hungry, so we saved you a piece of pie each. I'll heat it up while you have your showers."

Once they'd disappeared upstairs, well out of earshot, Emma raised an eyebrow at the five wily women sitting at the table, looking as innocent as the two little girls they'd been teaching to make scones. "Phew. That was close."

Chelsea huffed. "If there is one thing I've learned over the years, it's to tell Sullivan and Morgan men only what they need to know." She wiped chocolate off her nine-month-old son's forehead. "Another trick is to appear affronted or ask questions instead of answering theirs. It's all in the wording."

"Just like their challenges," added Ali. "If Reid ever makes a bet with you, run it past me or Chelsea before you accept. Those guys are experts at saying something that sounds clear when it's anything but."

"They sure are." Chelsea shook her head. "Remember that time my brothers agreed to race your brothers to the top of Eagle Rock. Reid put up Zeus as an incentive."

"I remember." Chelsea shook her head. "Riley and Jake were frothing at the mouth. They both wanted to win Reid's horse."

"What happened," asked Emma.

"Reid beat them all." Ali smirked. "He'd found a hidden entrance to the rumoured internal caves on Eagle Rock a few years before. Let me just say, it's extremely difficult to climb up the overhanging rock shelves at the top of the mountain. They were gob smacked to see Reid standing on top waving at them. Jake was ropeable and swore Reid had cheated but he couldn't figure out how, until …." She grimaced. "We almost lost our lives in a fire."

"I heard about that. You are so lucky. It would have devastated so many if you died." Emma rubbed her sore shoulder. "How do I hide this from Reid? If he sees bruises, he'll know you've been teaching me to shoot."

"Keep rubbing in that liniment." Kathleen pulled Emma's T-shirt collar aside and peered at her shoulder. "I don't think it will bruise. You only took that one kickback. The trick is to hold the rifle butt firmly against your shoulder and lean forward slightly to counterbalance the recoil."

"Lots of tricks. Got it. Can we practice again tomorrow, while the men are building the fence and working on the cottage? I've put my parents off visiting until next weekend and I've been banned from going near the cottage until it's repaired and cleaned."

"Shouldn't be a problem." Therese brushed her white curls behind her ear. "We will pack the boys a cooler full of sandwiches and cakes. No need to come home for lunch then."

Hannah looked at her elderly mother-in-law. "Therese, we were lucky James had to go to Mildura. He wouldn't approve of us teaching his niece to shoot. Thank goodness he's not due back until tonight."

They all jumped as heavy feet came thundering down the stairs. Riley and Jake ran into the kitchen, both pulling on clean T-shirts.

"What's happened," asked Ali, blocking their way.

Jake kissed his wife then shifted her aside. "Jerry Eckford just phoned. He thinks Bob Farrell is camping on Eagle Rock. They saw smoke. Reid and Hunter have gone to check."

"On their own?" Emma jumped to her feet. "It could be a set up."

"Don't panic." Riley's sharp tone drew her attention across the kitchen. "Reid and Hunter know what they're doing. Stay here until I tell you it's safe to go home." His gaze skimmed over the other women. "If you lot want to protect Emma then please stay on the right side of the law."

"Or?" asked his mother.

"Or I'll arrest the lot of you," vowed Riley, before following Jake out the back door.

Emma's heart pounded. She didn't want to lose Reid. Looking at the women who had all become so very important to her, she had to admit she was impressed. Not one of them had batted an eyelid as they watched her cousins run across the yard to Riley's police cruiser.

"Right." Kathleen rubbed her hands together. "As we now have the afternoon together, let's get this show on the road. "We will need a look out upstairs again."

"I'll do it," volunteered Chelsea. "Joel and Ellie need a feed and nap anyway. Then I can help Mum and Grandy with the other children."

"Thank you, dear." Kathleen's eyes lit with devilment. "Aleisha and I will set up new targets in the barn. We'll have to move the hay bales back into place to absorb the bullets." She pushed her chair out and stood. "Emma, you may never lift a rifle again in your life, but you will certainly know how to use one once we are done with you."

"My goodness, I'm trembling in my boots." She looked down at her navy and pink runners. "Well, I would be, if I had boots on."

"That's the first thing we need to fix." Chelsea handed her son to Aunt Hannah and ran into the laundry. A moment later, she was back with a pair of new riding boots. "I was going to give you these for your birthday, but no time like the present."

Emma blinked away tears as she stared at the riding boots. "Thank you, Chelsea. They will be much better than my runners. One of these days I might ask Reid to find me a nice placid horse."

"About that." Aleisha's lips twitched. "I was going to suggest the perfect gelding for you before you fell pregnant. So, once the baby is born, he will be our gift to you." She waved at the circle of women. "His name is Sir Walter. He's eight years old and sixteen hands high. Very quiet with beautiful manners. At the moment he is residing in one of my stables."

"Yikes, Ali. It's been a long time since I've ridden but I can't wait to meet Sir Walter." She laughed. "He's like a gift I can unwrap but not use, at least for a while. Who needs enemies when I have friends like you girls?" Emma grinned to show she wasn't serious. "Thank you."

"It's our pleasure." Samantha came around the table and hugged Emma. "It's six years since I arrived in Bindarra Creek with my brother. Both of us were a bit lost and alone. We only came because of a promise we made our dying mother." She wiped a tear away. "Not one day goes by without me counting myself as the luckiest girl alive. Being a part of *this* women's circle is a big part of that. You are one of us. We will always have your back, Emma."

"Thank you, Sam." Emma wiped away her runaway tears and smiled at her circle of women and the two little girls frowning at her. "I love you all."

"Jasmine, why is Aunty Emma crying," asked Elise.

Jasmine shook her head. "I think she hurt her back, or it's hoorons. My daddy told Uncle Reid, hoorons make girls cry at lot when they are breeving."

Ali almost choked. "Darling, it's hormones and Daddy is referring to ladies who are going to have a baby. However, we don't say a lady is breeding. That went out in the dark ages."

Hannah's eyes danced with merriment. "Jazzy, your daddy, and mummy are vets, so they talk about animals breeding, not breeving. Daddy got confused." She turned away, no doubt to muffle her laughter, as Emma noticed everyone else was doing.

Jasmine nodded gravely then passed Elise a grey cut out

of a pastry dog. "Daddy gets confused a lot. He thinks giving mummy a message will make her go to bed early, but he doesn't tell her the message, and he reads my books too fast." She rolled her eyes at Elise. "My books are more important than a message, but Mummy must like them, because she beats Daddy to bed."

Emma bit her lip, trying to hold in her laughter at Ali's flushed cheeks.

"My daddy gives mummy foot messages," whispered Elise. "He doesn't say anything either, but she likes him rubbing her feet."

Jasmine looked at Elise consideringly then lifted her chin stubbornly. "Well, I'm not going to bed without a story. Not for a silly message."

"Me either," agreed Elise. "Can we eat the puppies and rabbits now?"

"No!" came from every adult mouth in the room.

Emma's grandmother lifted the tray of pastry cut outs from the table. "Raw pastry will give you tummy aches. You two go wash your hands. I will put these in the oven, and you can eat them later."

"Thank you, Grandy." Elise and Jasmine jumped down from their chairs and ran off to the bathroom.

Grandy smiled. "Those two are going to give their fathers a run for their money when they're older."

"They already do." Ali kissed her sons on their heads then opened the back door. "Come on, Emma, we have work to do. Gran, bring your rifle."

"Don't forget the suppressor and earmuffs," called Emma. "I don't want to deafen myself or my baby." Emma joined Ali on the back verandah. They pulled on their boots before descending the back steps, following the brick path to the garden gate. They crossed the gravel yard to the huge barn, which had been built after the old one burnt to the ground two years ago.

As Emma helped Ali set up the targets and hay bales, she couldn't help feeling this was some kind of turning point in her life. Here she was with her family, both blood relations and in-laws. If she could convince Brenda to move to Bindarra Creek, it would be the icing on the cake.

Once they had their earmuffs on, Ali and Kathleen became hard task masters, continually adjusting Emma's stance, hand placement, and aim. Who knew there was so much to learn about shooting a rifle?

Emma had no idea how much time passed, as she'd been absorbed in hitting the bull's eye. Her arms ached and she'd love a cup of tea, but under Ali and Kathleen's tuition, she'd become addicted to hitting the centre black spot and pleasing them.

Out of bullets, she was lowering the rifle when a man's arm reached around her and gripped the barrel, effortlessly removing it from her hands. Her heart rate shot through the roof. Swallowing her terror, she pulled off her earmuffs and swung around to confront him.

"Reid?"

His furious gaze remained riveted on her as he passed the rifle to Hunter. "What the hell are you doing, Emma? Rifles are not bloody toys. They are weapons that can be taken then used against you, as I just demonstrated. You could have been shot. The baby could have been killed." He raised his hand.

"No." She reared back, raising her hands to block him.

His hand froze above his hair then fell to his side. "Jesus, Emma, I'm not going to hit you. I won't ever hit you. I meant to rub my head."

"Sorry." She lowered her hands as regret surged. "I know you'll never hit me, it was just instinct. I ... What are you doing here?"

He blew out a breath. "We were chasing someone and thought they might have come this way." He rubbed his forehead. "I'm sorry, I overreacted. Even though you're using a suppressor, we heard the shots as we approached. I feared you were at the mercy of a madman. You scared the shit out of me."

"I wasn't expecting you." She drew in a huge breath and glanced at Kathleen and Ali. They both wore guilty expressions and looked ready to take the brunt of the blame. She held up a hand to hold them back then lifting her chin, returned her attention to Reid. "If a madman had arrived, our lookout would have warned us."

He crossed his arms. "A lookout who failed to warn you of our approach."

"You're not a madman."

The sound of running feet drew their attention to the door where Samantha skidded to a halt. "Sorry, I was watching the front gate. They must have come in the back way from Tulachmhor."

Reid raised an eyebrow. "Some lookout."

Emma shrugged. "Why would you fear a madman had us at his mercy?"

Reid sighed. "Because we think Bob Farrell took a few shots at us, before we chased him into Akuna National Park."

"We lost him," added Hunter. "We thought he might double back to Tulachmhor or escape through Hickory Ridge and come up to the house."

"So it was Bob Farrell?" It was a relief in one way, but Emma wrapped her arms around her abdomen, suddenly feeling vulnerable and exposed. She swallowed the giant lump in her throat and grimaced. "You've all grown up on the land. You know this area like the back of your hands. You've been taught from an early age how to ride and shoot. I'm floundering here. I have a baby who I will defend to my last breath, but how am I supposed to do that without knowing what you all know?"

"Emma." Reid went to hug her.

"No." Emma backed away. "What if you're incapacitated? What if I'm the only person standing between you and a man with a grudge or a charging boar?"

"What?" Reid looked at his grandmother. "I might've known you were behind this."

"Emma is right." Kathleen glared at Reid. "She'd never forgive herself if she did nothing while you were gored to death or shot dead by Bob Farrell."

"Gran, that's not going to happen." Reid went to run his hand through his hair again but stopped mid-air. "Gran, I want you and Emma to move into town until the police have Bob Farrell in custody."

Kathleen's lips thinned. "Therese and Hannah are just as vulnerable as we are, plus all the kiddies are often here. What about all the visitors wandering around town next week? Should we ask for the Organic Festival to be postponed? Maybe the Sullivan and Morgan women should gather up the children and move further afield. Armidale or perhaps Queensland?"

"There's no need to be sarcastic, Gran." Reid sighed. "I don't want either of you hurt."

Emma nodded. "I get that, Reid, but my life is here with you. I don't want to be living miles away. What if you need me?"

"I don't need you on Tulachmhor. I can look after myself."

Emma recoiled, choking back her pain. A knife stab to the heart couldn't have hurt more, but she refused to stand here and let him tear her apart. She wouldn't. Dragging in a deep breath she lifted her chin. "That is becoming more and more obvious. What was I thinking? This was never going to work. Goodness, I can't believe I'm going to do this again, but—"

"No!" Reid dragged her into his arms. "Don't you dare walk away from me. I won't let you go. We belong together."

Oh God, not again. Searing pain tore at her heart. "I won't stop you from seeing the baby, Reid, but—"

"This is not about the baby. This is about us. You and me. I'm trying to protect you."

"Protect me." Hope bloomed. "Then don't send me away." She clutched his shirt, praying he'd see reason. "Let me help you, please."

He threw his head back and stared up at the rafters, the pulse in his throat beating furiously. After a moment he lowered his head, gave her a look she couldn't decipher then held out his hand toward Hunter. "Give Emma the damn rifle. Let's see if our grandmother and sister are as good as they think."

"Your call." Hunter passed Emma the rifle then crossed his arms. "I'm not sure this is a good idea, bro."

"We'll see." Reid stalked to the target frame, where he tore off the sheet full of holes and replaced it with a fresh one. "Let's make this a real contest. You and me. Closest shot to the bull's eye decides where we stay until Bob Farrell is caught."

"Hang on, we need to clarify a few things." Ali's eyes lit with mischief. "How many shots do you each get?"

Reid raised an arrogant eyebrow. "One shot each."

It sounded above board, yet Ali now had her hands on her hips. "Distance to targets?"

Reid's lips twitched. "The length of the barn." He picked up the target stand and strode to the far end of the barn, which didn't faze Emma as she practiced that exact shot earlier. Once Reid had a few hay bales spread behind it, he strolled back, grinning as if he'd already won. "Would you like to go first?"

Emma's gaze shot to Ali, who was biting her lip. She still

didn't trust Reid, so Emma wouldn't either. "Let me get this straight. We each get *one* shot at *that* target, and the closest shot to the bull's eye decides where we will be living until Bob Farrell is caught. But … we share the same bed every night?"

Reid growled low in his throat. "You've been hanging around my sister too long. Fine, we can stay with your parents in Armidale, and I'll drive to Tulachmhor every day."

Emma shook her head. "I don't want to leave Bindarra Creek. This is our home. My place is here with you. We are supposed to be partners."

"Damn it, Em, if something happens to you, it will kill me."

"That works both ways, my love."

"Fair enough, but when I win, we're moving into town. Take your shot."

"Deal." Emma placed the earmuffs over her ears then raised the rifle. She took her time, finding her balance, fitting the butt to her shoulder, and lining up the sight. Once she felt comfortable, she calmed her breathing then held her breath and pulled the trigger.

Ali ran to the target. "Bull's eye. You did it, Emma. Woohoo, what a woman."

Emma calmly held the rifle out to Reid. "Your go, darling. I guess if you hit the bull's eye, perfectly, we will need a shoot-out."

"Yes, we will." He ignored the rifle she held out and paced back to a stack of hay bales near a stable door, where he picked up a rifle with a scope.

"What? That's cheating." Emma looked to Ali, who shrugged helplessly. They had no choice but to stand back and wait for Reid to take his shot.

He raised the rifle, sighted the target, and fired.

Ali ran back to the target and leaned in. "Sorry, Reid, you are the tiniest bit off centre. Emma wins."

Reid didn't even bother checking. Instead, he handed his rifle to Hunter then took the rifle out of Emma's hands and passed it to Kathleen, before pulling Emma into a hug. "You're amazing, Emma. In one day, you've become a proficient shooter. Hitting a bull's eye at that distance without a scope isn't an easy feat."

"I had two excellent teachers." Emma grinned at Kathleen and Ali. "Thanks, ladies. I vote we stay on Tulachmhor." She was stretching up to kiss Reid when a gasp stopped her.

Sam pointed towards the drive. "Police, and they're in a hurry by the looks of things."

They all rushed to the barn's entrance to see a police wagon churning up a dusty bloom as it raced towards them.

"Oh, God." Ali clutched Sam's hand. "You don't think something has happened to Jake or Riley, do you?"

No one said a word as the wagon skidded to a stop and Senior Constable Abby Taylor jumped out of the passenger side. Constable AJ Donaldson slammed the driver's door and ran to catch up as Abby marched across the yard.

"Reid. Hunter." Abby's gaze flicked to the rifle in Hunter's hands. "I need you to accompany us to the station for questioning."

"Why?" Reid pulled Emma closer. "What's happened?"

Abby shifted on her feet, not quite meeting his eyes. "We found a body."

Emma's stomach dropped. "Who?"

"Jerry Eckford thinks it's Bob Farrell. The body is yet to be formally identified."

Reid's hand tightened around Emma's fingers. "Jerry *thinks* it's Bob?"

"Yeah." AJ nodded vigorously. "Hard to tell because his face is a mess."

Emma clutched Reid as gasps filled the barn.

"Jerry said you took rifles when you went to check out a campfire on Eagle Rock." Abby's gaze shifted to the two guns on top of the hay bales. "I'll need to confiscate those rifles for forensic examination." Her gaze swept over everyone, stopping at Kathleen. "Mrs. Sullivan, I'll need that rifle too."

Kathleen glowered. "You can't seriously believe my grandsons shot that man? He probably fell and the gun went off."

Abby shrugged. "That is possible, but until we know exactly what happened, Reid and Hunter are ..."

"Under suspicion for murder," announced AJ.

CHAPTER 9

*R*eid stared at his brother-in-law and Abby Taylor across a desk, in the police station's only interrogation room. The last time he'd sat in this exact position had been thirteen years ago. The night of Ali's and Chelsea's high school graduation dance. The sergeant back then had torn strips of him and Jake for getting into a fist fight and destroying the graduation arch. After reading them the riot act, he'd marched them into the only cell. He'd even handcuffed their hands behind their backs to prevent them attacking each other again. He'd almost thrown their fathers in with them.

Riley rubbed his eyes. He looked as tired as Reid felt. "Are you sure you or Hunter didn't fire a shot, Reid?"

"Not a single shot. We've gone over this, Riley. Hunter and I took the rifles in case we came across a boar or brown snake."

"Jerry Eckford heard Hunter say, and I quote, *Stop by the house. I'm not going up there unarmed.*" Riley read from the open file in front of him.

"That's right." Reid leaned back in his chair, desperate to

give off a calmness he was far from experiencing. Knowing everything he said was being recorded electronically had him carefully considering his responses. "Eagle Rock is full of rotting tree trunks and crevices where a king brown could lie in wait, and the swamp round the back is a known hangout for wild boar. You know that, Senior Sergeant Morgan. Back in the day, it was one of your ancestors who lost a wagon load of pigs near Akuna National Park."

Riley smirked. "The way I heard it, your ancestors ran him off the road."

"It wouldn't have happened if your ancestor didn't take off with a prime load of pigs meant to go to Tulachmhor. There might have been a chase, but your ancestor was driving so erratically, he lost a wheel and ended up in a ditch. Then while the two men were trading punches, the pigs got away."

Abby cleared her throat. "Let's get back on track. Reid, what happened when you made it to the campfire?" She held her biro over a notebook.

"We didn't. We were a third of the way up Eagle Rock when someone fired at us from further across the mountain. We changed direction and chased him."

"Chased him where?" asked Riley.

"Into the Akuna National Park." Frustration ate at Reid. "We have gone over this until we are all blue in the face. I didn't shoot Bob Farrell and neither did Hunter. We took our rifles in case we met a mob of pigs. There's no way either of us would shoot a person."

"Not even if you thought that person allegedly baited and shot your dog? Or allegedly fired a shot at your fiancée last night," asked Abby.

"We intended to catch him and hand him over to the police. Jerry can confirm all this."

"Jerry Eckford has not given us a formal statement,"

answered Riley. "I sent Constable Donaldson out to Tulachmhor to bring him in, but the shearing quarters were empty. We haven't been able to contact Jerry on his mobile either."

"That's strange." Reid's neck prickled. "Was his ute there?"

"No," replied Abby.

"How do you know it was a man you were chasing?" Riley looked up from his notes.

"I… Okay, I assumed it was a man. The person wore a black beanie, dark trousers, and a khaki jacket. I can't think of any woman with a grudge against me or my family."

Abby tapped the table with her pen. "What made you think the shooter was Bob Farrell?"

"I dismissed him yesterday and he made threats."

"So why did you double back to Hickory Ridge?" She held her hands wide. "You knew we were on our way to Tulachmhor. Why didn't you go back and report you'd lost the person you were following?"

"We were terrified Farrell might go after Emma or the other women and children. They were together at Hickory Ridge. From his vantage point on Eagle Rock, Bob Farrell would have seen Emma and my grandmother drive over to Hickory Ridge. If he wanted to destroy me, as his actions indicate, going after my family and friends would do it."

"What do you think happened to him?" asked Riley.

"I have no idea. The person we were chasing was alive and running when we lost his trail." Anger burned in Reid's throat as he spat out the words.

"So it might not have been Bob Farrell?" Abby tapped the table with her biro, an irritating sound that grated on Reid's nerves.

Riley raised his hand. "Again, I must caution you, Reid. Everything you say is being recorded. Are you sure you don't want your lawyer present?"

"I haven't done anything wrong. Look, you've taken my statement. I've cooperated fully. Told you everything I know. What's keeping the Tamworth detectives. You said earlier that they'd be handling the case?"

"They were involved in a car accident," replied Abby. "That's why we are doing the interviews." She squared her shoulders. "Let's go over this once more. You said Jerry saw campfire smoke. You told him to call Senior Sergeant Morgan, which he did at 3pm. At which time you would have been collecting your rifles. Then you and Hunter started up Eagle Rock. What happened to Jerry?"

"I have no idea." Reid sighed. "Someone further around the mountain fired on us as we were climbing Eagle Rock. We assumed it was a man. He fired several more shots while we were in pursuit, but we *never* fired a shot. After we lost him, there were no more gunshots. He was either hiding close by or escaped into the Akuna National Park. We couldn't reach Emma or Chelsea on their mobiles, so Hunter and I detoured to Hickory Ridge to check on our families. We arrived at Hickory Ridge about 4pm. Tell me what I don't know."

Riley leaned back in his chair. "After Jerry Eckford rang me, he climbed up to the smouldering campfire. He found a body lying beside a swag, and items of clothing strewn everywhere. He met Senior Constable Taylor and I at the bottom of Eagle Rock then lead us back up to the campsite. We searched the immediate area but didn't find a gun."

Reid grappled with this information. "No gun?"

"No gun," repeated Abby. "We did notice an area of dirt that had been disturbed recently. On closer inspection we extracted a large amount of cash rolled up in a T-shirt."

Reid blinked at them. "How much cash are we talking about?"

"Why?" asked Riley.

"A few weeks ago, he badgered me for an advance on his wages, as he couldn't pay his rent at the caravan park."

"Almost ten thousand dollars." Riley raised an eyebrow. "Would you have that much money on hand at Tulachmhor?"

"No way. You're sure there was no rifle?"

"Not that we found," confirmed Riley.

The back of Reid's neck prickled again. "How soon after we left Jerry, did he find the body?"

"He said he drove to the bottom of Eagle Rock and thinks it took him about ten minutes to climb up to the camp site." Abby answered, watching Reid closely. "So, about 3.15pm. Why?"

"If Jerry found Bob already dead then who the hell were we chasing?" Reid looked down at the metal desk. "Someone was firing at us. Hell, maybe Bob had nothing to do with what happened last night. Maybe he was camping up there because …. Hell, I have no idea. If he had ten grand, it's not as if he couldn't afford his rent at the caravan park."

"Interview suspended at 18.27pm." Riley switched off the recorder then closed his notebook. "I think that's enough for tonight. Hopefully, the detectives will be discharged from Tamworth hospital in the morning. I will give them your statements, but they will want to interview you all themselves."

"Where are Emma and my grandmother now?"

"Your grandmother is at Hickory Ridge." Abby stood. "I suspect Emma is here, sitting in the station lobby, as she has insisted on doing for the last two hours. Chelsea picked up Hunter a while ago. Your father and Antonia are on their way back from Darwin too. Ali called them."

"I figured she would. Is that it? Can I leave now?"

Riley rubbed his jaw. "Stay at my place tonight, and what-ever you do, don't leave town." He opened the door and followed Reid into the hall. "I don't like this anymore than you do, mate, but I promise to get to the bottom of it."

"Thanks." Reid stared at the floor. "I know this doesn't look good, but we didn't kill Bob Farrell. If I'd caught up with him, I would have confronted him, but we would have brought him in alive. We were chasing someone with a gun, and that bothers me."

"It bothers us too, Reid." Abby slipped past them and left the interview room.

Riley clamped a hand on Reid's shoulder. "It bothers me too, Reid. Bob Farrell's body has been collected and we've cordoned off the campsite. Two forensic officers from Tamworth are conducting an examination now. With any luck they can tell us more. Get some sleep." He strode down the short hall to the front office.

Light footsteps rushed across the floor. Reid looked up in time to catch Emma as she threw herself into his arms. He buried his face in her soft hair. "Em."

"I've been so worried. There are all sort of rumours flying around town. Are you okay?"

"I'm fine." He hugged her tightly.

"Chelsea is furious with Riley for detaining you and Hunter."

"He's just doing his job. I don't know if Bob killed himself or not. The police say there was no rifle near the body, and they found a large amount of money buried nearby. All that aside, we were chasing someone with a gun and that someone is still out there. I'm wondering if Bob boasted about coming into ten grand and it got him killed, or …." Reid couldn't finish that thought. It was beyond comprehension.

"Ten grand?" Emma's face had gone deadly pale. "You think Bob was paid ten grand to hurt you or … me, and that person killed him?"

"It's a possibility. I need you somewhere safe."

"We will both be safe at Riley and Samantha's house."

He hugged her again. "Without you, I …."

"Shush, nothing is going to happen to me. I heard the detectives from Tamworth were in a car accident near Glenmeer. The car that almost hit them didn't stop."

"I see the grapevine is as hot as ever." Reid noticed AJ hovering and blew out a breath. "Let's get out of here. I assume you brought the car?"

"Yes, it's out front. I am not cancelling our wedding."

"That's my girl." Reid lowered his head and kissed her.

AJ cleared his throat. "Scuse me, Senior Sergeant Morgan has something to tell you. It's important." He pointed across the front office to Riley, who sat behind his desk, speaking on the phone.

"What now?" snapped Reid, tightening his hold on to Emma.

She sagged in Reid's arms. "Want to make a run for it?" Her anxious eyes flicked to the front entrance. "I don't want any more bad news.

"Then let's hope it's good news."

* * *

WITH LEADEN FEET and a stomach full of butterflies, Emma gripped Reid's hand as they crossed the office.

Riley waved them to the chairs in front of his desk. "Thanks, Commander. I'll be in touch."

Emma awkwardly lowered herself onto the seat Reid pulled out for her. "Thank you, darling." Her words and smile were meant to ease the tension she could sense emanating from Reid. His jaw did appear to ease a little as he took the seat beside her.

"Emma, Reid, that was my Commander in Tamworth. She spoke to Doctor Hanson's chief of staff. Hanson is on mandatory leave pending an internal investigation into allegations against him. However, he failed to attend an interview three days ago, and appears to have disappeared."

Emma's heart dropped as she clutched Reid's hand. "He could be here."

"We don't know that, Emma." Riley closed his notebook. "My commander hasn't been able to confirm if Doctor Hanson is of interest to police. Having said that, I would caution you both to be aware of your surroundings and contact me immediately if you sight Doctor Hanson."

"We will." Emma stood and forced a smile. "Thanks, Riley. We will be at your house if there's any news."

"No worries."

Once they were in the Landcruiser, Emma turned to Reid. "I've got a few questions to run past you." At Reid's questioning glance she continued. "If Bob killed himself then where is the gun?"

"Someone must have taken it."

"Agreed. Do you think Jerry might have taken it to protect you from being blamed?"

"Maybe, but where is Jerry? Did he go after the guy we were chasing? Is he lying out in the National Park injured or dead? Hell, I don't want to cast suspicion, but he tells the police we went to get our rifles then he disappears. Is he caught up in something dodgy?"

"I don't know." Emma crossed her arms, hating the thought that something might have happened to Jerry. She couldn't let the fear overtake her. They needed answers and talking it out helped. "Why kill Bob? Was it for the money the police say he had buried nearby, or something more sinister?"

"I don't know." Reid started the engine then pulled out onto the road. "Where did he get ten grand? He cried poor to me."

"Maybe he won a scratchy and boasted about it at the pub. No, that juicy titbit would be all over town and we would have heard about it. What if he did mention it to someone down on their luck or passing through town? They might have gone after the money and things got out of hand."

"It wouldn't be handed over in cash. It would have been deposited into his account. Even so, I'd have thought Bob more the type to take the money and skip town." Reid rubbed his eyes. "Why camp on Tulachmhor? Why bait and shoot Gypsy? Why take a shot at you? Why try to burn down the cottage?"

There was another possibility. Emma shivered. "What if Bob was paid to spy on us? I'm wondering if by sacking him, you took away any future spying income, so he decided to get even, but then the person who hired him decided to get rid of him."

"That's a scary scenario, Emma."

"I know, but Riley said Glenn has disappeared. What if he paid Bob to cause problems on Tulachmhor and spy on me? What if it was Glenn who shot at me, thinking it was you? He could have killed Bob to stop him talking."

"Crikey, Emma, that's a hell of an accusation, but if it's true, we're in big trouble. I'll call

Riley and run it past him." Reid drove around the round-about then into Mt Ingalls Road. He swung into Riley and Samantha's long drive, parking in front of the garage.

Reid jumped out and ran around the Landcruiser's bonnet to help her out.

Sensor lights lit up the garden and path to the historical home's back porch. Emma glanced around the dark shadows of the garden. She hated feeling so vulnerable and exposed, but until the shooter had been arrested, they were all in danger.

CHAPTER 10

*A*nother false alarm. Emma yawned and ambled back to her office, leaving Scarlett to escort Deidre and Andrew King out of the maternity ward and down to the lobby. She couldn't blame Andrew for ringing her at the ungodly hour of 2am, pleading for her to come to his wife's aid. Deidre was in her early forties, and they'd been waiting years for their miracle baby. She just wished Deidre's Braxton Hicks contractions calmed down before they set off true labour.

A whisper of sound had Emma looking over her shoulder, expecting to see a night-duty nurse, Reid or Dodge, the night security guard. The hall was completely empty. With all that had happened over the last thirty hours or so, her imagination flared to life. It wasn't rare to have no patients in the maternity wing, but for some reason the ward had an eeriness about it tonight.

She stood perfectly still, barely breathing as she listened for … something. It could have been an echo from somewhere else within the hospital. It was possible Reid had fallen asleep in the visitors lounge just outside the maternity ward.

He had to be exhausted. She certainly was. She'd grab her bag and then they could go back to Riley's and get some sleep.

Unable to shake the trepidation, she picked up speed. Her office was at the other end of the maternity wing, well away from the nursing station, linen rooms, nursery, and lift. She passed the door to the emergency stairwell, her lungs seizing when she realised it was held open several inches by a broom handle. She swallowed, her heart thundering in her ears.

Why would anyone ...? She kicked the broom clear and pulled the door shut. It was called a fire door for a reason. Emma backed away from the door. Reid would see the Kings leaving. With all the weird things going on, he'd come looking for her any minute. The cleaner could have left the door propped open, planning to clean the maternity wing once everyone was out of his way. Maybe he got side-tracked and forgot to remove the broom. That was a plausible explanation. It didn't stop the crawling sensation creeping up her spine.

She shivered. "Plausible but unlikely." Her murmur echoed in her own ears.

Alert to the faintest sound, she paced to her office, closing the door, and locking it behind her, cutting off all light except for the sliver under the door. She was about to flip the light switch when the sliver of light dimmed. Someone stood outside her door. Her imagination was going into overdrive. It had to be Scarlett or the cleaner. Where was Reid?

Heart in her mouth, she swallowed, unable to drag her eyes away from the bottom of the door. She jumped when the handle vibrated under her hand. "Who's there?"

When no one answered, Emma closed her eyes and dragged up every ounce of courage she had. "I said, who's there?"

The door shuddered, sending terror shooting through every nerve in her body. Her silent stalker moved away, the sound of leather soles slapping against the vinyl flooring. A door slammed further down the hall. Emma flipped the switch and ran to her desk, wrenching open her top drawer and rummaging for her phone. It wasn't there. Perspiration broke out across her forehead. She scattered files and medical articles across the desk, lifting everything to search underneath. Her cylinder of pens crashed to the floor, scaring the daylights out of her. Her breath came in ragged gasps. Her phone wasn't anywhere.

"Desk phone." She hit the direct line for security, dragging in deep breaths. "Come on, answer."

A shrill alarm blocked any chance of hearing. Emma slowly lowered the phone. "That's the fire alarm." She sank onto her chair. This was no coincidence. Her stalker had set off the fire alarm, but did that mean there really was a fire, or … he wanted her to leave her office? Quickly, she pressed an outside line and punched in Reid's number, praying he hadn't been knocked over the head or worse.

He picked up on the first ring. "Emma, what's happened? The maternity doors are locked. I can't get through. Did you set off the alarm?"

"No!" She covered her other ear to drown out the alarm. "I've locked myself in my office. Someone was outside, rattling the door. They wouldn't answer me. It's possible they set off the fire alarm, but I don't know if there is a fire or not."

"Stay put. I'll find a way in. Stay on the phone. Hell, this is why I didn't want you coming into the hospital."

She flinched at his harsh tone. "I couldn't not come in. I told you, Deidre King is going through a high-risk preg-nancy. It was a false alarm, but the signs are all pointing to an early labour, which means a premature baby."

A loud banging came down the phone line. "Stay in your

office, Emma. I'll be there as fast as I can. How close is the fire door to your office?"

"It's down the hall. I found it wedged open so shut it."

"Where is your midwife?"

"Scarlett is seeing the Kings out. She took them down in the lift, so she must be in the lobby by now. As the lift is outside the maternity doors, she can't get back in either."

"Okay. In that case she will have been evacuated. Do you have your mobile with you?"

"No. I left it on my desk, but it's not there."

"Stay on the line, sweetheart. I'll text Riley. Will this phone reach your bathroom, and can you lock the door?"

"Yes."

"Good. Go there now."

"Okay." She pushed back her chair then hesitated. If she dragged her desk in front of the door and wedged it somehow, it would prevent anyone getting into her office. At least until Reid could get there. The desk was metal based and lightweight so she wouldn't hurt herself. Decision made, she placed the phone and handset on the floor then pulled the desk over to the door. Her gaze fell on the metal coat rack in the corner. "Perfect."

She wedged the feet against the base of the wall and top against the short side of her desk. Her panic subsided, replaced by anger and determination. It should hold. The alarm was giving her a headache, but she could live with it. Without taking her eyes off the door, she picked up the phone and backed into her small ensuite. "Are you still there, Reid?"

"Yes, just texting Dodge for a key to these doors."

"Be careful." Her gaze flicked to the high window. She might have been tempted to climb through it if she weren't pregnant and on the second floor. It could be a hoax. She couldn't smell smoke, but there could be a fire on a lower floor or in the older part of the hospital. "Reid, is there really a fire?"

"I don't know. Dodge is checking it out and the fire brigade are on the way. We can always get a ladder to your office if necessary."

She stood in the doorway of her bathroom, ready to slam and lock the door if need be. Her breath caught as a piece of paper shot under the door. *Are you kidding me?*

"Reid, someone just pushed a note under the door." She hurried over, snatched it up and scuttled back to the bathroom.

"Leave it," called Reid.

"Too late." Her heart pounded as she unfolded the white parchment. As she read the roughly scrawled words, blood rushed from her head and she sank to the floor, dropping her head as best she could between her knees.

"Emma! Emma! Are you okay?"

"Sorry." She took a deep breath. "It's from Glenn. He's here."

"Read the note to me, Emma. What does it say?"

"'There isn't anywhere you can hide that I won't find you.' He's here, Reid."

"Do you recognise the writing?"

She stared at the scrawl. Glenn hadn't been one for writing love notes or long messages but would add items to her grocery list. Like most doctors, he had notoriously bad handwriting, and tended to capitalise his letters, but she couldn't be positive. "I think it's his writing."

"Dodge is coming up the stairs now. We won't be long."

I need something to protect myself. Emma's gaze flicked around her office, snagging on the lead crystal vase her mother had given her last Christmas. It would certainly damage a person's skull. That thought reminded her of her beloved Beetle and her eyes filled with tears. Anyone who knew her well, knew what that car meant to her. This was personal.

She jumped back as the door handle rattled.

"Emma, it's me. Unlock the door."

"Reid." Relief and tears overwhelmed her. "I'm coming. Give me a minute. The desk is in front of it." Knocking the coat stand away, she pushed the desk sideways then unlocked the door. It opened immediately and Reid pulled her into his arms. Riley and Dodge were behind him.

"Emma." Reid's voice shook, his hold so tight, it hurt.

Suddenly the alarm stopped and there was blessed silence.

She pulled the crumpled note from her pocket. "This was pushed under my door. I think it's from Glenn. He's crazy."

"I'll check the stairwell," called Dodge as he ran off.

Riley pulled on disposable gloves then took the note. He read it then pulled out a zip lock bag and slipped it inside. "I'll get Abby to bring the wagon up to the rear delivery dock. We'll go back to my house and work out what we're going to do. I'll need to take your statements too. It might be best if Emma goes into a safe house out of town."

"No. It's too risky!" Reid glared at Riley. "The safest place for Emma is Tulachmhor homestead. We can see anyone approaching and it's far enough away from Eagle Rock that only an army sniper would have a hope of hitting us. We can set a trap for Hanson."

Riley shook his head. "I think Emma should leave town."

"This is bullshit. We have to protect her." Reid stepped away from Emma and slapped his palm against the wall.

"May I say something?" Emma waited until both men were looking at her. "I'm worried our families are at risk too. Samantha and the kids are home alone during the day, as are Chelsea and the twins. Ali and Jake have a business to run. People and animals depend on them. Jasmine and Elise go to pre-school. They could be snatched. What about your parents and grandmothers? There is a nut roaming around killing people. If he wants to hurt me, he only has to target any of you. We can't all leave town. I suggest you organise a search party as well as set a trap for him."

Riley ran a hand through his hair. "You're right. Everyone in the family could be vulnerable."

"Sarge." Abby charged through the end doors. "AJ saw someone in a balaclava running away from the hospital, but he lost them, and the main switchboard's phone line has been cut through."

"Damn. Has Kel found any sign of smoke or a fire?"

"No, but the alarm lever in the doctor's lounge was pulled down."

"Right." Riley looked along the hall in both directions. "Abby, I need you to bring the paddy wagon to the back delivery dock. Back it up nice and close. Then I want you, AJ, and Dodge to do a thorough search of the hospital. Make sure everyone is accounted for. Once it's safe to return, staff and patients can re-enter."

"Are we looking for someone in particular?" Abby's cool, assessing eyes flicked over Emma and Reid before returning to Riley.

"Doctor Glenn Hanson. You have his description."

"Yes." Abby straightened her shoulders. "I'll meet you in the loading dock." She strode off.

Riley rubbed his jaw. "We could move our families to Tulachmhor and organise round the clock surveillance. I'll ask the commander for extra police." Riley drew his scary-looking handgun. "We'll take the fire stairs. Stay behind me." He strode down the hall.

How had her happy life here turned into this nightmare? Emma held on to Reid's hand as they followed Riley, who checked the stairwell before descending the cement steps.

She drew in deep breaths, desperate to calm her racing heart.

Once they were on ground level, Riley opened the emergency exit door several inches and peeked through. "Clear. Abby is backing the paddy wagon in now. Wait for my signal." He slipped through the doorway, leaving a heavy silence behind him.

"Everything is going to be okay, Em." Reid held her tight against his side. "I won't let anything happen to you."

"I know." She jumped as the door opened again. Riley waved them through. "Straight into the wagon. It won't be comfortable, but I'll do my best to avoid potholes."

Abby opened the rear door of the twin cabin wagon for Emma. "You okay, Emma?"

"Yes." She smiled at Abby. "I was afraid Riley intended transporting us in the back, where the baddies go." Her attempt at humour fell flat. Not surprising as Reid and Riley seemed to be on tenterhooks, looking around nervously as they climbed into the wagon.

Riley slammed his door then looked over his shoulder at her. "Good to go?"

"Yes." Once she had her belt on, Emma cuddled closer to Reid and looked out the side window. Abby stood next to a control panel, her hand hovering over a huge red button. "What's she doing?"

"Once we exit the delivery dock, Abby will close the roller door." Riley started the engine and drove through the wide doorway. "It's dark, but we don't have cloud cover tonight, so don't plaster your faces against the windows. That way, if anyone is watching, they won't be able to identify who is with me."

Even so, Emma shrunk lower in the seat as Riley drove between the hospital's brick entrance pillars. During her relationship with Glenn, she'd spoken of her closest cousins.

Would he remember Riley was a cop and Jake a vet? Would he recall Chelsea was a kindergarten teacher and the Morgan family had a cattle property outside Bindarra Creek? She'd taken him home to Tamworth a couple of times, but he'd never met her cousins. Only her immediate family. *Oh, God. Her parents and Lindsay and baby Otis could be at risk too.* Emma squeezed Reid's hand.

"What the hell?" Riley raised his arm to block the blinding green light illuminating the windscreen.

"It's a bloody laser pointer," yelled Reid.

Riley slowed. "Can you tell where it's coming from?"

"Maybe the Akuna Motel or RSL carpark."

Emma clutched her seat belt. "You'll have to pull off the road."

"That might be exactly what he wants us to do." Riley slowed the paddy wagon. "Hang on tight. I'm going to do a U-turn."

A gun shot boomed, and the windscreen exploded. Emma screamed.

"Down," roared Riley.

She couldn't get any lower and she was being crushed by an unmoving weight. "Reid?"

"I'm okay."

More gunshots boomed. The wagon veered, lurched, and slammed into something solid.

Emma's heart nearly exploded from her chest. She clung to Reid. "What's happening? Is Riley hit?"

"Only by glass," came Riley's furious reply. "You okay, Emma?"

"Yes."

"Get us the hell out of here, Riley." Reid's growling order resonated inside the cabin.

Riley gunned the engine, burning rubber as the tires squealed. "I asked my commander to investigate the allegations against Hanson, but she hasn't got back to me yet. After this attack, extra police will be here within a couple of hours. We'll get him, Emma."

Clammy, nauseous, and squished in Reid strong arms, Emma prayed for a miracle. This was far worse than a person with a grudge. This was a deranged killer.

"Stay down." Riley kept driving as he radioed his commander. After reporting their situation and asking for assistance, he contacted Abby to update her and AJ then he drove around the back of the police station. "This is the safest place for the moment." He jumped out and opened Emma's door. "Hell, Emma, you don't look so good."

She was hit with refreshingly cold air, but it was too little too late. "I don't feel so well." She gagged. "I need to get out. I'm going to be sick." She pushed away from Reid, escaping the confines of the police wagon. She'd only taken a couple of steps when her stomach spasmed and she threw up over the concrete path. Instantly, a contraction hit, causing her to gasp.

"Let's get her inside." Reid swept her up in his arms and ran up the path.

"This is my fault." Emma clung to Reid as Riley unlocked the back door. "Everyone is in danger because of me."

"Emma. This isn't your fault." Reid lowered her to a chair in the meal room. "You couldn't know Glenn Hanson would lose his mind. No one could."

Riley's phone pinged and after locking the door behind them, he withdrew his mobile from his pocket and read a text. "That's if it is Glenn Hanson." His grim stare fixed on Reid. "Jerry Eckford withdrew ten grand last week."

CHAPTER 11

The sun was just rising as Reid crouched in front of the huge fireplace in the lounge room of Tulachmhor House. He fed the flames with kindling as he shot glances at Emma. She'd closed herself off, huddled in the corner of the plush four-seater sofa, cradling a cup of camomile tea in her hands. He could understand her not wanting to talk, she'd been nauseous since throwing up at the police station.

He placed a couple of logs on the fire then stood. "That should warm the house."

She didn't answer, seemingly lost in thought as she stared into the orange flames. Occasionally she'd glance at the other end of the room, where the others were congregated around the massive dining table. They were debating whether to flee Bindarra Creek or stay and fight. Their raised voices made it impossible not to hear every word. The women seemed to be winning the argument to stay.

Sam and Ali had lent Emma a pair of thick socks and winter pyjamas. They hadn't been enough to chase away her shivers though. Reid crouched down in front of her. "Hey,

Em. We're safe. The house is locked up. Gates are padlocked. Fences are electrified. Your uncle is monitoring the cameras. Riley's got police stationed outside, and us guys will take shifts staying awake. No one will get close."

"Thank you." She cleared her throat. "I'm so scared one of you will be hurt. It's churning my stomach. I wish I'd never met Glenn."

"If you hadn't, you would have stayed in Sydney and married some other guy. We can't change the past, Emma, but if it weren't for Glenn's narcissistic tendencies, we wouldn't be together now. You wouldn't have attended that fateful New Year's Eve party in our barn. I'll never regret falling in love with you, Em. You've changed my life for the better."

"I know, but none of you would be in danger, if it weren't for me."

"This is not your fault, love." Reid took the empty mug from her then sat on the sofa and drew her against his chest, wrapping his arms around her. "We haven't come this far to let anyone retreat and lick our wounds. Glenn Hanson obviously has a screw loose and needs professional help. Once the police arrest him, everything will go back to normal. It's a hell of story to tell our grandchildren."

Emma's big brown eyes filled with tears. "The only way to safeguard all the people I love, is for me to lead Glenn away from Bindarra Creek. I couldn't live with myself if something happens to any of you."

Reid shook his head. "The chances of him getting close to any of us is minimal."

"What about my family?"

"I've spoken to your dad and your sister. They wanted to join us here, but there isn't enough room. For your peace of mind, I've asked them to visit your paternal grandparents in Inverell. With luck, it will only be for a couple of days."

"Thank you." Emma straightened and met his gaze. "We need to set a trap for him."

He exhaled. "Riley won't allow it. Too many things can go wrong. There's an APB out for him and extra police have been sent to Bindarra Creek. They will find him, Emma. We have to sit tight and let the police do their job."

"It's not that easy, Reid. Glenn managed to get in and out of the hospital without anyone noticing. He got too close to me. I don't know whether it's revenge for leaving him, or he blames me for the path his life has taken. Is his plan to hurt you, or kill me? It's scary, but I can't just sit here and wait for him to make his next move." She turned back to stare into the flames.

Her resolve worried Reid. "He won't deny us our future, Emma. I won't allow it."

"*We* won't allow it." She pushed up from the sofa. "I'm for staying here and fighting. Are you with me?"

"You know I am." He came to his feet.

With a flick of her ponytail, she took his hand and padded across the loungeroom.

Reid fought a smile as he pulled out a chair, sat and pulled her onto his lap. Emma was going to make one hell of a wife and mother. Even though exhausted and frightened, she would fight to her last breath for those she loved. He met her challenging gaze and nodded. *Yes, Em, I'm with you. Always.*

Reid wrapped his arms around Emma then turned his attention to Jake, who was attempting to argue his point with the women.

"You will all be safer with the children away from here." Jake crossed his arms. "Go to the coast for a few days."

"No." Ali glared at her husband. "Jake, together we are stronger. Apart we are vulnerable."

Reid cleared his throat. "The ladies are right. We should stay together, but." He held up a hand as the other four men exclaimed and swore. "Hear me out. This guy is after Emma. He can't get close to this house without being seen by us and the police. That means we have a stalemate, which could last days, weeks or even months, but he needs to stay somewhere. I suggest we discreetly put his description about town, especially the caravan park, motels, pubs, and any private B&B's."

"Good thinking," mused his grandmother. "I'll ring my CWA friends."

"I have given the extra police Doctor Hanson's description and we already have a door knock under way." Riley looked around the table of faces. "The problem is, we can't stay locked up in this house for weeks. Nor will my commander justify an on-going police presence."

"We won't have to," chimed in Samantha. "We can still go about town, run the farms, and go to work. We just don't go anywhere alone. Emma is never alone."

Resignation flitted across Riley and Jake's faces. They knew when they were outnumbered. A sense of relief flooded Reid. If Emma had left town, he would have gone with her, which meant finding someone to help his father manage Tulachmhor.

"That reminds me. Has anyone seen Jerry?" Reid glanced around the table.

Everyone shook their heads.

"Okay, does anyone know why he withdrew ten grand?"

Again, everyone shook their heads.

Hunter frowned. "You don't think Bob stole that money from Jerry, do you?"

"I don't know what to think." Reid stared at the ceiling. "It's unlike him to keep secrets."

"Ouch." Emma winced, her hand going to her belly.

"What's wrong?" Reid spread his fingers over her belly. It was as hard as a rock. "Is that normal?"

"Yes, it's a Braxton Hick's contraction. Normal at this stage of pregnancy." She took in a deep breath then let it out slowly. Her belly softened under Reid's hand. "It's gone."

"Emma, did you know Glenn Hanson has a gun license?" Riley held his mobile in his hand but was watching Emma closely.

She frowned. "We never discussed it, but I assumed he did, as he belongs to a clay pigeon shooting club. He didn't keep a rifle at the apartment though. And he didn't go very often as his workload was too hectic. When he had a weekend off, he preferred to relax and catch up on articles that interested him."

Riley place his mobile on the table and scribbled in his notebook. "Do you know if he was a good shot?"

"I never saw him shoot, but he once told me he was the clay shooting champion at his private school and he had a few trophies from his club."

"So, he knows how to handle a rifle." The concern was clear in Hunter's voice. He rubbed his fingers back and forth over his chin. "We have a handful of unexplainable break-downs and odd things happening here on Tulachmhor. There is Gypsy's baiting and shooting. A possible intent to shoot Emma. The cottage fire, which Kel tells me, could be arson. One dead body, but no real proof who the killer is. We know there is an internal investigation into Hanson's behaviour while on duty, but no evidence he's using drugs. We have a note, which may or may not have been written by Hanson. Ten grand was found buried near Bob's body. Jerry withdrew ten grand several days ago and is now missing. We have the attack on Vince Stark that might or might not be associated with the vandalism of Emma's Beetle. We have someone who entered the doctors lounge and set off the hospital fire alarm. We know someone wearing a balaclava ran from the hospital. They might be laser pointer, who almost ran me off the road, and Hanson is missing." Hunter shook his head. "Have I forgotten anything, Riley?"

"I can't comment, mate."

Emma raised her hand. "Glenn Hanson rang my parents looking for me. Oh, and my friend Brenda, said he's been asking about me."

Riley's head snapped up. "Who exactly is Brenda?"

"Brenda Barker. We met during my internship before I started dating Glenn. She is a midwife, specialising in the care of premature babies."

"I see. Do you think Hanson might target your friend?"

Emma reared back. "I don't know. He didn't like me spending time with her."

"Hmm. Did Hanson have many friends?"

"Not close friends. He had colleagues who thought highly of him, but he didn't like socialising with people he worked alongside. He was close to his brother, who moved to Holland to take up a research grant before I met Glenn. He's an immunologist."

Riley shook his head. "Not anymore. He died from a brain aneurism two months ago."

Emma gasped. "That's terrible. Their parents died when Glenn was at uni. I don't think he has any other family."

Riley scratched his head. "Emma, from where I stand, you don't seem to have had much in common with Hanson? You are outgoing. He sounds like an introvert. You are empathetic and genuinely close to your patients. According to staff in Hanson's orthopaedic ward, he did not have a good bedside manner."

Emma screwed up her nose. "He used to be empathetic and attentive." She winced, her free hand clutching her belly. She looked at Reid. "Another Braxton Hicks. It's nothing to worry about."

Reid wasn't so sure.

Emma's attention returned to Riley. "When we first started dating, Glenn would watch rom coms with me, even though they weren't his thing. He loved running and did it every morning."

"Running?" Reid met Riley's alert gaze. "The guy we chased was quick. I remember thinking I'd never seen Bob move that fast."

"Which explains how he got away from the hospital fast enough to get into position with that laser pointer," added Emma. "It wouldn't have taken much to find out where I'm living. There are plenty of well-meaning residents in Bindarra Creek who would happily point a visitor in the right direction. Either Tulachmhor or the hospital."

"You're right." Jake sat in an armchair with Ali half asleep on his lap. "They just have to say they were an old colleague or a relative. That's why I'd prefer you ladies and the children take a holiday."

"Me too," agreed Riley.

Samantha, who had been folding washing at the end of the table, slammed her palm on the table. "There's no guarantee this creep won't follow us. If us ladies are here, there is more chance you men won't take any chances. We don't want our children to grow up without their fathers." A tear ran down her face.

"Sammy." Riley pushed back his chair and strode around the table, wrapping his arms around Samantha. "Sweetheart, that's not going to happen. Look, the detectives from Tamworth should be here tomorrow, and they will take over the case."

"We have three visitors," announced James Morgan. He had a large monitor set up on the kitchen bench. "The friendly, busybody kind, along with one of the cops. Front door."

Reid checked his watch. *Six-fifteen. What now?* He stood

and placed Emma on the chair. "I'll head them off." He wasn't surprised to see Riley follow him.

Chattering female voices had Reid sighing. "I don't believe this." He opened the door and scowled at the three elderly faces beaming at him. "Hello, ladies. What can I do for you at this extremely early time of morning?"

Mrs. Pamela Brown, a notorious gossip stepped forward. "We have information."

"Really." Reid glanced at the sun just rising behind them. "You'd better come in."

Mrs. Brown brushed past him, her sweet sister, Mrs. Beatrix Fukuka followed then Ms. Edwina Lette, the town's self-proclaimed clairvoyant and flamboyant hippie. This morning she wore stripy leggings and a long knitted, hairy jumper. Her grey hair flowing free. Reid had a soft spot for Edwina and Beatrix, but Pamela Brown, he preferred to steer well clear of.

Edwina patted Reid's shoulder as she toed off her pink gum boots. "We rise early for Tai chi on Sunday mornings, but today we thought it wiser to convey our news." She flicked her hair and followed the other women down the hall.

"Just what we need," muttered Riley.

Reid entered the dining room to find the three elderly ladies squished in around the table, as happy as pigs in mud. The table had been extended on both ends and four more chairs added.

As usual, Pamela Brown spoke first. "We heard about the ten thousand dollars found on Eagle Rock."

Riley muttered an oath only Reid heard, before leaning against the sideboard. "Mrs. Brown, who told you that?"

Edwina Lette elbowed Pamela. "That's irrelevant, young man. What's important is where the ten thousand came from. Did you know Jerry Eckford withdrew ten thousand dollars from his bank account last week?"

"Yes."

"Oh!" All three ladies deflated momentarily then Pamela Brown perked up. "Have you considered he and Mr. Farrell were in cahoots?"

"Mrs. Brown." Reid straightened from the wall he'd been leaning against. He could just see that bit of gossip speeding along the grapevine. "Jerry and Bob didn't get on and why would Jerry be party to hurting the Sullivans? We've been neighbours and friends for years. He was more than happy to sell us his property before the bank repossessed it."

"Well, he does come from a family of criminals." Pamela gave a snooty shake of her head. "His mother was part of a scheme to get Chelsea married to her eldest son, who then tried to kill her. Lighting fires might run in the family."

"Mrs. Brown. Jerry isn't like his mother or his brother," argued Hunter.

"You're right, dear." Beatrix Fukuka blushed as everyone looked at the shy little woman. She gave a nervous cough. "But he is a descendant of Victoria Sullivan and Nathanial Morgan, who eloped because their families refused them permission to marry. They did it anyway and were cast out of both families."

Reid turned to his grandmother and Therese Morgan, who were sitting side by side at one end of the table. "Is that true?"

His grandmother frowned. "I remember reading some-thing about that elopement in the family history Frank compiled."

"I do too, Kathleen." Therese looked over the top of her glasses, at the large ceiling fan. "If I recall correctly, Jerry's great, great grandfather bought that land next to Tulachmhor in the late eighteen hundreds then claimed to be the only child of Victoria and Nathaniel Morgan. His claim didn't go down well and got shoved under the carpet by all concerned. Do you think Jerry holds a grudge against us?"

Riley sighed. "Grandy, please don't make assumptions. Rumours like this can destroy people's lives and reputations. Jerry Eckford is a good guy. I'm … sure of it."

"No, it can't be Jerry." Emma met Reid's gaze. "Jerry is too nice to be a killer or an arsonist. Maybe he heard the rumours and is afraid everyone will turn on him. What if he withdrew that money for … a holiday and Bob stole it? He could be afraid the police think he hired Bob to cause trouble and didn't know what to do so he took off."

Reid didn't want to dash the hope in her eyes, but until he knew for sure, he wasn't taking any chances. "Emma, actions speak louder than words. Jake checked the shearer's quarters while we were at the police station. Drawers were hanging open and Jerry's swag isn't there. It looks like he left in a hurry."

"Okay, well that doesn't look good, but as I said, he could have panicked." Emma's eyes flared. "What if Jerry went back to the shearer's quarters and Glenn was there?" She stood and padded over to Reid. "It could be Glenn who took the clothes and swag." Her fingernails dug into his arm. "He might have forced Jerry to go with him and ... killed him."

"We don't know anything for sure, Emma. He could well turn up today with a plausible reason for withdrawing ten grand and … taking off without a word."

"I hope so." Emma shuddered against Reid.

Reid glanced around the sea of worried faces. Could they all be barking up the wrong tree? Could Jerry be the person with a grudge against both families? Did he charge up Eagle Rock and shoot Bob Farrell while Hunter ran into the house for their rifles? He was a fit guy. It wouldn't have been difficult for Jerry to lose them, dispose of the rifle, then double back to the camp site to wait for the police.

Reid could read the same thoughts in everyone's faces. "Hang on a minute. We can't condemn Jerry without hard evidence. If he knew what we were thinking, he'd be devastated."

"You're right, Reid." Hunter scratched his whiskers. "But I'm not prepared to take that chance with Chelsea or our twins."

"Me either," stated Jake.

"Then there is only one solution." Hannah Morgan rubbed her hands together. "We unite and defend what's ours." She rubbed Emma's shoulder. "That includes you, love."

Looking around the faces of his family and friends, Reid knew Hannah meant business. He could see the same determination on each of the ladies faces. There would be no swaying them. To be honest, he was much more comfortable knowing they'd be here.

"Right." His grandmother pushed her chair back and stood. "You and Emma need sleep. The children will be awake in any minute and full of beans. I suggest we take it in shifts to entertain the children and patrol the house. I'm happy to take the first guard duty."

"I'll assist you, Kathleen." Therese Morgan clambered to her feet. "Those who haven't had any sleep should grab a few hours. We can drink tea while we watch those monitors."

"Not so fast, Grandy." Riley tapped a finger against his lip then seemed to come to a decision. "The extra police from Tamworth have this house and the front gate covered. There is no reason for you to go outside or answer a knock on the door. Understand?"

"Perfectly."

Riley turned to Reid. "If you could work out an inside

roster for tomorrow with Hunter, I'd be obliged. Dad's had a long drive back from Mildura and needs some sleep."

Edwina Lette rubbed her hands together. "Bindarra Creek is becoming a hive of intrigue and mystery. And it's going to get more intriguing over the coming months, mark my words." She pushed back her chair. "Come along, Pamela, Beatrix. We have work to do."

"Ms. Lette." Riley pointed a finger at Edwina. "You and your cronies are not to get involved, and I'd appreciate it if you would all refrain from saying anything to anyone about Jerry Eckford. This is a police matter, and the police will deal with it."

"Of course, Riley." She patted his cheek. "What would three old ladies like us know what to do with a killer?" She winked at Reid. "I already know you will save the day and I'm looking forward to your wedding, which with luck will happen before your baby arrives. But to be sure, I'd advise a quickie wedding asap."

Reid's gaze shot to Emma, who had her hand over her belly. At Edwina Lette's words, Emma bit her lower lip, the fear in her eyes only doubled Reid's apprehension. He picked up her hands. "Come on, Em. You need sleep."

She allowed him to guide her to his father and Antonia's part of the house. The large extension consisted of a sitting room, large bedroom, walk-in-robe and huge ensuite. They would have complete privacy. He made a note to add a walk-in-robe to their own new bedroom when they extended the cottage.

Inside the elegant bedroom, he pulled back the doona for Emma then stripped off everything but his jocks and climbed in his side. With his two nieces in the house, he wasn't taking any chances of being caught naked if they decided to crawl into bed with him and Emma.

Emma removed everything except her singlet top and

panties then turned off the lamp and slid in beside him. She rested her cheek against his shoulder and her hand over his heart. "It's so good to lie down. Can we stay in here forever?"

He chuckled. "Not unless you're prepared to share the bed with my dad and Antonia."

"No. I'm only interested in sharing a bed with you." She snuggled up closer. "Reid?"

"Hmm."

"Tell me about your mother?"

He automatically stiffened. "Emma, you need sleep."

"I want to understand. Please?"

He sighed heavily and stared up at the dark ceiling. "She tricked my father into marrying her. She said he'd got her pregnant at a party. He'd been dating another girl who didn't make it to the party. He got so drunk he couldn't remember much of anything. He was forced to marry my mother but turns out she wasn't pregnant. Years later she admitted he hadn't touched her that night."

"That's terrible. Poor Tom."

"Yeah, Dad tried to make it work, but behind his back she was beating me and Hunter. She locked us in cupboards, starved us as a punishment for making too much noise. Left us locked in the cottage alone to go off shopping or meet a lover. Dad would leave early, work the cattle and fields then come home late. He had no idea, and we were too scared to tell him. After Ali was born, our mother ran off for a long time then extorted my father to take her back."

"Blackmail?" Emma struggled up onto her elbow. "What could she possibly use to blackmail Tom?"

"She threatened to tell the authorities he was abusing her and molesting us."

"What?"

"Dad had no choice but to allow her back, but refused to share a room with her, and she couldn't physically hurt me and Hunter because we were much bigger. As we were then living in the big house, Gran was there to protect us, but it wasn't a happy childhood for any of us. Antonia was married to Dad's brother who died. We've always loved Anty. We wished she was our mother, and now she is our stepmother. End of story."

"I'm so sorry, Reid. No child deserves to be raised like that. I swear to you now, I will love any children we have, and I will do whatever it takes to protect them and you."

CHAPTER 12

*W*aking to find herself surprisingly refreshed and as warm as toast, Emma went to stretch than froze. Reid had her cocooned within his arms, her back against his warm chest, exactly the way they'd fallen asleep however many hours ago that had been.

Tulachmhor House was amazingly quiet for the number of adults and children within its walls. Maybe they were all in the family room on the other side of the house with the doors closed. She carefully reached out for Reid's phone and checked the time. Seeing it was almost two o'clock in the afternoon, she gasped.

"What is it?" Reid's fingers tightened on her hip as he came fully awake. "Are you okay? Is something wrong?"

"I'm fine. I didn't mean to wake you, but I saw the time and freaked."

"There's no rush to get up. Ali snuck in while you were sleeping. She and Jake have taken their kids to the clinic with them today. Riley got a report a man matching Hanson's description was seen in one of the pubs last night, so he left early to go into town and look around."

"It's very quiet. Where is everyone else?"

"According to Ali, our grandmothers are cooking up a storm in the kitchen. Samantha and Chelsea are with their children in the family room and your aunt is watching the monitors."

"Where are Hunter and Uncle James?"

"Gone to check on Hickory Ridge. Don't worry, they have two constables with them." He kissed her gently, as if she were made of finely spun Venetian glass. It wouldn't do. Her pregnancy had sent her libido into overdrive and after the last couple of days without any intimate moments, it needed satisfying.

"Reid." She arched into him, at least as far as her abdomen would allow. "Kiss me properly. I have a need only you can take care of."

"Never let it be said I don't take care of you." He worshipped her throat with open mouthed kisses. "Better?"

"A little, although I feel a mite overdressed." Grinning, she whipped off her singlet top and panties then rolled over, pushing back against his erection. "That's better."

A deep chuckle rumbled against her ear as his large hand covered her breast, his thumb stroking across her taut nipple. "I do love you, Em." His warm breath tickled her skin as he layered kisses across her shoulder blade. "So much, it may take a while to show you."

"I'm not going anywhere." She turned her head, thrilled when he took her mouth greedily, sending a fiery pleasure deep to her core. A thorough loving was just what she needed. Within minutes, she'd been set alight, aching for Reid's touch.

* * *

HALF AN HOUR OR SO LATER, Emma picked up Reid's hand and kissed his palm. "Making love should come in prescription form. It makes everything better."

His chuckle warmed her heart. "Is that your opinion as a doctor or my soon-to-be wife?"

"Both, but you should always take your doctor's advice."

"I'll remember that." He kissed her shoulder. "We should get up."

"I know. I just don't want to face a day like yesterday."

A light knock had them both looking towards the door. Reid pulled the covers over them both. "Who is it?"

"Samantha. Is Emma awake?"

"Yes, why?"

"Your friend Brenda turned up at the police station. Riley didn't want to leave her in town in case your ex spotted her, so he brought her out to Tulachmhor."

"Brenda's here?" Emma threw the covers aside and scrambled into her pyjamas.

"Yes. She's been trying to ring you and texting since last night, but you didn't answer. She got worried, so jumped in her car and drove here. Someone at the bakery told her about the shooting so she went to the police station."

"Oh, my goodness." Emma threw Reid's T-shirt at him. "My phone is missing. Brenda would have been frantic."

"Why would you think that?" came Brenda's familiar sarcastic voice. "It's not like I'd be worried or anything."

"Sorry, Bren. Give me five minutes to shower and find some clothes."

"Please, I don't need details. I'll be in the kitchen with a strong coffee."

Reid had pulled on his clothes from yesterday and now grinned at Emma. "I think I'm going to like your friend, but she can't stay, it's not safe. If Hanson is here and he recognises her, he might go after her to hurt you."

"I know. Once we've had something to eat, I'll persuade her to continue on to her parents in Cobar. I don't want her in any danger."

"I'm sure Riley has explained that to Brenda. Oh, and Ali told me to tell you to borrow anything you need from Antonia's wardrobe. She won't mind."

"Thanks, I will. What are your plans for today?"

Reid opened the blinds and looked out across the paddocks. "As soon as Hunter gets back, we're going to take a couple of constables and check the boundary fences and gates. I promise not to get out of the cruiser unless it's absolutely necessary. By then the tracker and his dog should be here, so we will show him where we lost the person we were chasing. Riley will be with us."

"Okay, be careful." She stretched up kissed him. "I love you."

"Ditto, Em. I want to talk to Riley, then I'll come meet your friend."

Emma watched Reid pace across the bedroom with her heart in her mouth. If anything happened to him, she'd never get over it. She closed her eyes and sent up a prayer asking for his protection.

Once she'd showered and dressed, she rushed to the kitchen, excited on one hand to have Brenda in Bindarra Creek, but also terrified she'd become a target. Best to get her out of town as fast as possible.

Her friend sat on a stool at the kitchen counter, drinking coffee. She'd always been curvy, and liked to flaunt her assets, but the clingy low-cut tank top and shorts wouldn't keep her warm in this weather and would shock the strait-laced Pamela Browns of Bindarra Creek.

"Brenda!" Emma hurried across the kitchen and hugged her old friend. "It's good to see you."

"Yeah well. You haven't been back to Sydney in five years,

and when you wouldn't answer my calls or texts, I had to do something."

"Someone stole my phone, and my brain was in overload. You look fantastic."

"Thank you." She leaned around Emma and smirked. "Am I right in assuming this handsome devil is your fiancé?"

Emma glanced over her shoulder at Reid, standing in the doorway, looking sinfully sexy with his five o'clock shadow thing happening. "Yes, he certainly is." She drew away from Brenda and held out her hand to Reid. "Reid, this is Brenda. Possibly the best midwife in the southern hemisphere."

"Wow, that's some plug. Thanks, hon, but you exaggerate." Brenda shook Reid's hand. "Nice to finally meet you, Reid. I've heard nothing but good things about you. You've got my heart-felt thanks for making this girl so happy."

Reid released Brenda's hand and drew Emma against his chest. "I'm the one who needs to thank you, Brenda. Without your help, we probably wouldn't have crossed paths. I knew Emma was special the first night I met her. The only regret I have is keeping her at a distance for so long. The last two years have been the happiest I can remember."

"Oh, that is so sweet." Brenda raised an eyebrow at Emma. "Any more like him in town who are single?"

Emma laughed. "Maybe, but I got the best one."

"Hey!" Samantha pointed a plastic dinosaur at Emma. "I got the best one."

"Not even close," called Chelsea as she placed toasted rolls on the counter. "Hunter is by far the most handsome man in town."

"In your eyes, love." Aunt Hannah smiled at Emma. "For what it's worth I consider Riley and Jake to be the best looking. They take after their father."

Brenda chuckled. "Emma's cousins, the twins, right?"

"Right," grumbled Chelsea. They are my brothers.

Brenda winked at Emma. "So, who is the guy you want to introduce me to? Jerry something?"

If it was possible for the temperature in the room to drop several degrees, it did. When no one spoke, Brenda gave Emma a what-the-hell look. "Did I say something wrong?"

"No, Bren." Emma gritted her teeth. "I thought Jerry would be perfect for you, but I might have been wrong. Aside from that, you can't stay."

"Sorry?" A flush rose in Brenda's checks. "You want me to leave?"

"Yes. No." Emma pulled out of Reid's arms and grabbed one of Brenda's hands. "I don't want you to leave, but there's been some scary things happening. Someone could be targeting me, and I don't want you to get hurt, if that person decides to go after people I care about."

"Are you serious?" Brenda glanced around the room, obviously noting all the solemn faces watching her. "You are serious."

Riley, who had followed Reid in, strolled behind the counter and put his arm around Samantha. "Very serious, Brenda. Until we have more to go on, we aren't taking any risks. Unfortunately, as you spent some time searching for Emma this morning, your presence in town is common knowledge by now. That could make it dangerous for you to stay around."

"Wow." Brenda shook her head. "I thought Bindarra Creek was supposed to be a quiet little community where nothing much happens?"

"Usually it is." Emma gave a light shrug. "If I'd had my phone, I would have called you today. It's possible Glenn is my stalker, and he may have taken my phone."

Brenda blinked. "Glenn? Actually, I wouldn't put it past him. He's been strange since you left. He hasn't spoken to me since I refused to give him your new number. Please tell me you don't still use a swipe motion to unlock your phone or the same pin?"

Heat rose in Emma's face. "I could tell you that, but it wouldn't be true."

Brenda's mouth dropped. She looked across the counter to Riley. "If Glenn is Emma's stalker, it means he's probably read all our texts. He doesn't like me."

"Which is why you can't stay," announced Reid.

"I've been driving for six hours." Brenda rubbed her forehead. "I'm too tired to get back in my car and drive to Cobar now."

"Of course you're not driving to Cobar now." Emma scowled at Reid and Riley. "Brenda will be safe here at Tulachmhor for one night. I won't have her falling asleep behind the wheel."

"One night should be fine." Riley pinched a piece of cheese off the board where Sam was layering tomatoes, eggs, lettuce, and cheese on the buns. "What's at Cobar, Brenda?"

"My parents. I haven't seen them for several years. I had planned to visit them before the wedding, so having my company for a few extra days will make them ecstatic." She frowned at Reid. "Are you sure Emma will be safe here? It's sort of isolated."

"We've taken precautions and there's a lot of us staying in the house. We have external cameras, police at the gates and electric fences. Emma is safer here than anywhere else."

"It's true, Bren." Emma caught her friend's hand and squeezed. We are hoping the police catch … whoever is stalking me quickly, so things can get back to normal. Even so, nothing is going to stop me marrying Reid before this little tiger is born." She rubbed her hard-as-a-rock abdomen.

Brenda's gaze dropped. "Everything okay with the baby?"

"The baby is fine, but I've been getting minor contractions over the last 24 hours."

"You want me to check you're not dilating. I know you're the doctor, but trauma and anxiety can bring on labour."

"I'm good, but thanks for the offer." Emma smiled at her friend. "This isn't how I wanted to welcome you to Bindarra Creek, Bren, but I promise to make it up to you."

"I'm holding you to that. If Glenn *is* stalking you, I really do fear for your safety."

"Riley will catch whoever it is," pronounced Samantha. Now, who wants a hamburger?" She pushed a huge tray of burgers across the counter. "Help yourselves. There's plenty."

* * *

ONCE EVERYONE HAD EATEN their fill, and downed several pots of tea, Emma stood by the French doors and watched Reid leave with her uncle, two constables and Hunter. She prayed they'd be safe. With a heavy sigh, she turned back to the others. Babies, toddlers, and Elise crawled and played on the large rug. Chelsea had dragged in a huge cardboard carton, which she and Samantha intended turning into a cubbyhouse for the kids. The older ladies were already comfortable on the sofa with their knitting. Brenda hovered near the fireplace. She sent Emma a get-me-out-of-here look.

Laughing Emma joined her. Brenda wasn't into knitting, and she didn't know these women. "Come on, Bren. It's going to get very loud in here soon. We can catch up in Antonia and Tom's sitting room."

"Great." She followed Emma to the other side of the house. "Not that your family and friends aren't lovely, but I came here to see you."

"I know." Movement outside the window caught Emma's attention. A police vehicle pulled up at the front of the house and two police officers got out. Another walked down the path to meet them. The place was swarming with police. Riley wasn't taking any chances.

"So, tell me what's been happening at the hospital? Any changes?" Emma patted the sofa beside her. "I've missed our lunch breaks together."

It really was lovely to see Brenda, yet barely twenty minutes passed, and they were running out of things to talk about. Maybe it was because they weren't working together anymore or maybe Emma had changed since coming to Bindarra Creek. The city didn't interest her anymore and neither did the politics of a big hospital. She was about to suggest Brenda grab some sleep when a knock on the door stopped her.

Aunt Hannah poked her head around the door. "Sorry to disturb you ladies, I've just heard Jerry's ute has been found at Glenmeer. There's no sign of him, but the ute was parked near the coach stop. It's possible he caught a bus to Armidale or Sydney. Riley is checking."

Brenda frowned. "Why are you all so concerned with this Jerry guy? Is he another suspect?"

"Jerry is a farmhand on Tulachmhor, and he's gone missing. It's not like him." Emma didn't want to disparage Jerry. Not without hard evidence.

Brenda's lips twitched. "Maybe he heard you were lining up a blind date with me and he's not interested. It' a bit over the top to flee town, but it happens." She chuckled at her own joke, but there was a sadness to her eyes.

Noticing her aunt slip away, Emma shuffled along the sofa and put her arm around Brenda's slumped shoulders. "What about the guy you were telling me about? The one you broke up with, before we became friends."

Brenda pulled away, her mouth twisting into a grimace. "It's a no goer. He can't move on from his ex." She gave a strangled laugh. "I figured he'd come around. I mean, look at you and Reid. Neither of you wanted a serious relationship and now you're about to get married."

"It's not that we didn't want a serious relationship." Emma removed her arm and turned to fully face Brenda. "We'd both been through traumatic events. Reid's mother was violent and left him with trust issues. As for me …." She inhaled deeply. "After Glenn changed so dramatically, I was terrified of finding myself in another abusive relationship. I needed time alone to regain my confidence and self-esteem. Then I met Reid and we fell in love."

"I'm happy for you, hon." Brenda squeezed Emma's hand. "Pity about Jerry Eckel."

"Eckford." Emma forced a smile. "You grew up in the country, so how come you didn't go back to Cobar when you finished your training?"

"Ah, in Sydney there was a smorgasbord of men who didn't know me. Country towns can be restricting for a girl who wants to … try before she buys. I didn't want to scandalise my parents." Brenda looked out the window. "I do sometimes miss the wide, open spaces though." She yawned. "Is there an empty bed I can hog for a few hours?"

"Take that bed." Emma pointed through to Antonia and Tom's bedroom. "Reid and I have been sleeping there, but you can lie on top if you want and there's a warm throw on the chair if you're cold. I will make sure no one disturbs you."

"Thanks, hon." Brenda yawned again. "I appreciate it."

Pushing up off the sofa, Emma padded to the suite's outer door. "Sleep well, Bren. I'll see you later." She closed the door behind her and returned to the kitchen. The other ladies would probably appreciate a pot of tea and a biscuit about now.

The garden gate creaking had her looking out the window. Seeing Reid striding up the path was a sight for sore eyes. The other men were standing beside Riley's patrol car talking.

Reid kicked off his boots then opened the back door, his anxious gaze fixed on her immediately. She could sense his relief at seeing her. He tossed his Akubra at the hooks on the back wall then came around the counter and wrapped her in a bear hug. "Everything looks fine with the fences and gates, but I couldn't wait to get back to you."

"Me either." Their lips met in a desperate kiss. Emma clung to Reid, unwilling to let the love of her life go even for a second. She couldn't lose him. She couldn't.

He eased back. "Hey, what's up?"

She dropped her forehead against his chest. "It all just hit me. I'm terrified you'll get shot and I won't get to grow old with you. I'll never get to kiss you again. Never feel your arms around me or get to cuddle up with you in front of the fire. I can't abide the thought of our child never knowing you. A sob caught in her throat, quickly followed by a simmering fury. "I will not allow anyone to take you from me. Do you hear me?"

"Shush, love." Reid lifted her chin, so she had no choice but to meet his determined gaze. "We are safe here. No one can get close without being seen. Riley's commander has given him six cops to staff the gates and patrol outside this house. More have arrived from Tamworth and Armidale to check out the hotels, pubs, and caravan park. The army have offered troops if we need to search the National Park. It's only a matter of time before this guy is apprehended. As long as I know you and the baby are safe, that our families are safe, I can breathe easier."

Emma sniffed. "Reid, I need you." Her croaky whisper had him tightening his hold. He lowered his head to layer warm kisses down her throat. She pressed her mouth against his ear. "Our son needs you."

He reared back, his fingers digging into her butt, his questioning eyes locked with hers. "It's a boy?"

"Yes, and I want us to raise him together, which means you can't go galivanting about the farm. At least not until it's safe."

A huge smile spread over his face. "Do I get free rein to choose his name?"

She wacked his arm. "I should have known you'd find a way to bribe me." His wicked grin made her heart swell. "Fine. You can choose this time, but I'm warning you, Reid, it must be a normal name. Calling your horse Zeus is one thing. I won't agree to our son being named Hercules, or Horatio, or Hadrian."

"How about Jack, after my uncle?"

"Jack Sullivan." She gasped as the baby kicked. "I think he likes the name. Jack it is."

They came together for a deep, passionate, all-consuming kiss that seared Emma to the core. It had been this way from the beginning. She pressed closer, the fire within her veins building as she felt Reid's erection against her abdomen.

The phone in the hall trilled.

"We should take this to the bedroom," murmured Reid against her ear. His warm breath only inflaming her desire.

"We can't, Brenda's in there." The ringing stopped and Emma eased back. She could hear Kathleen's voice then the door opened. "Emma, Doctor Frobisher is on the phone. She needs to speak to you."

Reid took his time releasing Emma then stepped around her, so she stood in front of him, shielding the bulge in his jeans. "Emma's on parental leave. What's the problem, Gran?"

"Doctor Frobisher said it's about Deidre King."

"I'd better take it." Emma hurried to the hall and lifted the handset. "Jess, what's up?"

"I'm sorry to bother you, Emma. I know you're on leave,

but we've got an emergency, and your midwife, Scarlett, has gone down with a gastro bug."

"What's happened?"

"Deidre King was mugged this morning by a bag snatcher. Her husband brought her in, and I've been monitoring her. I thought all was well, but now she's in labour and I think her contractions are too close to risk sending her to Armidale. As she's your patient, and you have much more experience with premature babies, I'd appreciate you handling this."

Emma glanced at Reid. He wasn't going to be happy, but what choice did she have. "We may still have time to airlift Deidre King to Armidale."

"No can do. They're on another emergency, so is our only ambulance. The paramedics have been called out to a suspected heart attack on a property past Glenmeer,"

"Right. I'm on my way."

CHAPTER 13

Fast walking with a baby weighing on her bladder was not Emma's idea of fun. Neither was having Deidre King deliver her baby at thirty-three weeks, or Reid and Brenda protesting their displeasure as they followed hot on her heels into the hospital lift. "There's no choice. Deidre and her baby need me."

"Emma, this is madness," muttered Reid. "Can't she be airlifted to Armidale?"

"Apparently not. The rescue helicopter is on another job." The lift doors opened, and she paced to the maternity ward doors to key in her code.

"Okay, then what about Bindarra Creek's Ambulance Service?" Brenda ran ahead of Emma and blocked her way. "Surely the town's big enough to have one."

"We do, but there is only one ambulance and it's on a call well out of town."

"You have one ambulance?" Brenda blinked at her. "Seriously?"

"Yes." Emma dodged around Brenda. "Bottom line. Mrs.

King is my patient. I'm not prepared to risk the baby's life when I am perfectly capable of delivering it here in the hospital. You know better than anyone that premature babies can deliver quickly."

"Sure, but you have midwives. They can deliver the baby and send it by helicopter." Brenda grabbed Emma's shoulder. "You don't need to be here."

"Yes, I do, Brenda. I have one midwife and she is down with a bug. Once Mrs. King and the baby are on their way to Armidale, I will return to Tulachmhor." Emma frowned at the empty nurse's station and a plate with a tempting lamington on it. "Where is everyone?"

Ishya popped her head out of the double doors further down the corridor. "Doctor Fahey, thank God. Doctor Frobisher has been called down to emergency. Mrs. King is in our delivery suite. I've caught the same bug as Scarlett, so I can't get close to Mrs. King or you. Oh, and there's an urgent message on the top of the counter for you." Ishya clutched her stomach. "Sorry, gotta run." She ducked back behind the door.

"I met Scarlett early this morning when I came here looking for you. What kind of bug has she caught?" asked Brenda.

Emma sighed. "Gastro."

"You're joking." Brenda's mouth dropped. "Who is going to help you deliver the baby?"

"I'm hoping you will." Emma swiped up the white envelope marked urgent and kept walking as she glanced at Brenda. "It's an emergency. We have a duty of care to deliver this baby safely."

"Yeah, you're right. Come on, Doc, it will be just like old times." Brenda jogged down the hall, clicked one door back against the wall and ran around the corner. "It's 5.30pm now, so with luck we will be out of here in time for a late dinner."

Emma walked as fast as she could beside Reid. She stopped at a closed door and stroked his bristly chin. "With the emergency exit door locked, and you right here, and Riley outside the maternity ward doors, no one can get to me."

"All right, but I'm not moving from this spot." He lowered his voice. "If for any reason you feel unsafe, hit the emergency alarm."

"Okay." She stretched up and kissed him. "I love you."

"I'm counting on that. Go deliver that baby." He hugged her then opened the door to anguished cries, a shaky male voice demanding help, and Deidre's no-nonsense responses.

Emma closed the door behind her and bustled into the delivery room, plastering on her cool-as-a-cucumber face. "Hello, Deidre, just let me scrub my hands and find some gloves then we will see what's happening." She smiled at Deidre's puffy-eyed husband. "You are very lucky, because Brenda is a neonatal midwife, one of the best I've ever worked with, and the neonatal retrieval team from Armidale will be here as soon as they can."

"Who are they?" asked Andrew.

"A neonatal doctor and nurse." Brenda gave the Kings a thumbs up. "You are in good hands."

"I just want Deirdre and the baby to come through this." Andrew King's wet eyes implored Emma for an outcome she couldn't promise, but she could try to reassure them both.

"Deidre is healthy, and the second I'm organised, I'll check on the baby." She turned to Brenda, who already wore a surgical mask, fluid repellent apron and disposable gloves. "Bren, can you check the baby's heart rate?"

"I will but let me help you into an apron first."

"Thanks." Emma realised she still held the envelope marked urgent. She ripped it open as Brenda closed the back tabs of the apron. She pulled out a small business card and frowned. It was from a funeral home in Tamworth. Flipping it over, she gasped at the untidy scrawled letters of her name. She shivered as a chill invaded her whole body.

"Everything okay, Doctor Fahey?" The panic in Andrew King's voice snapped her attention back to the desperately scared couple.

"Fine."

She slipped the card back in the envelope then lifted her apron and slipped it into her pocket. Rage almost consumed her as she scrubbed her hands then pulled on a mask and gloves. She was being targeted. Her car, the fire, these pathetic messages. Possibly even the sabotage on Tulachmhor and Gypsy's baiting. The common link between everything was her and she'd had enough. At least her anger smothered her fear.

"Baby's heart rate is fine." Brenda moved the stethoscope to Deidre's chest. "Yours is a little elevated, Mrs. King. Relax, Doctor Fahey is here now."

Deidre nodded. "I'm trying, it's just that we've waited so many years for this baby."

Emma gave Deidre a reassuring smile then nodded for Brenda to lift the sheet. They both gasped at the sight of Deidre's grazed knees.

"How did that happen?" exclaimed Brenda. "Your knees," she clarified.

"A damn bag snatcher." Andrew scowled. "Dee went to wait in the car while I filled the trolley with our grocery bags. When I got to the car, she was sitting on the ground crying. He shoved a pregnant woman to the ground. Who does that?"

Emma was as astounded as Brenda. "Did you get a look at him, Deidre?"

"No, he … he wore a balaclava. I was so terrified he was going to kick me, that I curled into ball."

"I hope you reported it to police," muttered Brenda.

"We didn't have time." Andrew rubbed Deidre's arm. "I got Dee here as fast as I could."

Brenda shook her head. "Senior Sergeant Morgan is outside the maternity ward. We should tell him. I thought Bindarra Creek was supposed to be a quiet little backwater town where nothing bad happens?"

"It's not a backwater town." Emma ran her eyes over the birthing bed. Brenda hadn't wasted any time. She had it converted to a birthing chair with the bottom half lowered for Deidre's feet to rest on. Emma used her elbow to ease Deidre's legs further apart. "Let's see what this little cherub is doing."

Brenda turned back to the bed with a handful of swabs. "When Doctor Fahey has finished examining you, I'll clean your knees up a bit more, Dee. You've still got dirt in some of these cuts."

"Thank you. Doctor Frobisher had a nurse doing it, but then they were called away— oh, here comes another contraction, but it's low in my back."

Emma silently cursed. The absorbent bed mat was soaked, which meant Deidre's water had broken. The baby's head was engaged, and her cervix almost fully dilated. "Okay." She plastered on what she hoped was a cheerful smile. "Definitely not a false alarm this time."

"But it's too soon." Deidre panted through the contraction. "Can you stop it?"

"Too late, hon." Brenda met Emma's eyes. "How close are we, Doc?"

"Too close to offer Deidre any pain relief. The baby is in the perfect position and ready to come. We'll need warm towels and an IV of dextrose ready to go. The towel warmer is in the cupboard behind you. Everything else is in the sterile room next door."

"On it. Lift your bottom, hon." Brenda shoved a new giant absorbent pad under Deidre. "This is to absorb any amniotic fluid, Dee. You're doing great."

Deidre blew out a breath, closed her eyes, and relaxed back against the bed, clutching her husband's hand.

Brenda placed a box of disposable gloves on top of the treatment trolley. "I know it's a bit late, but do you want me to grab a foetal monitor, Doctor Fahey? That is if you have one here."

"Ha-ha, very funny. This maternity ward may be small, but we are fully equipped, and the staff are fantastic." Emma grinned at Brenda. "If you were to join us, you'd fit right in." Turning serious again she disposed of her used gloves and pulled on a new pair. "You might as well get the belt, it can't hurt."

As Brenda looked for the belt, Emma prayed the neonatal team would get here soon.

Once Brenda pulled on new gloves, she attached the electronic monitoring belt around Deidre's abdomen and an oximeter to her finger.

Andrew King watched on like a hawk. His greenish colour concerned Emma, as he looked ready to faint. He needed distracting.

"Andrew, the peg thing that Brenda attached to Deidre's finger is tracking her pulse. The belt has a Doppler device that monitors the baby's heart rate. The flat paddle is recording the tightening and relaxing of the contractions, and there's a tocodynamometer that tracks the frequency and duration of contractions. Deidre should be used to all this by now. How many false alarms have we had?"

"Five." Deidre gasped. "Here comes another contraction."

Emma checked Deidre's cervix then met Brenda's eyes and gave a nod. They were in for a quick birth. She prayed the baby's lungs and vital organs were developed enough to keep it alive. She'd never lost a baby and she prayed she never would.

The next ten minutes were intense and brutal on Deidre. The phone had rung once with Riley informing them the helicopter was on its way. Everyone in the room sighed with relief.

"Foetal heart rate is slowing," murmured Brenda.

"Is that bad?" Andrew looked at Emma anxiously.

Emma shook her head. "It normally slows as the baby's head compresses for birth. Deidre, we're going to sit you up further, so you're almost squatting. Andrew, if you wouldn't mind helping, Brenda." Emma turned away quickly, wincing as a powerful Braxton Hicks contraction hit. She took a couple of long slow breaths, turning back to her patient once her abdomen relaxed.

Brenda had the bed and Deidre in the right position. Emma disposed of her gloves and rubbed Deidre's shin. "One more big push on the next contraction, Deidre and then you can rest and hold your baby."

"Easy for you to say." Deidre closed her eyes again.

"You're doing great." Emma checked everything was ready then pulled on fresh gloves.

Deidre's eyes sprang open. "Here we go." She took a big breath and screamed out the contraction, and the baby, in a long, slow push, straight into Emma's hands, before sagging, exhausted against the birthing bed.

Emma quickly ran her eyes over the tiny baby, checking her colour, general condition, breathing and reflexes. Only then did she breathe a sigh of relief. "Congratulations, Mr. and Mrs King, you have a little princess."

"A girl." Deidre sobbed into her husband's chest. "Is she okay?"

"Her colour looks good." Emma patted the baby dry with a warm towel. "The important thing is that she stays warm, pink and sweet." Again, Emma wasn't sure whether she was trying to reassure the Kings or herself. "Leave the overhead light on, Bren, and tilt the bed back a little."

"You want me to get the IV ready?"

"Yes, please." Emma pushed the hospital gown off Deidre's shoulder, baring her skin to place the tiny miracle on her mother's chest. "We don't have a special crib here, but it's strongly believed that by putting a newborn on their mother's skin, it helps regulate their breathing."

"Won't she get cold," whispered Andrew, stroking his fingers ever so gently along the baby's back."

"Deidre's skin will warm her with all the heat she needs for now, along with a warm cover over both of them."

Brenda placed a warmed blanket over Deidre and the baby then put a woollen hat on the baby's head. She gave Emma the thumbs up as she placed another blanket in the warmer.

"What about the baby's airway?" Andrew frowned. "Why isn't she crying?"

"I'm watching her. Premature babies don't always cry," soothed Emma, slipping a pulse oximeter on the baby's ankle. She turned to the monitor. "See, your little princess is keeping her oxygen levels within range. What a clever girl. As for you, Deidre. You're a legend. Well done."

"Thank you, Doctor Emma."

"All good." Emma moved to the side of the bed. "Deidre, if you can express some colostrum onto your little finger, put it in the baby's mouth. She's working hard, using up her stores of sugar to keep herself warm and breathing. We need to replace the sugar to stop her becoming hypoglycaemic. We do that by inserting a tiny intravenous drip into her wrist, which will feed her a fluid called dextrose, but just a drop of your colostrum will help." Emma turned to Brenda and lowered her voice. I was hoping the retrieval team would be here by now."

"As they're not, you want to insert the IV, Doc?"

Another contraction had Emma wincing. "Give me a sec." Once it passed, she whipped off her soiled gloves and pulled on new ones, then got the tiny intravenous needle into the baby's wrist. She'd done her best and now could only monitor the baby. It was heaven to sit down, rest her legs, and let Brenda fuss over Deidre and baby.

A knock drew Emma's attention to the door. "I'll see who it is." She struggled to her feet, padded to the door, and cracked it open. "Hi, Reid. What's up?"

"The chopper just landed. Is your patient ready to go?"

"Soon. We're waiting on the placenta to come away, which won't take long. Do you know if there is a neonatal transport team on board the helicopter?"

"Yes, sorry, Riley asked me to tell you that."

"Great. Tell him to bring them in and I'll do the handover. How's Ishya?"

"She's gone home. Did everything go okay? Is the baby …?"

"So far, so good, but we need to get her to Armidale asap."

Reid hesitated. "Emma, Riley got a call from the paramedics. The heart attack call turned out to be a hoax. They arrived at the property only to find the owners in perfect health."

Emma stared at him. "What is going on in Bindarra Creek?"

"It gets more confusing. The bag snatcher was seen sprinting away by Paddy Cullen this morning. He said the guy was dressed in black and wore a balaclava, but the strange thing is, he threw Deidre King's bag away without stealing anything. Paddy picked it up, but the Kings had driven off, so he took it to the police station and reported the incident."

"That is so weird." Emma clutched the door frame as another contraction hit. "You don't think he mistook Deidre for me, do you?"

"I don't know what to think." He sighed. "One thing's for sure. I'm staying right here."

"Thank you, darling. Once I do the handover to the neonatal team, we can go home."

"Yeah. I'll be here if you need me." He pulled out his phone. "I'll let Riley know about the baby and check in with Hunter. Is there anything you need?"

"No, I'm good." Emma shut the door and plastered on her calm professional demeanour face. "Good news, Deidre. The neonatal retrieval team have arrived and once they stabilise the baby and examine you, they'll escort you to Armidale."

"Can I go with them?" asked Andrew. He hadn't stopped stroking the blanket covering the baby's back.

"I don't know, Andrew. You will have to ask them."

"Deidre is having some mild contractions," called Brenda folding the blanket back onto Deidre's stomach. "Do you want to deliver the placenta, Doctor Fahey?"

"Yes, then can you give Deidre a sponge bath so she's more comfortable?"

"Course I can." Brenda swung away to grab a dish and fill it with warm soapy water, leaving Emma to deliver and bag the placenta. They were just finishing up when a knock sounded and two women in scrubs and masks entered.

The doctor and nurse introduced themselves as Julie and Kerri, then assessed the baby and Deidre as they listened to Emma run through the delivery. It took forty-five minutes, but once they had Deidre settled in a wheelchair and the baby in a humidicrib, ready for transport, Julie took Reid's number and promised to ring Emma later. They couldn't take Andrew, so he decided to go home for Deidre's packed suitcase.

After they departed the maternity ward, Emma crumpled against the nurse's station. She gave Reid and Brenda a tired smile. "I need to wee, and I'd kill for a honey and camomile tea."

"No killing necessary." Brenda laughed. "Go make your tea, hon. I'll give the delivery room a scrub down and throw the used bed linen in the sluice room."

"That's not necessary, Bren. I'll message housekeeping and get them to take care of it."

"I've got nothing better to do." She pointed down the hall. "Go wee."

"Yes, ma'am."

A few minutes later Emma came out of the staff restroom as the double doors at the end of the hall crashed open. A wild-eyed man badly in need of a shave charged into the ward wielding a crowbar. "Glenn?"

"Emma!" Reid's bellow behind her unfroze her limbs. She considered making for the emergency exit, but she couldn't risk being pushed down the stairs by her ex. He stopped in his tracks and was staring at her abdomen. There was little left of the clean-cut, handsome man she'd left five years ago. He looked shabby and unkept, as if he'd been living on the streets, or in the bush.

"Back towards me," came Reid's low voice. "Don't make any sudden moves."

Easy for him to say, she wanted to turn tail and run. Holding Glenn's intense gaze, she backed away. Was he on crack or ice? If so, he'd be super strong. There'd be no

145

reasoning with him. He'd be delusional. He didn't look delusional. He looked exhausted and relieved.

He lowered the bar and took a step forward. "You're a hard woman to find, Emma."

Backing slowly, she tried to calm her racing heart. "Why are you here, Glenn?"

"Because you need to come with me." He frowned. "You're pregnant. How did I not know we're having a baby?"

"What?" Glenn had either lost his marbles, or he was drugged to the eyeballs. She needed to tread carefully. Movement behind him caught her attention. Riley and Abby crept stealthily into the ward.

Abby held a gun.

Riley put his finger to his lips then circled it in the air.

She assumed he wanted her to keep Glenn talking. Keep his attention focused on her. Swallowing her panic, Emma took another step back. If she could reason with Glenn, maybe Riley and Abby could overpower him before he hurt her or the baby. "Yes, I'm having a baby. You don't look well, Glenn. Would you like to sit down?"

His eyes darted between her face and abdomen, clearly confused. "You should have told me. Why didn't you tell me?" His gaze shot past her. "Who is he?"

She risked a glance behind, relieved to see Reid so close. Returning her attention to Glenn she tried to smile, terrified anything she said might trigger him to attack. "This is the maternity ward, Glenn. The man behind me is a new father. His wife and baby are in the room behind that door you're blocking. Would you please stand back so he can enter?"

Glenn glanced at the door to his right then took a step back. "Go in, but don't try anything." He waved the bar for Reid to pass in front of him.

The second Reid stepped in front of Emma, she stepped away. Her heart in her mouth as Reid braced his feet wide and faced Glenn, his broad shoulders completely blocked Emma's view.

"What do you want with Em ... Doctor Fahey?" demanded Reid

"It's none of your business," yelled Glenn. "Get out of the way."

"I'm not going anywhere."

"Police! Put the bar down, Doctor Hanson," came Riley's hard command.

"No, you don't understand. She's mine. Mine to p—"

Reid surged forward taking Glenn down hard to the floor. They both clasped the bar, rolling about as they struck out at each other with their free fists and elbows. Suddenly, they were both on their feet again.

Reid bent and drove Glenn against the wall with his shoulder, whacking the bar out of his hand. It flew across the floor narrowly missing Emma's feet.

Glenn hammered his fists into Reid's back then shoved him across the hall.

Reid bounced off the wall, raised his fists and leapt in front of Emma again.

Glenn let out an unearthly scream, clutched his head and collapsed to the floor.

"Holy hell." Reid clutched his right hand, pacing back and forth in front of Glenn's still body, muttering a string of coarse words that would have his grandmother chastising him.

Emma grabbed his arm. "Reid, your hand."

"Nothing an icepack won't fix." He wrapped his other arm around her shoulders and moved her well back as Riley and Abby descended on Glenn.

"Are you okay, Emma?" asked Riley as he pressed two fingers against Glenn's throat.

"I'm good." Emma looked down at Glenn's deathly white

face. "There's something very wrong with him. He could be on drugs, but that scream and the way he clutched his head, makes me think there's something else going on. We need to get him down to emergency." She reached over the nurse's station and pressed the emergency call button.

"I didn't kill him, did I?" Reid grimaced as he stared down at Glenn.

"No, he has a pulse." Riley stood. "I'm sorry. We got a call a man matching Doctor Hanson's description was in reception, so I went down the stairs to head him off. He must have been hiding near the stairwell and when I passed, made his way up here. With the doors locked and you up here with Emma, I thought she'd be safe."

"I couldn't let him hit Emma with that bar." Reid rubbed his eyes. "Why isn't he coming around?"

Emma chewed her lip as she studied her former fiancé. "Riley, when you get him down to emergency, have them do a blood count. If he doesn't regain consciousness soon, he needs to be transferred to Armidale for a brain scan."

Riley's head shot up. "Why?"

"His eyes would be glazed if he's stoned and there's blood trickling from his right ear. Glenn's brother died of an aneurism recently and I think his mother died of a brain tumour. On second thoughts, he should be transferred straight to Armidale for a brain scan, just to be safe. Get him onto a gurney and down to emergency."

A screech had Emma looking over her shoulder. Brenda stood there with her hand clasped over her mouth. She slowly lowered it, her eyes almost popping out of their sockets. "Is that Glenn?"

"Yes. He broke in here with a crowbar." Emma swallowed. "He thinks the baby is his."

Brenda took a step back, a look of horror spreading

across her face. "I didn't believe the gossip, but it must be true. He's on drugs. What if he followed me here?"

"He couldn't have, Bren. You only arrived this afternoon." Emma hugged her. "Brenda, Glenn coming here has nothing to do with you. We all have a choice in which path we follow, and must accept the consequences of our decisions, good and bad. Leaving Glenn was one of the best decisions I've ever made. Moving to Bindarra Creek was another. Glenn made the decision to come here. He is the one with the crowbar."

A mini stampede drew Emma's attention to the main doors as Doctor Frobisher, a wardsman, and two police officers rushed into the maternity ward.

Emma gave Jessamine a quick account of Glenn's behaviour and the family history she knew of as he was loaded onto a gurney. Then she turned to Riley. "You'd better take this." She handed him the envelope with the business card inside. "That was left for me at the nurse's station. I don't know if you'll get fingerprints, but it's worth a try."

"Another note?" asked Riley, his eyes going hard.

With the surge of adrenaline depleted, she started shaking. "No, it's a funeral home's business card with my name on the back."

"Shit." Reid cursed some more then wrapped his arm around Emma's shoulder. "We've got him now, Emma. It's over."

She nodded, her gaze falling on his swollen hand. "We need to get your hand looked out. Then we can go home." Knowing Glenn was in protective custody went a long way to easing her mind, yet something wasn't right. His erratic behaviour and confusion seemed at odds with the calculated attacks and sabotage. If he had a brain tumour it would explain a lot, but it didn't make him a murderer, an arsonist, or a vandal. It didn't make him evil, just obsessed. As Emma left the maternity ward with Reid, she tried to recall everything about Glenn's appearance and behaviour. She hadn't detected any evil intent. Had they got it wrong? A shiver ran down her spine. If Glenn wasn't the killer than it could be someone out to destroy Reid by hurting everyone and everything he care about. *Jerry?*

CHAPTER 14

*S*itting on a bed in the emergency department wasn't helping Reid's mood. He'd much rather be by Emma's side while the detective who'd finally turned up from Armidale interviewed her. Better still, he'd prefer her back at Tulachmhor. She was exhausted. A warm bath, food and sleep were what she needed. He winced. It wasn't a good idea to clench his fist. The pain killers had worn off and his hand was throbbing along with the beat of his heart. It was annoyingly repetitive.

Brenda bustled into Reid's cubicle. "Hey, hero-of-the-hour. How's the hand?"

"Bloody painful. Any news on Hanson's condition? No one will tell me anything."

"He was assessed by Doctor Frobisher and is waiting to be airlifted to Sydney. That helicopter crew are getting a workout today. They are on their way back from Newcastle now." She collapsed onto the only chair, looking tired and drained. "I still can't believe it. Glenn was an amazing orthopaedic surgeon. In the early days, Emma and I sometimes sat in an observation room to watch him work, and we weren't the only ones. To wash all that talent down the drain with drugs is incomprehensible."

She leaned back in the chair and closed her eyes. "When Emma hooked his attention, all the single female staff, and probably some of the male staff went green with envy. Glenn was a gentleman, always polite, and he had that knack of making a woman feel special, whether she was a patient or on staff. No one could believe it when Emma cancelled the wedding."

"She had good reason." Reid frowned at Brenda. "You knew that?"

"I knew something was wrong because Emma had become withdrawn. Where once she'd jump at the chance to go out for drinks or dinner, she came up with dull as mud excuses why she couldn't make it. When she dumped Glenn, I was as stunned and sceptical as any conspiracy theorist. I figured it was wedding jitters, but Emma played me one of his voice mails and frankly, it frightened me. I figured she needed to be as far away as possible." Brenda's eyes sprung open, the fury in them surprising Reid. "I never dreamed he'd come looking for her. It's been over five years, for Pete's sake."

"Yeah, well, hopefully the guy regains consciousness and gets the help he needs. I'm just glad it's over and we can get back to normality." Reid looked down at his bandaged hand. "There's just the mysterious disappearance of my farmhand and his withdrawal of ten thousand dollars to figure out."

"This would be Jerry, the guy Emma wanted to introduce me to?"

"Yeah. I've known him all my life. His family's property borders ours, but it was mortgaged to the hilt and the bank was about to issue a foreclosure notice, so we bought him out. He seemed pleased about it, but now I'm wondering."

"Why?"

"Long story short, the Sullivans and Morgans fell out almost two centuries ago, resulting in a feud that only ended five years ago."

"Emma told me about the feud. What's Jerry got to do with it?"

"Turns out his great, great, great grandparents were a Morgan and a Sullivan, who were denied permission to marry, so eloped. They were cast out of both families."

Brenda sat forward. "So, he could be behind the fire and shooting, not Glenn?"

"We won't know until Jerry turns up and Hanson regains consciousness. Riley and I aren't prepared to take any chances."

"Emma could still be in danger?"

"Possibly." Reid ran his good hand through his hair. "Hanson didn't know Emma was pregnant. That would suggest he didn't hire Bob. Otherwise, he would know about the baby."

"Maybe your dead farmhand figured that bit of information would cut off his income." Brenda stood and paced to the doorway. After peeping out, she came back to Reid. "How long has Emma been having strong contractions?"

"To my knowledge, they started last night. Should we be concerned?"

"Emma is under a lot of stress. She's been anxious about the baby, the wedding, you, and now Glenn. I noticed the baby has dropped, which in first pregnancies usually happens two to four weeks before the due date. It means the baby is in the vertical position with its head down towards the cervix. Stress and anxiety can bring contractions on. We need to keep a close eye on her."

"That's my plan, Brenda."

"What are you two cooking up?" Emma stood in the doorway, caressing her belly. "Should I be worried?"

"Nope, but you should be resting." Reid paced over and hugged her, careful not to bump his sore hand. "Is the detective done with you?"

"Yes, but we got side-tracked talking to the emergency MD. Glenn has regained consciousness and was asking for me. He didn't seem to know where he was and couldn't understand why he's under police guard. They did an X-ray while he was unconscious. Reid, he has a massive growth on his brain. It would explain his confusion and his need for pain killers." She grimaced. "It would also explain his change in character, mood swings and temper. I listened outside the room while the detective and Riley interviewed Glenn. He can't remember anything of the last five years. He thinks we're still together and insists he's never heard of Bindarra Creek."

Reid stiffened. "So, we don't know if he hired Bob Farrell?"

She shook her head. "We may never know. Glenn is being airlifted to Sydney for brain surgery. If he survives the operation, there's a high risk he may be left with brain damage."

Brenda gasped behind them. "You're saying this growth is what changed his personality? Turned him into a different person?"

"It's highly likely." Emma dropped her forehead on Reid's chest. "I should have realised something was wrong. He changed so drastically. The pain would have been immense, which is why he'd need strong pain killers. I can't understand why he didn't see a specialist."

Reid shrugged. "Maybe he was frightened. You said his mother died of a brain tumour and his brother died of an aneurism."

"Yes, but that's more reason to see a specialist."

"Not if he thought it was terminal," murmured Brenda. "If he sought confirmation, any specialist he saw would be honour bound to report it. Glenn wouldn't be allowed to operate, and he would have lost his private practice. Duty of care and all that."

"Exactly." Emma pushed out of Reid's arms. "Another reason to get things checked out. I know it would have devastated him to give up being an orthopaedic surgeon, but that's beside the point. I'm astounded he was able to operate at all."

Reid picked up Emma's hand. "When Hanson burst into the maternity ward, he said, *I found you.* Then he got side-tracked by your pregnancy. Now that I think about it, he didn't look as if he was about to attack you, but I could be wrong."

"Then why send me a funeral home's card with my name on the back?"

"There you are." Riley stepped through the doorway. "I just received the forensic report on your rifles. The only rifle that had been fired recently was Kathleen's and it doesn't match the bullet found in Bob Farrell's skull."

"So, they confirmed it was Bob Farrell?" Reid drew Emma under his arm.

"Yeah. His DNA was a match to a sibling we tracked down. His family hadn't seen him for years. From all accounts Farrell was in and out of trouble and no longer welcome in the family. He has priors for drunk and disorderly behaviour, theft, illegal procession of a firearm and intimidation. His last known address was a boarding house in Darlinghurst."

"Darlinghurst." Brenda's eyes shot to Emma. "St Vincent's Hospital is in Darlinghurst. Glenn must have hire him."

Emma's pale colour worried Reid. He looked over her head at Riley. "Are we done here? I want to take Emma home."

"There's one more thing." Riley glanced around, as if

checking for anyone within earshot. "There was blood on the crowbar Glenn Hanson was carrying. It's been sent off to forensics to see if the blood matches Vince Stark's."

Reid narrowed his eyes. "If it does than Glenn Hanson has been in town since Friday." He felt Emma shudder.

"Maybe longer." Riley lowered his voice as a nurse walked past the door. "I've got AJ looking for Hanson's car. It's possible he's been sleeping in it as he wasn't staying at the caravan park, pubs, motel, or any of the guest houses. There's an APB alert out for Jerry, but I think it's time we got the SES and army involved in the search, just in case."

"Hunter and I will check Tulachmhor and the Eckford place. You really think Jerry might have it in for our families?"

Riley rolled his shoulders. "I wouldn't have thought so. It could be a case of being in the wrong place at the wrong time. He might have seen someone or something that got him …."

Emma grunted and clutched her belly.

"Em?" Reid backed her onto a chair. "Are you okay?"

"That was a nasty one and way too low." She raised startled eyes. "Reid, I think … I think I might be in labour."

"You think?"

"Well, I've never gone through labour, but sharp pain in the lower back is a classic sign. We might be able to slow or stop the labour if I get bed rest, and intravenous fluids." She looked to Brenda. "I'll need 20mg of nifedipine too."

"On it." Brenda met Reid's eyes. "Get her on the bed and up to the maternity ward. She's not to walk and she can't have any stress whatsoever. I'll race up and get everything ready. Let me just advised the MD on duty?" She ran off without waiting for an answer.

Emma clutched Reid's hand. "Another couple of weeks will make a huge difference to the baby. If we can't stop *Jack* from being born, having Brenda on hand is the next best thing, but I need you with me."

"I'm not going anywhere, Em."

"I'll ring Tulachmhor." Riley pulled out his phone. "Let them know what's happening."

"Thanks." Reid picked Emma up and laid her on the bed.

She cupped his cheek. "No need to panic, darling. There is a good chance we can trick my uterus into relaxing."

"I hope so." Reid covered Emma with a blanket then released the wheel locks. "Relax, Em, and enjoy the ride."

Riley followed them all the way to the lift, his phone glued to his ear, first talking to Hunter then getting his commander's approval to organise a search party. They weren't taking any chances in case Jerry was in fact gunning for the Sullivans and Morgans. It might seem an amazing coincidence, given the fact Hanson had come looking for Emma, but too many things didn't add up. A little of Reid's tension eased knowing Emma had Brenda to help her and that Hanson was under guard.

They took the lift to the second floor's foyer. As Reid wheeled the gurney out of the lift, Scarlett Stark burst from the stairwell and ran towards them.

"Hi." She bent over her knees panting. "I was visiting Dad when I heard Doctor Fahey was in labour."

"Scarlett?" Emma lifted her head to look back. "You should be at home."

"I'm good, Doctor. Must have been something I ate. Don't worry, I'm here for you. I called the ambulance in case you need to go to Armidale."

"Thanks. How's Vince?"

Scarlett straightened and jogged to Emma's side. "Dad's feeling much better. He still has a headache but he's lapping up all the attention and Mum hasn't left his side."

"That's great." Emma smiled up at Reid. "Now we have two great midwives."

Scarlett shot Reid a penetrating look before returning her attention to Emma. "I heard your friend helped deliver Deidre King's baby, and that some guy tried to attack you. It's all over the hospital. Let's get you into the delivery room." She pushed open the damaged door to the maternity ward, holding it wide for Reid to push the bed through. Scarlett directed him down the corridor then opened a door to a room that looked more like a hotel suite than a delivery room. It was the same room he'd stood outside earlier.

"Okey dokey." Scarlett smiled. "Take the doc in there. I'll grab a few things and be back in a minute." She dashed off along the corridor.

Reid carefully steered Emma's bed through the wide doorway, careful not to bump the sides. Brenda stood at an IV stand, pressing buttons.

She looked over and smiled. He didn't miss the worry in her eyes. "Great. Can you lift Emma onto the delivery bed and get rid of that gurney, Reid?"

"Sure." He removed the blanket then lifted Emma onto the odd-looking bed and recovered her. "I'll be right back."

She reached for his hand. "I love you, darling."

"Love you too, Em. Don't go anywhere."

She rolled her eyes. "Highly unlikely."

Reid wheeled the bed outside the door and left it further down the hall then he leaned against the wall, closed his eyes, and took several deep breaths, willing his stomach to settle.

He jerked as the door beside him opened and the flaming haired nurse almost collided with him. He remembered her from school. In fact, they'd once got into a heavy kissing session at a party. Come to think of it, that was the last time he remembered seeing her. "After you."

"Thanks." She gave him a hesitant smile then led the way

back into the delivery room. "I ordered a plate of sandwiches from the kitchen, as I've been told none of you ate dinner."

"What are you doing here?" Brenda scowled at the midwife. "Don't come near Emma."

"It wasn't a bug. Must have been something I ate." Scarlett chuckled. "Maybe those yummy lamingtons you brought us." She turned to Emma. "Your friend came to the hospital this afternoon looking for you and baring delicious treats."

Brenda swabbed the back of Emma's hand. "If the lamingtons were off, you can blame Bindarra Creek's cake shop. I stopped in there for directions." She huffed. "I hope they weren't off, as I gave the rest to your grandmother, Emma."

"Can't be." Emma gently rubbed her abdomen. "I had one with coffee and I'm fine.

Scarlett shrugged. "It could have been the leftover curried prawns from yesterday that Ishya brought in for lunch. How are you feeling, Doc? Any more pain?"

"I had a sharp twinge in the lift, but nothing like earlier."

"Good. Let's hope it stays that way." Scarlett pulled a trolley closer then sorted through the items laid out neatly, ripping open packaging to reveal a catheter, IV tubing, a syringe with fluid in it and a see-through dressing cover and another swab. "Talk around the hospital is you have a stalker and he tried to attack you. Is that true?"

"I honestly don't know, Scarlett. There is so much that doesn't make sense."

"Hmm." Scarlett connected the syringe to the tubing then set it aside and pulled on some purple disposable gloves. "Unusual for you not to be doing this, Doc." Scarlett slipped Emma's arm through a torniquet and tightened it just above her elbow then palpated the skin on the back of Emma's hand.

Reid stood frozen, scared out of his wits as Scarlett picked up another swab then re-wiped the area thoroughly.

Behind her Brenda scowled, probably annoyed at being relegated to the background. He could sympathise with her.

Scarlett smiled at Reid. "If things calm down, you're welcome to stay tonight." She jerked her head towards an armchair in the corner. "That folds out into a bed. Your legs will hang over the end but it's better than sleeping in a chair or on the floor."

"Thanks." He winced as Scarlett inserted the needle into Emma's vein then released the torniquet. With a click, she removed the needle then twisted on the narrow tubing with the syringe at the end. Blood rushed into it. Reid's stomach churned. Blood had never upset him before. It had to be because this was Emma's blood. He'd swap places with her in an instant if it were possible.

Scarlett flushed the blood back along the tube then clamped the tube and disconnected the syringe. She secured the tubing and catheter to Emma's hand with the see-through sticky pad and peeled off the white edging. It was all done quickly and smoothly, leaving Reid even more in awe of Emma. She did this sort of thing every day. He could only imagine the anxiety of carrying so much responsibility. Holding so many women and babies' lives in her hands, yet Emma calmly went about her life without any outward sign of the load she carried. She amazed him.

"Rings on or off, Doc?" Scarlett held up a thin spool of tape. "I recommend you leave them on, and I'll tape them."

"Okay."

Once Scarlett had the IV connected, she looked to Brenda. "Sorry to take over. As the midwife on staff, I'm responsible if anything goes wrong. I've got the ambulance on standby outside emergency if we need it."

"Good." Brenda removed Emma's blanket and replaced it with a warm one. "I understand completely and would do the same thing in your place. I'm here if you need me." She passed Scarlett a small packet. "Emma requested 20mg of nifedipine. If she takes one now and another in thirty minutes, it might be enough to stop the labour."

"Let's hope so." Scarlett read the label then opened the packet and passed Emma a pill and cup of water.

Reid met Brenda's solemn grey eyes, giving her a nod of gratitude. "When it comes to Emma and the baby, I need you both to work as a team."

There was a knock at the door and Reid's mouth dropped as Edwina Lette shuffled in. "Ms. Lette, what are you doing here? How did you get in?"

"Pamela Brown and I were visiting Vince Stark when we heard what happened." She tapped her nose. "Riley has police guarding the lifts on each floor, so we used the stairs. Pamela had to distract the constable so I could get past."

Reid sighed. "You shouldn't be here, Ms. Lette."

She patted his arm. "I wouldn't be if it weren't important." Edwina smiled at Emma. "How are you, Doctor?"

"Um, I'm okay. Why are you here, Ms. Lette?"

"I had a vision downstairs. You are in grave danger."

"I will not have Emma upset by your … crazy visions or premonitions." Reid grasped her elbow and tried to steer the old lady towards the door.

Edwina batted him away. "Don't you manhandle me, young man. I'm here to warn you. My vision was clear. I saw Emma drenched and fighting her way through the forest. Running for her life."

"Emma's stalker has been caught, ma'am. You need to leave." Brenda's no-nonsense demand only succeeded in raising one of Edwina's grey eyebrows.

She ducked back to Emma's side. "I know that's what they're saying, but my visions are never wrong, Doctor. Maybe a little sketchy, but never wrong. You are in danger. Oh, and the baby will come early. Florence Miller has offered her services to marry you and Reid right now if you want. She's downstairs too."

"What?" Reid had taken as much baloney as he could stand. "If you are not out of here in ten seconds, Ms. Lette, I will carry you out and have Senior Sergeant Morgan lock you up."

"No, Reid. Wait." Emma held out her hand to him. "We intended to be married before the baby arrived. I know it sounds crazy, but I like the idea."

"You do?"

"Yes. We can hold a reception in two weeks. Let's get married, now."

He stared at her in disbelief. "But you've planned a beautiful wedding."

"How would you know? I've had to organise everything."

"Because … because I can imagine it through your excitement, whenever you tell me what you've organised." Reid brought her hand to his mouth and kissed her knuckles. "Emma, has this anything to do with Hanson?"

Colour stained her cheeks. "Why would you say that?"

"You've just found out he has a growth on his brain. A growth that probably changed his character. If they operate and … and it's a success, he might return to the person you loved."

She licked her lips. "Reid, what I felt for Glenn is nothing to what I feel for you. Why can't you trust me in this?"

"I understand that, but if he hadn't changed, you would have ended up marrying him." Sharp prongs drove into Reid's heart, but he couldn't seem to stop. "All I'm saying is there's no need to rush our wedding. You deserve the wedding of your dreams."

"I deserve your trust."

"Enough." Brenda glared at Reid. "No stress. Remember? I want everyone out of this room right now so I can examine

Emma." She turned to Scarlett. "Please see this lady and the one distracting the police officer down to reception."

"Certainly." Scarlett's eyes flicked back to Emma before she hustled Edwina out.

Reid's gaze returned to Emma. Her wounded eyes floored him. "Em."

"Please go for walk." She turned her face to the window where rain lashed against the glass. "Brenda will look after me."

"Em, it's not that I don't want to marry you. I do, but there's no rush."

"You don't trust me. Deep in your heart you think I will one day betray you, like your mother betrayed Tom. You don't trust me."

"No, that's not it at all. Please look at me, Emma."

She gasped and clutched her belly. "Please go, you're just making things worse."

"Em, I'm sorry. I ..."

"Reid!" Brenda gripped his arm and pulled him to the door. "Go for a walk or a coffee. Give Emma some space."

"I don't want to leave."

"By staying you are raising her anxiety levels and blood pressure. Go into the visitors lounge and figure out how to make this right. Better still, go down to the cafeteria and get us all a hot chocolate. Give me half an hour to examine Emma and make her comfortable."

"Okay." He looked back at Emma. "Call me, if ..."

"I will."

Brenda shut the door in his face, leaving him standing alone in the silent hall as terror sliced his heart to ribbons. He'd only wanted Emma to have the wedding of her dreams. He knew she wasn't like his witch of a mother. He did trust her. She was his life. He needed to fix this. He needed to prove he trusted her, but how?

He strode past the visitors lounge and out of the maternity ward, sending the police officer a scowl. "Don't let anyone past you. My fiancée might still be in danger."

He couldn't discount Edwina's vision. She had that uncanny knack of being right. He jogged down the stairs, his mind racing. He'd do anything to make Emma happy. To bring back her beautiful smile. If she wanted to get married tonight, then they'd damned well get married tonight. He had to find Florence Miller quickly and get back to Emma.

CHAPTER 15

"*H*on, we have a problem." Brenda pulled off her gloves, threw them in the bin then as Emma straightened her legs, covered her with the lovely warm blanket. "You've passed your mucus plug and your cervix is partially dilated."

"What? That's impossible. I've hardly had any pain."

"Do you remember that Indian woman who delivered premature twins with barely a grunt? She lay in a yoga pose and meditated, insisting she wasn't in pain, even though her water had broken. Then out popped the first baby, giving us all the fright of our lives."

"Yes, but that's very rare. My sister went through seven hours of labour."

"Everyone is different, hon. Your blood pressure is up too and …"

"And what? Brenda, I can tell by your eyes, there's something else."

"Bub's heartrate is up a little."

"Okay." Emma closed her eyes as another twinge hit. She took several calming breaths then opened her eyes. "With five weeks to go, I'm not risking the baby's health. Honest opinion. Do I have time to get to Armidale's neonatal ward?"

"I think so, if you stay calm."

"Let's do it. Ask Scarlett to find Reid and tell him to meet us in emergency."

"Right, I'll ring down to emergency now and make sure that ambulance is ready to go." She hesitated. "I want to come with you, in case the baby comes."

"Bren, I'm not leaving this hospital without you, but I need Reid there too."

"Phew." Brenda pretended to wipe her brow. "Rest. I'll sort it out with Scarlett."

Emma nodded and closed her eyes. She needed to practice what she'd preached to hundreds of women. Relax, calm her breathing, think happy thoughts. Meditation might work. She suddenly felt extremely tired, which didn't surprise her, and the twinges seemed to be easing.

She let herself sink into a comfortable dozy state, aware of quiet movement around her and the occasional whispers. She was in good hands, Brenda, Scarlett, and Reid would look after her. She just had to relax her mind and body. Reid loved her, she knew it to the bottom of her soul, but she needed him to trust her love, to trust she'd never betray him. Glenn hadn't trusted her. Maybe if he hadn't had a growth on his brain, things would have been different, but destiny had chosen another path for her. Destiny had led her to Reid.

She drifted through happier memories with Glenn. When they'd become friends then started dating. He'd been such a nice guy, yet even at their happiest, she hadn't loved him like Reid. She hadn't been consumed by heat and desire as she was with Reid. She looked forward to falling asleep in Reid's arms every night. He never left her in the morning without a kiss, except for yesterday, but he hadn't wanted to wake her.

Even if Glenn survived the surgery without brain damage

and returned to his old self, there was no way she'd leave Reid. He was her life, her soul mate, her partner, her destiny. How she could get that through his thick skull, she didn't know, but she would. They belonged together.

The bed jolted and she suddenly realised she was on the move, but her eyelids were too heavy to open. There was only one explanation. Scarlett or Brenda must have given her a mild sedative. It would be something safe, they both knew her views on those things. She felt a little kick up under her ribs and smiled. At least the contractions and twinges had disappeared. Jack was safe for now and didn't appear to be in any hurry to be born. She wasn't looking forward to five weeks bed rest in Armidale's maternity ward, but she'd do it for Jack.

Another jolt and a blast of cold air on her face had Emma cracking her eyelids. She was outside, under bright lights, being loaded into an ambulance. A soft male voice asked someone if they had the medical record and transfer papers. The bed jolted again as it was fixed in place. Emma floated in and out of her dreamy state. It was rather nice, but where was Reid? She wanted him beside her, holding her hand.

Another male voice rose sharply. "What now? We don't have time. Okay, make it quick."

Emma closed her eyes again.

A door slamming woke her more fully and she looked to the right expecting to see Reid in the chair. It was empty. The engine started as she tilted her head back, expecting to see Brenda or a paramedic who should be sitting there monitoring her vitals, or changing the IV bag, which was clipped to an IV pole. She was alone. *That's odd.*

A niggle of apprehension ran through Emma as she focused on the rear windows, and the doors to emergency, trying to clear the fuzziness in her head. The doors were getting small. The ambulance was leaving. Where was Brenda? Where was Reid?

She tried to wriggle but the straps over her chest and thighs kept her securely in place. Tilting her head back again she peered through the gap in the seats to the front cab. There was no paramedic in the passenger seat. Her eyes shot back to the emergency entrance to see Reid run out of the building. He stopped by the *Ambulance Parking Only* sign, his attention riveted on her departing ambulance. A paramedic jogged through the doors behind him then threw something aside and began waving frantically. Whatever he yelled had Reid sprinting past him. They were chasing her ambulance.

I've been taken. Oh my God, I've been taken.

Her heart rate shot up. She couldn't see the driver, but by the swerving of the vehicle they were taking the bends way to fast. She jumped as the siren roared to life. Lights from distant farmhouses flashed past. A Bindarra Downs Nursery sign flashed past. They were on Mount Ingalls Road, heading for Armidale, but she doubted that was the driver's destination. Her breath was coming in small gasps. She'd have a panic attack if she didn't calm down. Easier said than done.

Who had kidnapped her? Was it Glenn? Could she reason with him? Or was it Jerry, intent on taking his revenge on the Sullivans and Morgans? If he'd killed Bob and attacked Vince, what would he do to her? It didn't bear thinking about.

She began shaking violently. She was going into shock. This wouldn't do.

Think Emma, think.

They were on the main road to Armidale. Reid would come after her. Riley would jump in his souped-up highway patrol car and chase them with his own sirens screaming. He'd put out an alert and have roadblocks set up. Jake and Hunter would be in on the chase too. It would be okay. In the meantime, she had to remain calm. She needed to trick her uterus into relaxing. At least she had the IV giving her fluids. She twisted her wrist. The IV was definitely still attached. Her fingers touched a tiny carton. She gripped it and wriggled her hand from under the safety belt and blanket. Lifting the carton, she read the label. *Nifedipine.* Okay, she'd take another capsule. It had to be close to half an hour since she had the first one and that would give her three hours before she needed another.

The ambulance took a sharp turn, it's wheels squealing. Emma gripped the bed as the ambulance swerved, fishtailing several times before straightening. Then the siren stopped. She stared out the windows, unable to see anything but blackness and the rain hitting the glass. They were driving over bumpy ruts and hitting serious potholes. They'd left the main road. She twisted to look through the front windscreen, trying to swallow her panic as the beams picked up thick overhanging trees and foliage packed tightly together. They could be on one of the fire trails leading into the Akuna National Park.

Panic surged. *Reid and Riley will never find me in here. Not in time.*

Ranting mutters reached her, but she couldn't make out the voice due to the sleeting rain and eerie wind, reminding her of Edwina's vision. Bindarra Creek's psychic had seen Emma fighting her way through the forest. Running for her life.

Emma closed her eyes and tried to be brave. What would Chelsea, Ali, or Sam do? They'd been trapped in a cave with three men who planned to kill them and yet they'd escaped their captors. If Edwina Lette saw Emma fighting her way through the forest, then that's what she would do, but first she needed to get loose and remove the IV.

As the ambulance continued to slide over the dirt road

and hit every rut possible, she wriggled her left arm free then quickly removed the catheter, clamping two fingers over the small incision. The walls on either side held an assortment of emergency items, equipment, and meds. She skimmed over the defibrillator, oxygen masks, neck collars, boxes of sterilised gloves and monitors.

Her gaze fixed on a drawer of bandages and dressing pads above her. Reaching for a waterproof dressing pad, she peeled off the backing and stuck it over the incision, rubbing the edges to seal it.

The ambulance slid sideways, the back smacking into soft branches before surging forward. Coarse swearing reached Emma, but she still couldn't identify the low voice. Finding the strap release, she pressed the button and eased the belt away from her chest. Searching for some sort of weapon, she leaned over the side, her breath catching when her eyes locked on a paramedic. He was lying on the floor, his eyes closed. It was Chandra Bhandari, Ishya's husband.

That answered one question. The person driving wasn't a paramedic.

For two terrifying seconds, Emma waited until Chandra's chest rose then fell. He was alive but for how long?

She fumbled with the nifedipine packet, made more difficult by Scarlett's bulky tape around her rings. She squeezed one tablet free and swallowed it. The only way she'd be able to help Chandra was to get free and pray their abductor left him alone. There was nothing she could use as a weapon, except maybe the fire extinguisher, but she couldn't risk the driver hearing her dislodge it or him seeing her in the review mirror.

Emma gripped the sides of her gurney, fighting not to be thrown across the ambulance each time the vehicle slid or smacked into small saplings. She did another scan of the interior, her eyes spotting a tiny camera above the rear doors. She was pretty sure it only feed to the front cabin. Hopefully, it hadn't been switched on. Surely the ambulance had some sort of tracking device.

She would need to escape, but at thirty-five weeks pregnant, she couldn't jump from a moving vehicle, especially one skidding from one side of the dirt fire trail to the other. She would have to wait until it stopped, and she still needed a weapon and something to keep her warm, or she'd get hypothermia.

It was hopeless. She couldn't defend herself and the baby against a man much stronger than her. A man set on revenge.

Her gaze fixed on the three kits behind the front passenger seat. Oxygen kit, defib kit and drug kit. The last might come in handy. To the right of her bed, against the wall were drawers with basic meds, dressing and every sized needle. Above the drawers a telephone was mounted on the wall with a laminated list of numbers above it. Making a call would definitely attract the attention of the driver. She spied hypothermia blankets in another drawer. Her gaze returned to the med kit. All she'd need was a couple of vials of midazolam or droperidol. Both acted within five to ten minutes and would sedate her abductor if she could get close enough. The kit would also contain intramuscular needles. Better than nothing.

Edwina Lette's vision wouldn't leave her. While Emma had breath in her body, she would fight to save her baby son. She looked at the vehicle's side door. She would have to slide it open from the inside and run for her life, and her baby's life.

Thunder rumbled overhead as static, and a distorted voice came through the front cabin communicator. A radio operator was trying to communicate with Chandra.

Praying it would distract the driver, Emma released the safety belt across her legs. She slid off the bed, crouched low and crawled behind the front passenger seat. With the driver's attention hopefully focussed ahead and, on the radio operator, Emma checked Chandra's pulse, relieved to find it steady under her fingers.

A used syringe rolled across the floor. Her gaze flew back to Chandra. He'd been drugged. A saying her grandmother loved came to mind. *If it's good enough for the goose, it's good enough for the gander.* So be it.

She still couldn't see the driver's face as he wore a balaclava. He also wore a white coat, which he must have stolen from the emergency department. A terrifying, twelve-inch knife lay in the console, its blade covered in blood.

With her heart pounding in her throat, Emma squeezed as close to the side door as possible and braced her feet, which kept her from being thrown about. She opened the meds kit and rifled through, pulling out two syringes, sedation vials, and needles. She would have loved taking the paramedics slinger pack with her, but that would be in a locked compartment on the outside of the ambulance. She raided a few of the drawers, taking antiseptic wipes, bandages and two hypothermia blanket packs.

Without the warmth of the hospital blanket, she shivered. A thin hospital gown would not protect her from the pelting rain, chilly wind, or branches scratching her arms and legs. Bed socks would not stop sharp objects cutting into her feet. Brenda's need to make her comfortable would be a major hindrance out in the bush. The coward in Emma wanted to curl up and pray for a miracle. She almost succumbed.

A swift kick from baby Jack changed her mind.

She unzipped a bandage pouch and emptied most of its contents, before replacing them with the antiseptic swabs, a couple of dressing pads and a few sticking plasters. After stuffing the hypothermia blanket inside, she set about arming herself. The ambulance sliding in the wet gravel made it hard to fit the needles to the syringes and fill them with the sedative, but she persevered, breathing a sigh of relief when she accomplished the deed without losing her balance. Luckily, Chandra appeared to be wedged between the chair and gurney locking station.

The radio static and violent storm had saved her from being heard as she moved about, but the lashing rain and dropping temperature could well be her downfall once she left the ambulance. Her gaze fixed on a paramedic jacket hanging on the back of the observation chair. Almost in slow motion, she slowly reached for the hem and tugged as they slid around another corner. The jacket came free and fell across Chandra.

Emma drew it closer then shoved her arms through, thankful for the extra warmth.

Another round of curses from the front had her frowning. She inched forward to peep around the front seat. Her eyes locked on the driver's signet ring.

Incredulity and disbelief paralysed her vocal cords as well as her limbs, otherwise she would have cried out, giving herself away. While her abductor thought her heavily sedated, she had a slim chance to escape, but first she had to calm her racing heart.

Why?

That one word rolled round and round in her mind as she tried to make sense of it. The hatred spewing from her abductor's mouth stunned her. It didn't make sense. What had she ever done to warrant such loathing?

The ambulance fishtailed again then slid across the road. Emma braced her feet and clutched the door handle seconds before the ambulance slammed into something solid. The impact flung her forward then back. Her head slammed into the front seat. Her elbow smashed against the door. White powder from the front airbags filled the air, making it hard to breathe. Emma acted on pure instinct. Holding the pouch handle and syringes in one hand, she released the lock then slid the side door open, falling onto her knees into a squelchy pile of wet undergrowth.

A roaring from the front cab had her scrambling to her feet and running blindly, one hand out in front as branches whipped against her face and legs.

"Come back, you bitch! Come back or I'll kill you."

Not if I can help it. Emma flinched as something sharp dug into her foot, but she didn't stop. She changed direction several times, stumbling her way through thick foliage, and although soaked and freezing, she could only be thankful for the howling wind and drenching rain masking her escape. And the jacket covering her torso. She prayed her abductor was in no state to follow her.

A yell behind Emma buried that hope.

She needed to find a hiding place. Her hair and the front of the gown were plastered to her body. The back of her skull and elbow throbbed. She shivered uncontrollably.

The first sign of hypothermia.

She pushed on, her hand outstretched to fend off wet branches, struggling to hold in her cries as sharp twigs scratched her legs and face. It was so dark, but her loud panting breaths would surely give away her position.

"Argh!" The ground disappeared under Emma's feet. She landed on her butt in soft, mushy undergrowth. Before she could catch her breath, she shot forward, feet first, sliding downhill, jolting, and bumping over mushy, rough terrain as she tried to protect her abdomen.

Her descent ended with a second of being airborne then a resounding plop as she landed in thick sludge that splattered her face and chest.

Can't stop. Emma clambered to her feet, amazed to find she still held the pouch and syringes in one hand. "What is it with me and mud lately." She pulled the sticky gown down her thighs trying not to think of the damage her bottom might have suffered, or the possible infection from stagnant mud now that her mucus plug had come away. She trudged across the shallow mud to the opposite bank then feeling about with her free hand found exposed tree roots. She used them to crawl onto the bank.

She may as well be blind for the dark world she found herself in. Another hurdle she had to overcome. She had no idea of the time. At least the canopy above sheltered her from the driving rain. She crawled round the tree then rested against its trunk. The wide tree trunk would hide her presence, as long as her abductor didn't cross the mud hole.

A shiver racked her body. Her seconds of hurtling down the slope had raised her adrenaline levels, but now she was back to trembling uncontrollably. With shaking fingers, she unzipped the pouch and pulled out the compact hypothermia blankets. She tied one around her waist to protect her legs from the cold. Hard to do as her fingers were stiff. The other blanket she used to cover her upper body to stop the cold sinking into her bones. She sat on the edges to keep out the chilling wind.

Within minutes her breathing warmed the inside of her cocoon and she set about using the swabs to clean and disinfect her hands and everywhere she could reach. The nifedipine appeared to be working. She was drenched. Her teeth were chattering. Her skin was cool to touch, and she was incredibly drowsy. More signs of hypothermia.

The minutes ticked by as Emma strained to hear anything other than rolling thunder, blustery wind, and sheeting rain. She could feel her strength draining away. Huddling closer to the tree, she did her best to protect her unborn child.

Reid, I need you. Where are you?

CHAPTER 16

*R*eid leaned forward in his seat, his heart in his mouth. His knuckles whitened as he gripped the dashboard, his gaze searching the road ahead. Riley had the siren blaring and was certainly breaking the speed limit, but they should have caught the ambulance by now.

"How the hell did this happen?" Reid struggled to breathe.

"I don't know." Riley sounded hoarse. "I'm sorry, mate. I just don't know."

The radio crackled and Abby Taylor's voice came through loud and clear. "Senior Sergeant Morgan, Doctor Hanson is missing. He asked to use the bathroom and looks to have absconded through a window. Over."

Dread seeped through Reid's veins. He clenched his fists tighter as Riley barked questions at Abby.

"Who was guarding him? Over."

"A constable from Moree. He was found unconscious with a stab wound to the back. Over."

"Have you accessed the emergency entrance external video surveillance? Over."

"We're looking at it now. Okay, here it is. We're

watching Emma being loaded into the back of the ambulance by our local paramedics Chandra Bhandari and Colm O'Leary. Brenda Barker is with them. Colm is examining some paperwork and shaking his head. Now he's returning to emergency with Brenda. Chandra has shut the rear doors and he's opening the side slider and climbing inside."

Silence came over the radio for what seemed like hours then Abby continued in a sharp voice. "Someone in a balaclava and doctor's coat just ran out of emergency. They're approaching the side of the ambulance, carrying … a knife in their right hand. Climbing in."

Riley sped along the highway; his knuckles white where he gripped the steering wheel. Reid could only sit there, helpless as the vice around his lungs tightened, dreading Abby's next words.

"Perpetrator just climbed out of the ambulance, slammed door and is running around to the driver's side, climbing in. Ambulance pulling away. Reid Sullivan striding out of emergency. Colm O'Leary running out of emergency. Both of them chasing ambulance. Over."

"Thanks, Abby. Keep us informed. Over and out." Riley stared ahead. "Where is that bloody ambulance?"

The radio crackled again as a dispatcher identified himself. "Senior Sergeant Morgan, we are tracking the ambulance. It's turned off Mount Ingalls Road onto a fire trail. Over."

"Turn around," roared Reid.

Riley already had the highway patrol car in a wide U-turn. They screamed back towards Bindarra Creek. He flicked a button on his steering wheel and identified himself and his position. "Which fire trail? Over."

The dispatcher could only relay the approximate distance between Bindarra Creek and Glenmeer as the ambulance looked to be moving fast through nothingness. The trail wasn't charted on the Global Positioning System.

"It's heading into Akuna National Park." Riley sent Reid a quick glance. "We need to think logically. Hanson's in a bad way. He might have made a run for it, but he wouldn't know where the fire trails are. It's gotta be Jerry. He'd know every fire trail round here."

"Anyone who studied a map would know about the trails. It's Hanson. He's missing from the hospital and the only one crazy enough to do something like this." Reid swallowed. "Maybe he saw the trail entrance and made a snap decision to take it."

Neither of them said a word, each knowing what the other was thinking. They didn't have a second to lose. Riley got back on his radio, asking the dispatcher to send back up.

Several tense minutes later, Abby's voice sounded over the crackle of the radio. "Senior Sergeant, Doctor Hanson has been found in the emergency department's sluice room under a pile of sheets. He has stab wounds to his chest and arms. He's been rushed upstairs for emergency surgery. The nurse who found him said he kept mumbling that he'd tried to save Emma, and it was all his fault. Over and out."

"It's not Hanson." Reid couldn't make sense of it. "That leaves ... Jerry."

Riley slowed then swerved right, onto a fire trail. Cutting his siren, he jumped out and ran into the beam of the headlights.

Joining him, Reid studied the fresh, fishtailing, tyre tracks as the heavy rain dowsed them. "Look at the wheel span and slide marks." He pointed to the distinctive evidence of a recent vehicle almost losing control. "They came this way."

"I agree. Let's go."

Reid buckled in again, the tension inside the car heavy as Riley confirmed their destination with dispatch then concentrated on the fire trail, while Reid kept his eyes locked on the tyre tracks, cursing every time they showed the ambulance fishtailing around bends. He had to watch carefully as there were lots of trails leading off the main one.

"It doesn't add up." Riley slammed his palm against the wheel. "If Hanson hired Bob Farrell to spy on Emma, why would he kill him?"

"I've been wondering the same thing." Reid stared ahead, through the headlights and sheeting rain. "It is possible Jerry discovered what Bob was up to. Seeing an opportunity to exact his own revenge, he sabotaged Tulachmhor's windmills and anything else he could get his hands on. Hell, he could have untied Bob's dog."

Riley slowed for a sharp bend. "When you fired Bob, Jerry stepped up his agenda, by baiting Gypsy and setting the cottage alight."

"Yeah, but if he meant to bait her, why shoot her?"

"He could have fired off a couple of shots, thinking she was about to attack. One went wide and almost hit Emma."

Reid clenched his fists, wincing when pain shot through his bandaged hand. "Jerry was tipped to win the darts final, but he didn't make it because he had a stomach bug. What if he lied? Maybe the fire truck arrived before he could finish the job. When Hanson couldn't contact Farrell, he drove to Bindarra, and discovered his spy was dead."

"Okay." Riley nodded his head slowly. "But why would Jerry kill Bob? You said he pointed out the campfire smoke."

"Jerry knew Hunter and I wouldn't go after Farrell unarmed. It gave him the time to race up the hill, shoot Farrell dead then lead us on a wild goose chase, before doubling back to meet the police."

"Your theory is plausible, but I still find it hard to swallow."

So did Reid, but he couldn't think of any other explanation. "There! Turn left."

Riley spun the wheel, sending his patrol car into a slide. He hit the accelerator hard, and they fishtailed out of it. There were stacks of close calls where the ambulance looked to have almost gone off the trail and one where it did. Reid's gut clenched as the patrol car's headlights picked up a bunch of flattened saplings.

"There! Go right." Reid dragged in a deep breath as he squinted through the windscreen. "They can't be too far ahead. This trail leads to a picnic ground that borders the back gate of Tulachmhor."

"Why would he take her back to — shit!" Riley slammed on the brakes.

Reid went flying forward, the seat belt cutting into his chest as Riley slammed on his brakes. Ahead of them, the ambulance had left the fire trail and smashed through thick scrub, ending up sideways, the front and back wedged between a forest of saplings.

"No!" Reid leaped out of the patrol car and sprinted to the ambulance, ignoring Riley's yell to stop. The driver's door was wide open, the internal lights on, the airbags exploded. He ran to the back doors but couldn't open them because of branches. He fought his way through the dense scrub and saplings to the side door of the ambulance, also open. It only took a second to ascertain Emma wasn't inside, but a paramedic lay on the floor. He checked for a pulse.

Riley pushed through the foliage beside Reid. "It's Chandra Bhandari. Is he alive?"

"Yes. I'm going after Em."

"Wait. I'll radio in our location and request an ambulance from Armidale. Don't leave without me."

"I'm not waiting, mate. What would you do if it was Samantha?"

"Give me one minute, Reid. If he'd wanted to kill Emma, he would have done it already. Go shut the driver's door. The least we can do is make sure Chandra doesn't freeze to death."

"Come in, Senior Sergeant. Over." Abby's voice crackled through the tense atmosphere.

"Wait for me," ordered Riley. "You are no good to Emma dead." He ran back to his patrol car.

Reid slid the door closed then wrestled his way round to the driver's door. He'd just closed it when he heard Abby reporting another person missing. He strode to patrol car's open door.

Riley met Reid's gaze. "Who is missing, Abby? Over."

"Scarlett Stark. She was last seen in the emergency ward of Bindarra Creek Hospital. Her parents are frantic, because seventeen years ago, she didn't come home from a camping weekend. Before they could officially announce her missing, Jerry Eckford brought Scarlett home. He'd found her wandering in Akuna National Park. She was naked, concussed and had no memory of how she got there. Valma Stark told me her daughter couldn't bear the public humiliation if it got out, so she moved to Tamworth to live with an aunt. Vince Stark said rally driving helped Scarlett put it behind her. Over."

"Rally driving?" Riley straightened.

"Yes, but she wears a GPS tracker. It's showing her in the National Park. Over."

"Thanks, Abby. Over and out." Riley blew out a breath then handed Reid a torch.

"Hell." Reid's heart thundered. "We were there that night, Riley." A memory he'd forgotten rose in his mind. "Chelsea and Ali crashed the party, so you, Jake and Hunter took them home. Jerry and I stayed. Scarlett was younger than us, but she was drinking and dancing with a group of girls. I didn't realise they were underage until Jerry told me. We insisted they go home before they ended up in trouble. The girls Scarlett was with refused to leave and it caused a bit of a scene." He raked a hand through his hair. "I didn't know Scarlett disappeared that night."

"Sounds like her parents kept it quiet." Riley checked his gun. "Something obviously happened to her that night. She might have come back to Bindarra to settle a few scores. You and Jerry might be on her list for … whatever happened to her. She was in a perfect position to steal the ambulance."

"Maybe, but what's Emma ever done to her. No, I don't buy it. Let's go."

They shone their torches around, picking up one set of footprints and one set of patterned shoe prints going in the same direction. The tight band around Reid's lungs constricted. Emma wasn't wearing shoes. They followed the prints for several minutes then Riley pointed out only one set of shoeprints going forward. They searched around until Reid spotted footprints going off to the right. "I'm going this way."

"All right but be careful."

"You too." Reid kept his torch down, searching for flattened grass and footprints in the saturated leaf litter, anything to stay on Emma's trail. His hair shirt and pants were plasters to his skin. He had to wipe the rainwater out of his eyes just to see.

The trail ended at the top of a drop-off and Reid's heart plummeted. Emma's descent was clearly obvious, like a toboggan on a mud slide. He gripped the torch then edged over the drop and let gravity take him, fighting to keep his body on her trail, while directing the torch downward and whacking branches out of his way. It wasn't a pleasant ride.

Nor was the landing. He flew off a bank and into thick, sloppy mud. Surging to his feet, he whipped out his shirt and wiped the front of the torch so he could search the shallow mud for any sign of Emma, relieved when he found gouge marks on the opposite bank.

She'd got out of the mud hole, which meant she could still move. He shone the torch up on the tussocky bank and over the trees lining it, praying for a decent trail to follow. How she'd manage to escape at all was beyond him, but to do it in pitch black, sheeting rain and freezing wind, left him in awe. He had to believe her abductor's footprints indicated they'd kept going through the bush. Because the thought of anything happening to Emma tore his soul apart.

A crackly growl escaped his throat. She had to be freezing to death.

He dragged himself out of the mud hole then staggered round a tree and almost fell over a bulging, silver, hypothermic blanket. "Emma!" He dropped to his knees, pulling the silver wrapping aside, revealing her pale face. She was shivering, her teeth chattering. "Emma!"

Her eyelids fluttered then she groaned, turning away from the light. "Too bright."

"Sorry." He flicked the beam to low, placed the torch on the ground then ran his hands over her arms and legs. "Are you hurt, love?"

"A few bruises and scratches. Am I dreaming, Reid, or are you really here?"

"I'm here, Em." He tucked the silver blanket around her as best he could then scooped her off the ground, exchanging places, so he was sitting against the tree with his precious bundle across his thighs. "Riley's trailing your kidnapper. For the moment we'll stay here. Help isn't far away." He flicked off the torch and kept his voice to a low whisper. "Who took you, Em?"

"It doesn't make sense. She sobbed into his chest. "She has a knife and wants to kill me. Why does she hate *me*?"

So it is Scarlett. "We think it's revenge for something that happened seventeen years ago, but I'm here now, and she's not getting near you. We just need to stay hidden and quiet until help arrives. I'm not risking your safety." Reid tucked the silver blanket around Emma.

"What are you talking about?" Emma's teeth chatted as she pushed the thin material away from her face. "You knew her seventeen years ago?"

"Not well. Someone had the idea to pitch a bunch of tents at a picnic ground not far from here and party. There were lots of people I didn't know. We sat around campfires, listening to loud music and dancing. Those with licenses came by car. Hunter and I raced Riley and Jake here on horseback."

"That's a long ride."

"Not if you use the fire trails. Ali and Chelsea had followed us, so the others took them home. I hung around for a while, danced with a pretty girl I'd seen around school. We were making out when Jerry interrupted. He'd found out she and her friends were underage. Jerry offered to drive them home, but they didn't want to leave the party. I didn't know her name."

Emma squirmed on his lap, trying to get closer. "That's rather awkward."

"It was just a few kisses and dancing." Reid sighed. "I only just discovered she disappeared that night. Jerry apparently found her a couple of days later wandering about, so he took her home and the whole thing was hushed up."

"She never told me."

"Apparently, she had no memory of what happened and left Bindarra Creek fearing humiliation. I didn't even notice she hadn't returned to our school."

"Why would she? Brenda comes from Cobar."

"Brenda!" Reid whacked his head on the tree. "Ouch. I'm talking about Scarlett Stark."

"Oh! …. What? … Scarlett didn't abduct me." Emma shuddered against his chest. "It was Brenda."

"Bren—" A high-pitched squeal reached them. "Shush." Reid reached for the torch.

Emma stiffened in his arms as rustling and grunts reached them. He lowered his lips to whisper in her ear. "We have company. Stay very still. Don't make a sound."

Grunts, more squeals and dozens of hooves were growing louder. Coming closer.

The last thing he needed was a wild boar goring Emma and the baby. The thought churned his stomach. He surged to his feet, holding her against his chest as he tried to decern the direction of the potentially deadly threat. Turning, he whispered, "We're on a feral pig trail. They're coming from the left, along the bank. We need to get out of here before they reach this mud hole." He prayed the scent of humans would scare them off, but a wild boar was just as likely to charge.

Emma began to struggle out of her blanket. "Do you know where we are?"

"Yeah. There's an old picnic ground not far from here. Tulachmhor is about an hour's walk away."

"It might as well be a week. I can't feel my legs." Emma's teeth were chattering.

He had to get her to the picnic ground fast. "If you can hold the torch, I'll carry you." He figured they had a couple of minutes at best before the pigs arrived at the mudhole.

"Keep the beam low and pointed ahead if you can." He placed the torch in Emma's shaking hand then lifted her against his chest. This wasn't going to be a walk in the park.

The low beam shot all over the place but gave him enough light to find his footing in the well-worn, muddy trail. The chilling wind hit him in the back and legs, bringing the stench of pigs. The wind's direction did little to relieve his mind. Feral pigs had an acute sense of hearing and could pick up odours from miles away. They would be aware intruders were in their midst.

The minutes dragged as Reid attempted to protect Emma from overhanging branches, but the threat of being gored had him leaving the trail and thrashing through vegetation as fast as his legs would carry him. It was a hellion task not to slip and drop his precious bundle. He'd had a few close calls. It didn't help that Emma got heavier with each minute, but he dared not slow his punishing pace. She hadn't spoken since leaving the mud hole, yet she'd had the sense to hook the torch cord over her arm, so she didn't drop it.

He staggered into the overgrown picnic ground, surprised it wasn't crammed with police and emergency vehicles. To find it empty meant the causeway had to be too deep to cross, which meant he'd have to carry Emma to Tulachmhor. At least the clouds were starting to clear, leaving only misty rain.

Sirens shrieked in the distance, but without a phone he couldn't redirect them to Tulachmhor. He juggled Emma higher and made for the only remaining picnic table and the dilapidated structure housing it. At least the roof and three sides would give them a reprieve from the rain and wind. He needed a minute to rest his cramped arms before the trek to Tulachmhor.

He lay Emma on the table, groaning as he straightened out his aching arms.

She stirred and rolled onto her side. "Reid?"

"I'm here, Emma." He propped the torch beside her, pointing up to the rusted tin roof and giving them some light. A sixth sense told him, something or someone stood behind him. He turned slowly, ready to leap onto the table if he faced a feral boar. He didn't even make it halfway round when pain exploded in his head, and he fell to his knees.

Emma screaming his name over and over ripped his heart to shreds, but for the life of him, Reid couldn't stop the blackness closing in.

He'd failed Emma when she needed him most.

CHAPTER 17

"What is wrong with you, Brenda?" Emma clambered off the table and dropped to her knees on the long grass beside Reid. The light from the torch lit up the metal roof and immediate area. "Why are you doing this?"

Her best friend of seven years laughed hysterically before throwing a thick piece of wood into surrounding bush and pointing the terrifying knife at Emma. "You want to know why, Miss perfect, goody two-shoes? He was mine first. Mine!"

"Who was yours first? I don't know who you're talking about."

"Glenn." Brenda slashed at Emma, only missing her by a couple of inches. "He was dating me, then you sashayed into the cafeteria with your blonde hair and big brown eyes."

"Why didn't you say something?" Emma leaned closer to Reid and wrapped her arms around her abdomen to protect her baby.

"What could I say. The man I'd loved for three years, who'd finally started dating me the week before you arrived, dropped me the minute he set eyes on you. He left me sitting at a table to rush over and introduce himself. And you! You acted as if he wasn't the best thing since sliced bread. You hooked him with your disinterest."

"Brenda, I said hello. I didn't know who he was. I'd just arrived to do my residency. I wasn't looking for a boyfriend. I was focussed on settling in and learning everything I could."

"Yeah, right. You knew by playing hard to get he wouldn't be able to resist the challenge."

"No, that's not true." Emma felt for Reid's pulse, relieved to find it. She ran her fingers lightly over his head, anger rising when warm liquid ran over her fingers. He needed stitches. She had to stall until Riley found them. "Brenda, I wasn't interested in dating Glenn, not even when I found out he was on the orthopaedic team. I appreciated his offer of friendship but that was it."

"That's crap. You batted your eyelids at him, playing the innocent and he fell for it." Brenda slashed the knife through the air, back and forth, her agitation palpable.

"That's not true, Brenda." Emma shuddered. The cold air was making her bare legs sting. Her feet were numb and that knife was coming far too close for comfort. "If you felt this way, why did you approach me? Why become my friend?" Keeping her eyes glued on Brenda, Emma crawled over the top of Reid, gaining some much-needed space.

"Because I needed to be near Glenn. I figured he'd grow tired of you soon enough. He wasn't into innocents. But you kept him dangling and the fool fell for you. How do you think I felt when you moved in with him? How do you think I felt when you told me he'd asked you to marry him, but you weren't even sure you loved him?" Brenda screamed the last question. "You made him fall in love with you. He never stopped loving you."

"How could Glenn love me, if he was having an affair?" Emma scanned the ground for a stick or a rock. There weren't any.

"He wasn't having an affair. I made that up, hoping you'd leave him. I spent months trying to get him to dump you, but nothing I did worked."

"What do you mean? What did you do?" Emma could only stare at Brenda in shocked disbelief. Was nothing what it seemed?

"I was the one who told him you had lunch with a male colleague. That you were too focussed on your career to settle down, but he dismissed it as nothing. You had everything I wanted, but it wasn't enough." Brenda spat the words out. "You broke Glenn's heart. He kept asking me if I'd heard from you. He'd beg me for information. I told him I'd heard you were working in another state, that you had a new boyfriend. It didn't matter. He wanted to contact you and fix things. Nothing I said put him off."

"I left him because he didn't trust me and turned violent. You know that."

"Lies." Brenda circled Emma and Reid. "If you'd loved Glenn properly, you would've known he had a tumour. Got him to a specialist. Instead, you made up lies and left him to get worse, while you got on with your happy life here. But it wasn't enough, was it, Emma? You wanted one more fling with Glenn for old time's sake, didn't you?"

"I don't know what you're talking about Brenda. I love Reid."

"Please don't make me vomit." Brenda kicked Reid's leg. He didn't make a sound. "You just had to come back to Sydney to see Glenn. One more time to dig your knife in deeper."

"Brenda, I haven't seen Glenn since I left Sydney five years ago."

"Liar. You came to Sydney for two medical conferences. I know because you were seen."

Emma's throat tightened. She was dealing with a psycho. "Yes, that's true, but they were quick trips, and both times you were away, running marathons."

"How convenient. I tried to tell Glenn you weren't worth it, but he got angry. He accused me of lying. That I'd done everything I could to poison you against him. When I said you were pregnant, close to full term, he freaked out. He said if it was true, you should have told him you were carrying his baby. That's when I figured it all out."

"He's delusional, Brenda. The tumour is affecting Glenn's brain."

"I knew you'd say that. I gave him one more chance to forget you, and come back to Sydney with me, but he refused. He said I was a poisonous witch. Me!" She gave Emma a malicious smile. "He tried to stop me, you know, but I showed him." Evil radiated from Brenda as she paced back and forth, glancing periodically about the area. "If I can't have him neither will you."

"What have you done, Brenda?" Emma's gaze locked on the bloodstained knife.

"I stabbed Glenn in the back. He's dead."

"Oh my God." Emma clutched her chest, her fingers colliding with the medical pouch she'd stuffed inside the jacket. "Please, Brenda, let me see to Reid. He has a head wound. I think you've cracked his skull."

"That was the idea, hon. In this temperature, he'll be dead soon enough, so it's not going to make any difference." She slashed again, nicking Emma's hand as she tried to protect her face. Blood ran down her arm.

"Brenda, you bring babies into the world. If you kill me, you kill an innocent baby."

"Oh, I don't intend to kill you just yet, Emma. I plan to deliver Glenn's baby first."

"It's not …." Emma clamped her lips shut and held her cut hand. There might still be a chance to save Reid and the baby. She needed to keep Brenda talking until Riley got here. She'd heard sirens. They had to be searching for her. Dare she scream to reveal their exact location? Or would that be enough to provoke Brenda to attack?

"How did you know we'd end up here? I have no idea where we are."

"Actually, I thought I'd lost you and that damn cop cousin of yours almost caught me. I had to dump the white coat and hide. Once he turned back, I stumbled on then lucked out when I saw your torch light waving about. I've been scouting these trails for four days because there's a back way onto your fiancé's property. The National Park makes a great place to disappear and hide bodies. Imagine my delight when Reid led me here. It's ideal really." Her high-pitched cackle turned Emma's stomach.

Keep her talking. Riley will find us. "Did you have anything to do with Bob Farrell's death?"

"Stupid fool. He was happy enough with the twelve grand I gave him to spy on you and do a little sabotage for me, but then he got himself fired. The fool decided to exact his own revenge. I had planned to set him up for your death, but I couldn't risk the police catching him alive. Pity he died without revealing where he'd stashed the money. Still, when I heard Jerry Eckford had withdrawn ten grand, it gave me a new scapegoat."

"You're responsible for Jerry's disappearance?" Bile rose in Emma's throat. Lovely Jerry, who everyone assumed was the villain. Ensuring she kept her hands out of view beside Reid, Emma pulled the bandage pouch handle off her wrist and unzipped it. "Where is he, Brenda?"

"Where no one will find him until I want him found."

"Brenda, emergency services will be here any minute. Run. I'll say I don't know who abducted me. We're close to Tulachmhor. You can escape."

"Do you think I'm stupid?" She continued to pace. "I've been here nearly a week, watching you go about your happy little life. I've checked the local maps and run all the fire trails, while I worked out how to get rid of you. I know exactly where Tulachmhor is."

"A week?" With her heart pounding a million miles a minute, Emma unzipped the jacket and pulled out the pouch.

"I've been staying at a Bed and Breakfast in Glenmeer. Nice old lady who loves to gossip. She's been most helpful. I had planned to bring you to a shack I found in this National Park. I was going to deliver the baby and say you died in childbirth. Its DNA would prove Glenn was the father and with Reid Sullivan dead, Glenn would get custody. He would have been so grateful that I'd saved his child, and he would have welcomed me to help him raise it, but you were too heavily guarded."

Brenda kicked at a rock viciously. She didn't seem to care that Emma was dabbing Reid's head with antiseptic wipes. "Then I came up with the idea of laxative filled lamingtons. I tested one on Jerry when I arranged to meet him in Glenmeer. Silly fool believed I'd been given his number by a friend, whose name I couldn't remember. We had lunch. You're right, he's a nice guy. It wasn't hard to trick him into meeting me again. The laxative worked so well, he had to rush off. I gave your midwife and the other nurse laxative dosed lamingtons too."

She halted her pacing and glared at Emma. "Unfortunately, Scarlett recovered sooner than expected. Down in emergency I handed one paramedic a laxative-laced hot chocolate to drink while he waited for your transfer papers, which I made sure were incomplete."

Emma could only stare, dumbfounded. "It was you who vandalised my Beetle."

"Oh, that was so gratifying. Slashing the tyres of a pathetic old car you loved more than Glenn. If that fat security guard hadn't got in the way, I would have kept going, but he came poking about the Men's Shed, so I had to come back later that night to finish the job."

"You hit Vince over the head."

"I did." Brenda looked down at Reid. "Check his pulse."

"Why?"

"I can't risk leaving here until I know he's past saving."

"It's thready. He needs medical attention. Brenda, listen to me. Reid doesn't know who took me because I didn't know."

Brenda narrowed her eyes. "You're lying."

"I'm not. I saw the paramedic unconscious and only got a glimpse of the driver's white coat and balaclava. I thought it was Glenn. I'm telling you the truth, Bren. I woke up confused and couldn't figure out what was happening. When I saw the paramedic, I panicked."

Brenda looked about again then pinned Emma with cold eyes. "If you were so panicked, why did you think to grab that jacket and a medical kit?"

"The jacket fell on me. I was cold. There were things strewn all over the floor. I must have picked the pouch up on instinct because I was bleeding from the IV incision." Emma pulled out a bandage, intending to wrap it around Reid's head.

"Don't." Brenda crouched down, holding the knife to Reid's throat. "I need him found like this."

"Please, don't hurt him, Brenda. Please." Her voice cracked and wobbled as she held her hand out to Brenda. "I beg of you."

"I won't cut him if you do what you're told. But only because it suits me. I know you're dying to know my plans." She chuckled menacingly. "I've made it look like Jerry stabbed Glenn then stole the ambulance. It's the perfect set-up really. Jerry planned to abduct you in revenge against the Sullivans and Morgans. Oh, yes, I took note of that piece of information and his ten grand withdrawal. It was the icing on the cake. The police will figure Jerry killed Reid and took you to a shack, where remorse finally caught up with him. They will conclude Jerry shot himself in the head, with the same rifle used to kill Bob Farrell, leaving you in labour."

"You killed Jerry?"

"Not yet. I need the post-mortem to show he died tomorrow morning. He can't get away, hon. I've got him heavily sedated and tied up. He's not going anywhere. Oh, and the bar I used to hit the security guard I planted in Glenn's boot. The same bar he was welding when he broke into the maternity ward to save you."

"Save me?"

"Yes. He figured out what I was up to."

Emma's mouth dropped open as horror crept through her freezing veins. She gripped Reid's cold hand, praying for a miracle. This was the stuff of nightmares or a thriller movie. It wasn't her life. She did another quick scan of the area, searching for something she could use as a weapon. Wasted effort, which only left one option. She needed to keep Brenda talking. "How can you deliver the baby if I'm not in labour? We stopped it."

"You were never in labour, hon. I lied about the mucus plug and your cervix dilating."

"But I felt pain in my lower back."

"I admit that was a bonus. A nice long walk should get things started and if it doesn't, I'll break your water."

"You're putting the baby's life at risk."

"Glenn's baby will be fine. I plan to tell the police I heard what had happened and ran to my car, hoping to catch the ambulance. Once I stow you away, I will go back distraught and terrified on your behalf. Tomorrow morning, I will go running in the National Park, desperate to find you, after hearing the ambulance was found near here. I will be the person who finds you in time to hear your confession and deliver Glenn's baby. You even insist on signing over legal guardianship of the baby. Sadly, I'm not quick enough to prevent you jumping off a ravine."

Emma was shaking so badly she could barely speak. "Why would I do that?"

"Because if you don't, I will drop the baby off the ravine." Brenda smirked. "As for your reason for jumping, you felt responsible for the death of the baby's real father, Glenn, and the man you tricked into asking you to marry him, Reid Sullivan."

Reid's fingers stiffened under Emma's hand.

How much had he heard? He couldn't possibly believe she would betray him or trick him into marrying her. She wasn't anything like his mother. She pressed on his chest, praying he wouldn't move. He didn't have the strength to protect himself. She needed to move away from Reid. She needed to distract Brenda.

"I'm not about to sign over the baby or take my own life. No one would believe it of me." Emma put her other hand over her abdomen, terrified for her baby.

Brenda bent over and pushed the blade's point against Reid's neck. Instantly, a thin trickle of blood trailed down his skin, enacting Emma's worst nightmare.

"Stop! Okay, I'll sign anything, just don't hurt him."

"Good decision, hon." Brenda stood again. "Let's go. Bring the pouch." She glanced away, across the dark picnic ground.

Emma pushed the torn antiseptic wipe packs and a

bandage roll under Reid then picked up the pouch and slid the handle over her wrist. "Aren't you worried the hospital's cameras will identify you?"

"Nope. Balaclava, remember." Brenda grabbed Reid's torch off the table.

After struggling to her feet, Emma slid her hands into the jacket's pockets to grip the syringes and flick off the safety caps. The second Brenda got close enough, she'd try to knock the knife out of her hand then stab her with the syringes and plunge every drop of sedative into her body. Her only consolation had to be Brenda was just as cold and wet as she was. Emma stumbled out of the shelter, shuddering as she was once again exposed to the cool breeze and misty rain. What she'd give for her warm boots, gloves, coat, jeans, and woollen hat.

Brenda walked slightly behind her, still wearing the black balaclava, and shining the torch light just ahead of Emma's feet.

"Oh my God, you are the bag snatcher. You knocked Deidre King down on purpose."

"Correct." Brenda smirked again. "I knew if I could get her back into the hospital without transport to Armidale or Tamworth, you wouldn't hesitate to check on her. One thing I could count on. You've always put your patients first, hon."

"I don't see what you gain from this, Bren. The Sullivans will fight you for custody."

"Not when they discover you deceived Reid, and the baby was never his." She poked the deadly knife at Emma, pricking her elbow.

"Ouch."

"Move. There's a narrow trail just up to the left."

Gritting her teeth, Emma prayed Reid wouldn't believe Brenda's lies. She couldn't bare his last memory of her to be that of a lying, cheating witch like his mother. She gripped the syringes and withdrew her hands, allowing the jacket's sleeves to hide them as she listened desperately for any sound of approaching vehicles.

Nothing. The sirens had long since faded, leaving only rustling branches, an eery wind and the crunch of their footsteps. She winced, a sob escaping as a sharp stick speared through the wet sock into the sole of her foot. At least her feet weren't completely numb.

She stumbled on, shaking uncontrollably, her teeth chattering, and her head pounding. It was a bit late to have an epiphany, but she suddenly realised if she'd been carrying a rifle, she wouldn't hesitate to use it now. Under the right circumstances, anyone could become a killer. She would, to save the man she loved and the child they'd created together.

The point of a needle pricked the inside of her wrist, reminding her she wasn't done fighting for her family yet. Bile rose in her throat at the thought of Brenda raising Jack. It wouldn't happen because the baby's DNA would prove Reid was his father. Emma's resolve grew, forcing aside her discomfort and terror. While she had breath in her body and a heartbeat, she would fight. An inferno of raw fury twisted and swirled from deep within her core, rising through her body, warming her frozen limbs from within. She would strike out at the first opportunity. Every muscle tensed. Ready. Waiting.

They were going downhill when a loud, revving engine broke the silence. It was coming fast, getting louder somewhere above them. Brenda swore and whirled around, searching the narrow trail behind them.

It was now or never. Emma kicked the back of Brenda's knee as she drove the two needles into her back, pressing the plungers into the syringe and shoving with all her strength.

Brenda crashed face-first into the undergrowth, howling and twisting to get free. With a snarl of rage, she came up on her knees, elbowing Emma hard in the chest and sending her flying onto her back.

Winded, Emma fought for breath, managing to struggle to her knees as Brenda raised the knife and came at her, screaming. "For that, I'm going to cut the baby out."

"No!" Emma threw herself aside, hunching into a ball and rolling to escape. She cried out as the ground dropped from under her and she went sliding feet first down another steep, wet bank. If there was a river at the bottom, she'd never survive the freezing water. Grappling for something to slow her down, didn't help. The narrow track had become a mud slide. All she could do was protect her abdomen and pray for a soft, earthy landing.

CHAPTER 18

Clutching at a steel post, Reid dragged himself to his feet, his vision a mixture of fuzzy shadows and blurry objects. The pain in his head was nothing to the agony ripping through his heart and soul as he stumbled into the picnic table. *Gotta save Emma.*

He hadn't heard a lot of Brenda's vindictive plan, but enough to piece together what he thought she'd done, all in revenge for Glenn Hanson preferring Emma. Remaining still while she outlined her scheme nearly killed him, but even lifting a finger had taken enormous effort. If he'd tried to do more, she'd have slit his throat without a crumb of remorse. He had to get help for Emma and Jerry, but with all the rain, the closest fire trail would be impossible to cross, especially on unsteady legs. Not even an emergency vehicle could cross the fast-flowing causeway. He could try to retrace his steps to the feral pigs watering hole, except he no longer had a torch and it would take too much time.

Time, they didn't have. He had to find the shack. His stomach lurched, nausea rising so fast he barely had time to lean forward before throwing up. He wiped his mouth on his jacket sleeve as dizziness threatened to overwhelm him. He'd never fainted in his life and couldn't start now. Thankful for the clearer sky, he stumbled forward, he made for the edge of the picnic ground, in the direction Brenda had forced Emma. He'd give anything to have Hunter or Riley and Jake with him.

He searched his memory for shacks in the area, dismissing any that were too far away. It had to be within walking range. The only thing that came to mind was a humpy he and Hunter had built as teenagers, before they'd discovered the caves inside Eagle Rock. They'd stolen most of the materials from one of the picnic ground shelters. The flooring, door, and window, they'd scrounged from an abandoned cottage on the edge of town. That humpy had been their safe places when their father was away, and their mother was in one of her rages. He hadn't been near it in twenty years, but with the clouds clearing he could use this trail to get there.

He caught a low branch to steady himself, listening hard as a high revving engine caught his attention. It was some distance away but coming fast from another fire trail. A fire trail that ran close to Tulachmhor. He almost fell to his knees in gratitude. It had to be Jake or Hunter on one of the quad bikes. As the vehicle got closer, Reid frowned, staring at the entrance of the dark trail. It didn't sound like a quad bike. Whatever it was, it was coming towards the old picnic ground extremely fast. At the first sight of headlights, he staggered across to the middle of the park, raising his arms to wave down the vehicle, praying it kept coming.

A beat-up car tore into the park, skidding to stop in front of him and splattering him with bits of gravel, grass, and mud. The driver's door flew open, and Scarlett Stark jumped out, wearing a helmet. "Reid! Where's Emma?"

"Gone." He reached for the hot bonnet to stop himself

falling on his face. "Brenda has her. They went that way." He pointed at the overgrown track. "I need you to phone for help."

"I can't. The battery is flat."

"Damn." Reid shook his head, trying to clear his vision. "Please help me find Emma."

"That's the plan. Are you okay?"

"I've got double vision, but I can manage. She plans to kill Emma."

"We won't let that happen." Scarlett ran around the car, opened the door and helped him over cross bars and into the front passenger seat, which hugged him like a child's safety seat. More than a little confused, he watched her buckle him into a five-point harness-like contraption. She shut the door and ran off. He heard a back door slam then she was throwing herself into the driver's seat and buckling herself into a similar contraption.

"Put this on." She handed him a helmet. "Keep your hands inside the roll bars."

He did as she commanded, while noticing there were no internal linings and a fire extinguisher buckled to the floor under his legs. "This is your car?"

"It's my rally car. Ms. Lette's vision worried me. My mother reckons she's never been wrong. Hang on for the ride of your life." She hit the accelerator and spun the car towards the dark bush track, lighting it up as she smashed aside branches and shrubs, sliding around puddle filled corners then accelerating out of it.

"Slow down, Scarlett, before we go over the edge or run Emma down."

"No chance of that. They've left the trail and taken a track to the left."

"Wow." He flinched as she wiped out a row of saplings. "How do you know?"

"GPS." She pointed to a screen on the dashboard. "Emma's wearing my tracker ring. I slipped it on her finger after I inserted the IV. Figured if she had a stalker, we couldn't be too careful, and I lied about the prawn curry. The only thing I ate for lunch was half a lamington. Andrew King rang in to apologise for taking the last one. He told me it was Karma, because he was hit with a bout of gastro on the way to Armidale Hospital."

"Brenda poisoned you and Ishya?"

"That's my guess. She did it to get us out of the way."

Reid held onto the sides of the seat as Scarlett slid around another bend, his eyes glued to the small screen. "She's got Jerry Eckford."

"What?" Scarlett sent him a startled glance before returning her attention to the track.

Reid held his breath, releasing it when they slid around the next bend. "She plans to kill him and make it look like a suicide. Thinks he'll be blamed for my farmhand's murder and this abduction. They're heading for a small shack at the bottom of this hill. You'll need to pull up in about … ten seconds."

"I know where it is." She took another corner in a slide then slammed on the brake, unbuckled her harness, and leaped out of the car. "Meet you at the shack."

Reid struggled to get the harness undone then out of the confounded rally car. Throwing the helmet on the seat, he stumbled into the thick foliage towards the hidden shack. A streak of lightning lit up the night followed instantly by a mighty crack of thunder. He broke into a lopsided run.

He found the door hanging open and under the soft glow of a torch, discovered Scarlett on her knees untying Jerry's hands. He looked to be unconscious.

"Wake up, Jerry." Scarlett shook his shoulder. "Wake up."

"That won't work, Scarlett. He's heavily sedated. Where's Emma?"

"Not here." Scarlett held out her watch. "Take this. I've got the GPS on. Follow it and you'll run into her and that woman. Be careful. I'll get Jerry to the car."

"Thanks, Scarlett. I owe you big time." He ran back out into the dark, heading up hill into the scrub, glancing from the tracker to the darkness above, listening for the slightest sound of approaching feet. Hard with the rumbling thunder all around.

The tracker showed Emma to be stationary. Reid's heart pounded as he scrambled up the steep incline. He stopped every couple of minutes to check the tracker and listen. Brenda had forced Emma to descend through thick, scrubby bush. She was close, but still not moving. He sank low and crawled forward on his hands and knees, praying harder than he'd ever prayed in his life.

He heard Emma's cowed sobs before he saw her huddled in a ball at the base of a boulder. There was no sign of Brenda. Warily, he crept forward, searching the dark as he reached out and touched Emma's shoulder.

"No!" She struck out with a sharp object, clipping his shoulder, and knocking him on his arse. If not for his jacket, she would have torn his flesh.

"Emma, it's me." He caught her wrists before she sliced his face open. "I've got you."

"Reid?" She collapsed against him, sobbing into his chest. "I didn't. I never. It's your baby. I'm not like ... your mother."

"I know, love. I know." He held her tight, fighting his own tears. "Are you hurt?"

"She ... cut me, but I ... think I'm okay."

Reid searched the darkness. "Where is she, Emma?"

"I don't ... know. I injected two ... vials of sedatives into her, but ... it didn't stop her. Brenda was going to ... to cut the baby out. She's ... crazy. I tried to ... to dive to the side and ended up rolling down ... this hillside. Oh, Reid, what if I've hurt the baby?"

"More likely you saved both your lives. I'm so proud of you, Emma, but we gotta get out of here. You're freezing and I'm worried Brenda will slog me again."

"No chance of that. By now she's either heavily sedated or ... dead."

"Good. Let me help you down the hill." He lifted Emma to her feet then put an arm around her waist. Her whole body shook violently. "Easy does it."

"How did you ... find me?"

"Scarlett put her GPS ring on you."

"What? Why?"

"She didn't like the idea of a stalker taking you. She also knew about the hidden shack at the bottom of this slope. I think she may have been held there when she disappeared seventeen years ago."

"Oh no." Emma clung to him. "Maybe ... she's come back to ... to expose her abductor."

"Or get even." Reid hoped to hell Scarlett wasn't gunning for Jerry.

They struggled on down the slope, reaching the shack to find it empty. Reid scooped Emma up in his arms and strode along the flattened trail. It looked like Scarlett had dragged Jerry to the car. Emma's shivering was a major concern. He had to get her warm. He didn't know a whole lot about hypothermia, but he prayed Emma and the baby came through unscathed. To lose the baby would haunt Emma for the rest of her life.

He stepped onto the dirt road to hear Scarlett huffing and puffing as she dragged Jerry through a mud puddle towards the car.

"Let me help." He opened the front passenger door and

placed Emma into the seat, then shut her in. "I'll lift Jerry's shoulders. You lift his legs then I'll back into the car."

"That'll work."

With a few grunts and Scarlett's help, Reid managed to lift Jerry into the rear shell of the rally car. He left Scarlett to buckle Emma in and braced his back against a roll bar and his feet against the metal hub. "No rally driving this time, Scarlett, but follow this dirt road. It ends at the back gate of Tulachmhor."

"Where's Brenda?"

"Don't know. Don't care."

She started the engine, put the car into gear and took off like a bat out of hell. He'd hate to see what she considered fast driving. "I couldn't wake Jerry, but he feels like a block of ice."

Reid gripped the roll bar. "So does Emma. I'm trying to decide if we should go straight to the hospital or stop at the house for dry clothes and blankets first."

"No choice." Scarlett glanced over her shoulder. "I don't have enough fuel to get us into town."

"Right. We'll go up to the main house and get these two into dry clothes then take them to the hospital." Reid felt Jerry's neck, his worry increasing at the thready pulse.

Scarlett slowed for a corner. "I guess you're wondering why I wear a GPS ring."

"I figure it's something to do with your disappearance seventeen years ago."

"You knew about that?"

"Not until tonight. Your parents reported you missing so Riley Morgan did some digging. I'm sorry, Scarlett. I should have taken you home that night."

"Not your fault. I guess it's hot gossip by now."

"Sorry." Reid rubbed his sore shoulder where Emma had walloped him.

"It's okay. I don't remember much about that night or the next two days. Some girls I thought were my friends played a cruel joke on me. We'd had a few drinks, but I remember them suggesting a midnight swim. They took my clothes and ran off. I saw them coming back with a group of guys, so I jumped into the river. The rest is a blur of weird memories. When I recovered, my parents told me it was Jerry who brought me home."

"Who were the girls?" Reid barely contained his fury. He made a silent vow to track each of them down and give them a tongue lashing for their malicious behaviour that night.

"Not your concern, Reid. We can't change the past, be we can learn from it."

Emma reached out a shaking hand and touched Scarlett's shoulder. "You … could have drowned or … been raped. The girls … who set you up … should be made accountable."

"They will." Scarlett patted Emma's hand. "It's called karma. We're at the gate, Reid."

He glanced out the front window at the large metal gate gleaming in the high beam of Scarlett's headlights. "I don't have keys. We're going to have to climb it and walk."

"Forget that. I've got bull bars." Scarlett reversed her car then revved the motor. "Hang on to something."

Reid grasped a bar and Jerry, holding his breath as Scarlett drove straight at the gate, smashing it off its hinges and off to the side. "Wow. You've done that before, haven't you?"

Scarlett chuckled. "No, but I've always wanted to. I'll need directions."

"Follow the tracks around the base of Eagle Rock. That's the mountain on our right."

"I've always wanted to climb to the top of Eagle Rock."

"Anytime you want, Scarlett. We'll come to another gate in about five minutes. Don't drive through that one. It's not chained."

"Got it."

They passed through five gates before reaching the Tulachmhor homestead, where to Reid's relief the lights were blazing, which meant the fire would be as well. Two people ran out onto the rear verandah. "It's Dad and Antonia." Emotion almost swamped him as he climbed out over the roll bars.

His father ran across the yard and embraced Reid, thumping his back hard. "Son."

Reid couldn't reply as a rush of grief clogged his throat, made worse when Anty hugged him from behind.

"Hello, Mr. and Mrs. Sullivan." Scarlett slammed her door. "You probably don't remember me. I'm Scarlett Stark. My mother told me you got married a few years ago. I bet that rocked the grape vine gossips." Scarlett didn't wait for an answer as she ran around the car. "We'll need help moving Jerry and the doc inside."

Antonia and Reid's father didn't say a word as they watched Scarlett warily, which surprised Reid, until he realised why. "Scarlett helped me rescue Emma and Jerry. It was Emma's friend, Brenda, who abducted them. That woman is seriously deranged, but at the moment she's lying in the National Park heavily sedated. We need to alert Riley and the others before the sedative wears off."

"Oh!" Antonia released Reid. "That's a relief. Hello, Scarlett. You were a lovely child. I often wondered why you left town. We had no idea you'd been through such a harrowing experience."

Scarlett's gaze shot to Reid. "So much for keeping my past a secret. The grapevine must be burning hot tonight."

"I'm just glad you found Emma." Antonia kissed Reid's cheek. "I'll let Riley and the boys know you're here. They're all out searching for you and out of their minds with worry." She ran back to the house.

"I'll get Emma." Reid strode around the car to the door Scarlett held opened. He lifted his precious fiancée into his arms then made for the house. Weariness dragged at him, and Emma seemed to have tripled in weight. He carried her through the kitchen and down the hall to the lounge room, where several logs burned inside the wood heater. The warmth radiating from it was heaven to his frozen limbs. He'd love to put Emma in a hot shower and warm pyjamas, but he didn't have the energy to carry her to the bathroom just yet. He lay her on the thick rug in front of the fire, relieved when she sighed in appreciation.

"Thank you, darling."

His stepmother ran in behind him and sank to her knees beside Emma. "I've brought a blanket. Oh, my goodness, love, you're frozen. We need to get you out of this wet jacket. Why are your legs bare?"

"Hospital gown." Emma's teeth still chattered, and her hand shook in Reid's. "Need to get … warm, fast, and then to … Armidale Hospital."

"We can get you warm, love, but the heavy rain has washed out Wallaby Creek Road. Tulachmhor and Hickory Ridge are completely cut off."

"Oh, that's … not good."

"It'll be okay, Em." Reid stripped off her jacket and the hospital gown, wincing at the knife cuts on her hand, arm, and shoulder. They didn't look deep enough for stitching but were seeping blood. More of a concern was the bluish tinge to her lips, arms, legs, and abdomen. Antonia helped him wrap Emma in the woollen blanket. "Stay with her, Anty, while I help Dad bring Jerry inside."

"No need," called Scarlett. "We've got him."

Reid looked over his shoulder, relieved to see his father and Scarlett shuffle through the door then lay Jerry on the couch. "Thanks. Dad, are you sure the ambulance from Armidale can't get through Wallaby Flat's Road?"

"Yep. It felt spongy when we crossed over earlier. I checked it about half an hour ago. The washout's too wide and deep for any vehicle to cross. We're lucky we didn't get stuck in it."

Emma's fingernails dug into Reid's hand. "I need a warm bath."

"Use the one in our ensuite." His stepmother wiped Emma's wet hair away from her face. "How's the baby, love?"

"I don't know." The desolation in Emma's eyes clawed at Reid's heart. "Stay with her, Anty. I'll run the bath and come back for her when it's full."

His father followed, handing over his phone. "Talk to Riley while the bath's running then have a shower. You can borrow some of my clothes."

"Thanks, Dad. Where is everyone?"

"The ladies and children are over at Hickory Ridge with a police guard. We thought it safer. The men are out searching for you. You okay, son? That's a nasty wound on your head."

"Yeah." Reid paced to his father and Antonia's bedroom. As warm water filled the enormous bath, Reid brought Riley up to date and learned a few things he didn't know. When they were finished talking, Reid stripped off his saturated clothes and ducked into the shower, closing his eyes as warmth chased away the chill invading his body. It didn't block the desolation in Emma eyes or his own fear for the baby's wellbeing.

CHAPTER 19

*H*er nightmare was over. Speaking was beyond Emma as warmth seeped through her body. Heaven on earth. At first touch, the water burned the souls of her feet, bringing forth a scream. To be so close, yet unable to bear the temperature had been torture.

Poor Reid. He'd made the water lukewarm, yet to her it might as well have been scalding hot, plus her feet and legs were badly scratched. Gradually, Reid added warm water then joined her in the large bath. She lay between his legs, her back against his chest, neither saying a word. It was an awkward silence. The wall between them would only get thicker if she didn't smash it down now. Fight for their happy ever after.

"Reid?"

"Hmm."

"I've never betrayed you. The baby is yours. His DNA will prove it."

"I don't need a DNA test done, Emma. I believe you."

"No. I insist. I don't want you one day down the track throwing this in my face."

"It won't happen, Emma. I love you."

"But do you trust me?" She twisted to meet his hooded gaze. "Those two conferences I attended in Sydney were important. I flew down the night before, stayed in my hotel room, attended the conferences, and flew straight back the next day. I didn't go out to dinner, and I didn't run into anyone I knew from my old hospital. Reid, I have never been unfaithful to you. I love you."

His chest expanded then he exhaled. "Emma, you are my life. There isn't anything I wouldn't do to make you happy. I know you're not like my mother. You appreciate everything I do for you. You aren't demanding. You don't throw tantrums. You care about the people in your life, and my family love you. I was a fool to fear otherwise. I do trust you, love. You're an amazing woman and you will make an amazing mother."

His softly spoken words sunk deep into her heart, filling her with joy and bringing tears to her eyes. There was only one thunder cloud on their horizon. She sniffed back a sob. "I did my best tonight to keep our baby safe, but he hasn't moved. Not since just before the ambulance crashed."

Reid's fingers shook as he stroked her cheek. "Whatever happens, we will face it together, Em. We must believe he's a little fighter, like his mother. Positive thinking, remember."

"You are going to make an amazing father, Reid." Emma covered his hand. "After I tumbled down the hill, I had a few strong contractions and worried my water would break any minute, but it didn't. Brenda lied. She was my friend, Reid, and she lied. She's hated me the whole time."

"I know, love, but it's behind us now." Reid kissed Emma then urged her to lie back against his chest again. "I spoke to Riley. The Tamworth police have arrived with all-wheel drives to access the fire trail Scarlett used. Riley said it's in bad shape due to the heavy rain, but if Scarlett got through, they will. He promised to ring as soon as they find Brenda."

Emma shuddered. She never wanted to see that woman again. "How's Jerry?"

"Still heavily sedated. Dad and Scarlett are going to drive him down to Wallaby Flat's Road then an Emergency Services crew will stretcher Jerry across the washout to a waiting ambulance that's come from Armidale."

"I'm so glad he wasn't the culprit or out for revenge. Brenda boasted how she laced lamingtons with laxatives to get Jerry, Ishya, and Scarlett out of the way. Why do you think Jerry withdrew ten thousand dollars from his account?"

Reid kissed her shoulder. "According to Riley, someone left ten grand in cash and a note on Scarlett's back porch. The note stated the money was to go towards her new rally car. Vince and Valma assumed it was one of their parents who preferred not to be seen as having a favourite grand-child. Riley suspects the money came from Jerry. It's possible he felt guilty for not seeing Scarlett home safely during that party. Vince plays darts with Jerry. He told Riley that Jerry asked about Scarlett. He hadn't known she was back in town or that she was saving for a rally car. Vince hadn't thought about it at the time, but several days later the money appeared on their porch."

"Wow." Emma caught Reid's hand and raised it to her lips. "You saved me twice tonight. Thank you, darling. It might take a while, but I will overcome my fear of stockyards and cattle. I plan to make you a fabulous wife. A wife you can be proud of."

"I'm already proud of you, Emma. You don't need to go near the stockyards." He layered a path of kisses from her shoulder to her ear. "I will always be proud of you, no matter what."

"Yes, but if Jack wants to hang around stockyards, then so will—Uh!"

"What?" Reid sat up so suddenly a wave of water sloshed over the side of the bath.

Emma smiled for the first time in what felt like weeks. Clutching Reid's hand, she held it high on her abdomen, tears of joy running down her face as Jack kicked his tiny feet. "He's alive."

"Told you he was a fighter like his mother." Reid wrapped his arms around Emma and her huge abdomen then nuzzled her neck. "Two years ago, Edwina Lette predicted we'd have three children."

"Yes, she did. Right after you kissed me in front of that crowd at Riverside Pub, shocking the whole community."

He chuckled against her throat. "We weren't the only ones to shock the locals that night."

A soft rap sounded on the door. "It's just me," announced Antonia. "Tom and Scarlett have taken Jerry to the ambulance. Scarlett is going with him to the hospital. Oh, and Tom asked me to tell you, Dr Frobisher came along with the paramedics and wants to examine Emma."

"Great. That saves us dragging Emma back to the hospital." His eyes shone with love as he smiled at Emma. "We'll be out in five minutes.

"Oh, two more things," added Antonia. Riley is on his way to take your statements and I'd be delighted if Emma would call me Anty."

"I would love to. Thanks, Anty." Emma kissed Reid's arm. "I guess it's time we get out of this lovely bath."

"Yeah." Reid helped her up and over the edge. "Anty left a warm nightie for you and we're sleeping in her bed again tonight. Best not to be climbing up and down stairs."

"I hope Riley isn't too long. I just want to curl up with you and close my eyes."

Reid towelled her dry then applied antiseptic and band aids of all sizes to her deep scratches and cuts. There were many, especially on her feet and legs. He bandaged the knife cuts on her hand, arm, and shoulder, before helping her into an old-fashioned nightie and orange bed socks, sending them both into a fit of giggles. They had to be Kathleen's.

As Emma ran a wide-toothed comb through her wet hair, Reid dried off, dressed then did his best to blow-dry her hair. He'd never make a hair stylist.

Once Emma was propped up in bed with a thick doona tucked around her, Reid went to find Doctor Frobisher. Emma closed her eyes and breathed deep. It had been a very long day and she was beyond exhaustion, but until she knew Brenda had been taken into custody, she wouldn't relax.

The door opened and Jessamine Frobisher marched in wearing her trademark black pants and white blouse. "Hello, Emma. You gave us a terrible scare. What a night."

"Hi, Jess. How is Glenn Hanson?"

"He's been stabilised and flown to Saint Vincent's. Poor guy. How he functioned with a tumour that size, I don't know, but he's in the best place now. I patched him up as best I could and he's scheduled for emergency surgery as soon as they get a team ready."

"Good. I hope … I hope it's successful. Do you know if Chandra is okay?"

"Yes, the paramedic is fine. Let's have a look at you. Anything you're concerned about?"

"I'm getting a few contractions, so I'd appreciate you checking my cervix then I'd like to borrow your stethoscope to listen to the baby's heartrate myself."

"Your fiancé said you were cut with a knife? I'd like to check the wounds and your feet."

"Thank you. I appreciate you coming out here, Jess. I know you've had a long day too."

"No problem." Jess checked Emma over thoroughly before allowing her to listen to the baby's heartbeat, which sounded perfect and brought tears to Emma's eyes. She handed back the stethoscope and snuggled down into her doona again. Jess was around twenty-eight, a couple of years younger than Emma, but they were friends, both of them now an integral member of staff at the hospital.

"Thank you, Jess, can you examine Reid's head. He took a huge hit with a piece of wood, and I know there's a wound."

"I'll do it now. You get some rest."

"I will. See you at the wedding."

"You bet. Bye, Emma."

The door had barely closed before it opened again, and Antonia popped her head around it. "Riley's here, Emma."

"Send him in."

"Hey." Riley strode over to the bed and kissed her forehead. "You gave us a hell of scare, Emma. I've heard of keeping your friends close and your enemies closer, but with friends like Brenda, you went and killed two birds with one stone."

"Not funny, Riley. I'm sorry I ever met Brenda. Have you found her?"

"Not yet. We've called in extra police to help with the search. Reid said she had a knife and she used it on you both."

"Yes. She admitted to killing Bob, lacing lamingtons with laxatives, vandalising my car, attacking Vince, kidnapping and sedating Jerry and she thought she'd killed Glenn. She even told me she was setting Jerry up to take the blame. She intended to frame him for my death too and make his death look like a suicide."

Emma drew in a breath. "Riley, Brenda intended to keep my baby. She'd convinced herself Glenn was the father."

"Hell. You'd better start at the beginning." He pulled out his notebook then sat on the edge of the bed. "Take your time, Emma. If you forget something, I'll add it in later."

"Wait!" Antonia padded into the room carrying a loaded tray. "Emma can eat then answer your questions, Riley."

A tantalising aroma assailed Emma. She hadn't eaten anything since lunch. Her tummy growled. "That smells delicious, Antonia."

"Luckily, I had chicken vegetable soup in the freezer."

Riley fidgeted with his pen. "Emma, do you want Reid present for this interview or not?"

"Yes, I'd prefer him here."

"He won't be a minute." Antonia placed the tray across Emma's lap. "Doctor Frobisher is putting a couple of stitches in his head." Antonia patted Emma's sore shoulder. "You two have certainly been through an ordeal over the last two days."

That was the understatement of the year. Emma took a bite of the toasted sourdough smothered in butter and sighed. "Delicious." She picked up the soup spoon.

As she ate, Riley bounced his knee impatiently. Finally, with her stomach full, and Reid sitting beside her, Emma picked up her hot chocolate and leaned back in the pillows. "For any of this to make sense, I will have to start at the very beginning on my first day at Saint Vincent's Hospital."

* * *

IT WAS ALMOST 2am when Riley's phone rang. Emma watched intently as he took the call then wrote in his notebook.

Closing the notebook, Riley grimaced. "What a tangled web." He scratched his head. "Brenda Barker has been found and taken to the hospital. She'll stay under police guard until the sedatives wear off and she can be transferred to Tamworth for questioning. Police found a knife in her hand and a rifle in that shack, along with a box of sedatives.

Constable Donaldson will stay in the house with you tonight, just in case."

Reid's arm tightened around Emma. "I have one concern, Riley."

"Go on."

"Whoever Hunter and I were chasing was fast. They knew where they were going and how to use a rifle. Brenda Barker has never been to Tulachmhor. Could she have a partner?"

"I can answer that." Emma covered a yawn. "Brenda is a marathon runner. One of her favourite things is to sprint along beaches and she does cross country marathons too. She said she's been here almost a week, checking the trails in Akuna National Park and watching Tulachmhor. As for the rifle, she grew up on a property in Cobar. I remember her telling me she used to go pig shooting with friends."

"Right." Riley scribbled in his notebook again. "I've spoken to her parents. The family has been estranged from Brenda for years. Apparently, she was thrown out of the family home after attacking her sister with a rolling pin."

"Why?" Emma lifted her head from Reid's shoulder.

"A guy Brenda fancied asked the sister to go steady. Mr. Barker said it was the last straw. He refused to elaborate but told me the family haven't spoken to Brenda since."

"Wow." Emma blocked another yawn. "I'm concerned about Jerry."

Riley tucked his notebook into his pocket. "He's going to be fine. Oh, and Abby Taylor sent me a text, confirming it was Jerry who left the money on Scarlett Stark's back porch."

"He's a good guy." Emma squeezed Reid's hand resting on her abdomen. "Jerry is going to hear there was an APB out on him. When he discovers he was suspected of killing Bob and everything else we've thought he's done, he's not going to take it well. In fact, I wouldn't be surprised if he packs up and leaves Bindarra Creek. Is there a way to withhold that information?"

"Hell, you're right," muttered Reid.

Emma looked from Reid to Riley. "Can you withhold that information?"

"It will come out in the enquiry." Riley pinched the bridge of his nose. "Jerry's going to feel like *we* betrayed *him.*"

"Hopefully, once he hears the full story, he will understand." Emma wasn't sure she believed her own words. In Jerry's place, she'd be devastated. She yawned again, finding it hard to keep her eyes open.

"I'll call by in the morning." Riley paced to the door. "Dad, Tom, Hunter, and Jake are going to get the tractors going at first light and repair the road, at least enough that we can use it. Call me if you need anything."

"We will." Reid climbed out of bed, crossed the room, and locked the door after Riley. After shucking off his trackpants and T-shirt, he climbed back into bed and switched off the bedside lamp.

Already lying on her side, Emma pushed back into the warmth of his chest, smiling as his arm came around her abdomen and he spooned her with his body, wrapping her in warmth.

"Love you, Em."

"Love you too, darling." Emma placed her hand over his on her abdomen and the baby within, grateful all was well. The last couple of days had pushed her out of her comfort zone yet forced her to face her demons and fears head on. She had a little way to go, but Reid would help.

Best of all, she could finally let go of the past and look forward to their future with joy and anticipation.

EPILOGUE

"*I*'m getting married once and once only." Reid glared at the smirking faces of his brother and the Morgan twins. His best man and groomsmen. Who would have thought it? They'd all been through this and survived, so he would too. It was the waiting that bothered him most. He needed to be doing something with his hands so he wouldn't keep checking the vestry window. Not that he feared Emma wouldn't turn up at the church. Well, yes, that was his biggest fear, but only because she'd had a couple of severe contractions yesterday and he'd expected her to be on time today. He strode back to the window and checked the road.

No wedding cars yet. "Where are they? Emma insisted on bringing the wedding forward a week because she wanted to be married and have a honeymoon before the baby arrives. This is Edwina Lette's fault."

"Don't you all look very smart."

"Speak of the devil," muttered Reid. "Hello, Ms. Lette.

She almost bounced across the vestry and took his hand. "Sorry, dear. I just need to check something." She turned his hand over and frowned. "That's the strangest thing."

"What is?" He pulled his hand away and checked his palm. Other than a few new calluses and healing scratches it looked the same as always.

Edwina shrugged her thin shoulders. "Last night I had a vison of you and Emma with your family ten or so years from now. It didn't add up, because two years ago I read three babies in both your futures. Must have been a glitch."

Goosebumps ran down Reid's spine. This hippy, joint-smoking psychic had proven her visions true too many times to take her words lightly. He shot his brother, and the Morgan twins a plea for help. He did not want to know about glitches. Emma was looking forward to adding two more children to their family down the track.

Edwina cackled. "Down panic, boy. I called by Riley and Samantha's house to take a quick peek at Emma's palm. By the way, she is glowing, and her dress is beautiful. Where was I? Oh, yes. Emma's palm is the same as yours. Definitely a glitch. I've never known that to happen before, but she bore the news well."

He frowned. "So, instead of three children, we're having two, or is it just one?" That would disappoint Emma. He didn't want her disappointed on her wedding day.

"Pwush." Edwina tapped his arm. "You can't rub out children. Another two lines have appeared. You and Emma can expect five children and they're going to run you round in circles. Good luck." She pranced out of the vestry like a fairy queen who'd shown him the pot of gold waiting for him at the end of a rainbow. His for the taking.

"Five?" Wonder spread through Reid. "Em and I are having five children." He slapped palms with Hunter then turned to Jake and Riley Morgan. "Sullivans out do the Morgans again."

"Yeah, yeah." Jake strolled over to the window. "Betcha they're all girls."

Reid scratched his chin. "Wanna put your money where your mouth is, mate?"

"Hmm. As Riley, Hunter and I had girls first and our wives would know the sex if Emma knew, I'm willing to treat Gypsy free for the rest of her life, if Emma has a boy first."

"Done." They shook hands.

"Hang on. What are you prepared to wager," challenged Riley.

"Nothing. Emma's having a boy. I think I might call him …Jack."

Jake and Riley looked at each other and laughed then both spoke at once. "Jacqueline."

"Whatever." Reid swallowed his grin. Having Gypsy treated for free was a big saving. "So, Riley, any news on Glenn Hanson?"

"Yeah. He's out of the induced coma and talking. He has little memory of the past five years and according to his specialist is horrified by the way he treated Emma. The tumour wasn't malignant and as he hasn't harmed anyone, no charges will be brought against him. He has sent a letter of apology to Emma but understands if she doesn't want to see him."

"Does Hanson know she's getting married today?" enquired Hunter.

"Yes. He's accepted she's moved on and although disappointed, is okay with it."

"What about Brenda Barker?" Jake turned from the small window he'd been looking out. "Any news on her?"

"Yes. The hearing is set for next March. The judge stated Glenn Hanson should be well enough to attend by then."

"Anyone heard from Jerry?" asked Hunter.

Reid and Jake shook their heads. Everyone looked to Riley.

He sighed. "Jerry picked up work out at Blue Orchard Park. He's helping the McKenna's with their horses. He'll come round. We just need to give him time."

"On another subject. Do you know where Emma is taking you for your honeymoon?" Riley chuckled. "Or is it still a secret?"

"I do. Emma is taking me to Port Stephens for a week. We're staying in a house overlooking the beach and she's booked a whale watching cruise."

"Nice." Jake's lips twitched. "Not too much dancing tonight or you might not make Port Stephens."

"They're here," announced Hunter.

Reid ran to the window, jostled by the other three as they all tried to get a glimpse of the wedding party. A grin spread across his face as his two sisters and sister-in-law were handed out of a horse drawn carriage by Paddy Cullen, looking very spritely in a grey suit. Ali, Samantha, and Chelsea looked stunning, with their hair caught up in pink and white flowers. They wore white cowboy boots and knee length gowns in a bold shade of … "What colour is that?"

Riley elbowed him. "I'm told it's fuchsia."

Dodge Myers and Angus McGregor lifted Jasmin and Elise down then stood back as the two little girls twirled around, showing off their frothy, fuchsia dresses, and cute little boots. "Now I understand why Emma wanted us to wear blue jeans, riding boots and Akubras."

Jake chuckled. "No tie is a win in my book."

As the church was packed with family, friends, and a good portion of Bindarra Creek locals, the crowd on the other side of the street had to be out of towners, here for the Organic Festival and Scavenger Hunt. Reid didn't care. They were welcome to watch the ladies arrive. Cheers went up as another horse drawn carriage arrived. "Damn it, I can't see her." He pressed his cheek to the window. "Nope, she's just out of view."

"Okay, gentleman. Time to take your places." Florence Miller stood in the doorway pointing a finger at them. "No peeking. Come on." She waved them past her and into the church. "Much better."

Reid took his place closest to the aisle and adjusted the collar of his blue shirt. The four Akubras sat on the pew behind. If he'd been wearing a tie, it would be strangling him by now. The navy embroidered waistcoat was bad enough.

The soft cords of a violin started up, followed by a flute and piano. He looked up to the choir loft, surprised to see several violinists, a guitarist, and other musicians. He recognised the melody as it was one of his grandmother's favourites. Beethoven's Ode to Joy. Emotion welled.

Reid looked down the aisle as Elise and Jasmine started down the carpet. Elise carried a basket of rose petals, giggling as she tossed handfuls up in the air. Jasmine carried an air of importance as she held Gypsy on a pink lead. His brave dog had a garland of flowers around her collar. Jasmine and Elise were cute little imps dressed as angelic fairies. He could easily see them ruling the pack of Sullivan and Morgan offspring through the next fifteen years.

Interesting times lay ahead indeed. Reid's five nephews and youngest niece were at Tulachmhor being babysat by Kaylee Myers and two of her friends, overseen by Sarah and Anthony Luchetti. Antonia's elderly parents were more than happy to let the teenagers manage the babies, while they sat on the verandah in the sun.

Samantha came down the aisle next, smiling from ear to ear. Then Ali, who winked at Reid. Who'd have thought the Sullivan siblings would find love and settle down? Antonia, the mother they'd always wanted, took pride of place in the front seat with Reid's father and grandmother. He gave them a nod, his lips twitching when his father dabbed a handkerchief at his eyes.

Reid looked back down the aisle as Chelsea stepped through the door. Halfway down the aisle, she raised an eyebrow then stuck her tongue out. He chuckled. Just what he needed to loosen the tension in his shoulders. His gaze fell on Scarlett Stark and her parents. She gave him the thumbs up.

He looked across to the other front pew, where Emma's mother, sister and brother-in-law stood with baby Otis. A sprained ankle prevented Lindsay being Emma's matron of honour, but it couldn't be helped. Mrs. Fahey smiled at him and wiped a tear away. Another knot of tension unrolled in Reid's shoulders. The Faheys hadn't been pleased with Emma's decision to get married in Bindarra Creek instead of Armidale, yet at the end of the day, they wanted her to be happy, so all had worked out.

She'd told him she was changing a few things, but this was amazing. It was Emma through and through. The fully catered reception out at Tulachmhor was set to be a boot scooting hoot, with several country and western singers and a band ready to rock the night away. Behind the Faheys stood James and Hannah Morgan and Emma's grandmother, Therese. Beside her stood Edwina Lette and her posse of friends. The pews were lined with familiar faces.

The music suddenly changed to the traditional wedding march, so loud it echoed throughout the church and sent goosebumps down Reid's legs. He drew in a deep breath and waited for his bride to appear.

Then she did, on the arm of her father, and carrying a massive bouquet of colour that completely concealed her pregnancy. Her hair was piled on top of her head in large curls. She wore a crown of cream flowers, which matched the lace covering her shoulders and the soft looking layers that fell beneath the flowers almost reaching the floor. She'd said she was wearing chiffon, which meant nothing to him. It looked fragile and feminine and ... so Emma. She wore no veil. Her stunning, melting chocolate eyes shone with happiness and love. The final knot disintegrated, and Reid's heart swelled with pride as she joined him in front of the altar.

"You look magnificent, Em. You're a fairy princess."

"No, Uncle Reid. That's me and Elise," whined Jasmine. "Aunty Emma is just a normal princess, and you are the handsome prince who has to kiss her."

Chuckles filled the church.

Reid winked at Jasmine. "I'll get right onto that, Jazzy."

Reverend Florence Miller stepped forward and welcomed everyone, thanking the congregation for bearing witness to his and Emma's union. Most of it went in one ear and out the other as Reid looked at Emma. She really did glow.

Once her father stepped away, Emma slid her hand into his and squeezed. "You look very handsome, darling. How are you holding up?"

"I'm good. No! I'm great. You're an amazing woman, Emma. I've got to be the luckiest man alive. You are everything to me. Everything. I love you."

She blinked furiously, even as she smiled radiantly. "You are everything to me too, Reid. What I feel for you is too big to contain, so I won't." She stretched up and touched her soft lips to his cheek. "I love you."

"Beautiful sentiments," proclaimed Reverend Miller. "Now, let's get you two married before you do me out of a job."

Laughter and cheers filled the church. With so many friends and family surrounding them, Reid couldn't help but count his blessings. There was only one person missing, who should be here. Reid made a silent vow to fix things with

Jerry. To show him he was valued and a vital part of the community, and hopefully it could be achieved by Christmas. Afterall, wasn't Christmas a time for healing and bringing people together?

Emma squeezed his hand, her stunning smile filling him with happiness and optimism. Everything would work out. How could it not? This was Bindarra Creek.

The End

Thank you for purchasing my book, **Protecting their Destiny,** and for supporting this wonderful series. I hope you enjoyed meeting or reacquainting yourself with the Morgan and Sullivan families, as well as many of the eccentric and wonderful characters in Bindarra Creek. My other books in this quirky town are: **Tempting Fate, Date with Destiny, and A Twist of Fate.**

About the Bindarra Creek Series

Welcome to Bindarra Creek, a struggling country town where people work hard and love deeply. Set in the picturesque tablelands of New England, Australia, Bindarra Creek is a fictional, rural community full of romance, intrigue, adventure, drama and suspense.

To date there are four multi-author 'series' set in the Bindarra Creek world all written by best-selling Australian romance authors. A fifth is planned for late 2022 – **A Bindarra Creek Christmas.**

A Bindarra Creek Mystery Romance – released from July 2022

Amulet of Death – Suzanne Gilchrist (aka S E Gilchrist)
Beyond the Gate – Rhonda Forrest
Protecting their Destiny – Erin Moira O'Hara
Only She Knew – Linda Charles
Secrets of River Cottage – Annie Seaton
Forgotten Secrets – Susanne Bellamy
A Perfect Danger – Phillipa Nefri Clark

Bindarra Creek A Town Reborn

Take Me Home – Suzanne Gilchrist (aka S E Gilchrist)
In the Heat of the Night – Susanne Bellamy
No Looking Back - Linda Charles
Worth the Wait – Annie Seaton
With Every Breath – Lauren K. McKellar
Stealing Her Heart – Simone Angela
A Twist of Fate – Erin Moira O'Hara
Promise Me Forever – Juanita Kees

Bindarra Creek Short & Sweet

What's in a Kiss – Linda Charles
My Forever Valentine – Sandie James (not available)
Pearls and Green Beer – Susanne Bellamy
Full Circle – Annie Seaton
Date with Destiny – Erin Moira O'Hara
A Letter From the Queen – Lee Christine
Love's Sweet Challenge – Suzanne Gilchrist (aka S E Gilchrist)
The Widow Maker – Lauren K. McKellar
Out of the Blue – Noelle Clark

Bindarra Creek Romance

Bindarra Creek Makeover - S. E. Gilchrist
Shadows of the Heart - Lee Christine
Second Chance Love - Susanne Bellamy
The CEO Mechanic - Sandie James (not available)
Reach for the Stars - Kerrie Paterson
Home to Bindarra Creek - Juanita Kees
Stolen Sanctuary - Stacey Nash
Tempting Fate - Erin Moira O'Hara
One More Day - Linda Charles
The Vine - Lauren K. McKellar
The Ghost of His Past - Simone Angela
Joanie's Dilemma - Marianne Theresa
Buckley's Chance - Noelle Clark

Full details on buy links for all books in Bindarra Creek world can be found at www.bindarracreekromance.com

ACKNOWLEDGMENTS

My appreciation and heartfelt thanks to my wonderful team who consistently help me deliver the best books I can.

The brilliant Juanita Kees for her exceptional editing skills, guidance and delightful sense of humour.

My critique partner, Suzanne Gilchrist, who is always available for a brainstorming session or a chat. You continue to motivate me with your enthusiasm.

Annie Seaton for my lovely cover, and Cindy Pearson, an amazing proofreader.

My special thanks to midwife and author, Fiona McArthur, for her help with pre-natal babies. And to paramedic, Matt Graham for his help with my ambulance scene.

And lastly, my fellow authors in the Bindarra Creek Romance series. You ladies rock.

About the Author

Erin Moira O'Hara grew up in the Blue Mountains of Australia, with a garden backing onto native bushland, hidden caves and fabulous lookouts. Weekends were spent exploring, climbing trees and creating secret bases. Her love of reading began with visits to the local library as a child, where she became absorbed in a world of intrigue, fantasy and action-packed adventures.

The moment Erin read her first romance; she was hooked and dreamed of her own hero and writing romantic adventures. She now lives close to Lake Macquarie, the largest, coastal, saltwater lake in Australia. The family home overlooks bushland and is surrounded by birds and an acre of ever-growing gardens. She shares this paradise with her husband, three eccentric hens, two spoilt cats and one adorable dog called Murphy-girl.

Erin's writing encompasses everything she loves best—intrigue, suspense, passion and romance.

Reviews are appreciated, as they help readers find books and increase a writer's visibility.

If you would like to know more about Erin Moira O'Hara, please visit her website. www.erinmoiraohara.com